St. Mary's Dating Agency

Agency

Book #4 Max & Olivia Series

Books In This Series

Operation Underpants (2016)

Claudia (2017)

Operation OBE - Over Bloody Eighty (2018)

St. Mary's Dating Agency (2020)

Operation Origami - The Ire of Claudia (2021)

Operation Snowflake (2021)

Other books by Mark A. Biggs

Above and Beyond: 2nd edition (2014)

Love Letters From Dresden: Book #1 Artōrius Series (2019)

Silent Trail: Book #2 Artōrius Series (2024)

St. Mary's Dating Agency

Mark A. Biggs

Copyright

A CIP catalogue record for this book is available from the National Library of Australia.

First published in Australia 2020.

mbkbooks

62 Sunnybrook Ave

Warragul Victoria 3820

Australia

Dedication

To John Moss and the League of Retired Gentlemen, my
curmudgeonly friends

Note:

The quoted email romance script was used by scammers to perpetrate catfishing
and romance frauds. They were cited in court evidence.

Acknowledgment:

The words of the late Right Reverend John McIntyre, former Bishop of
Gippsland, were used with the agreement of his widow, Jan McIntyre (pg. 299 &
300)

Disclaimer:

This story is a work of fiction.

Book Cover:

Cover design by Craig Braithwaite, aussiepics.

CHAPTER 1

PI-SKI

As Edith rushed past and up the steps of the St Mary's Anglican Church in Pi-Ski, Cornwall, late for Sunday morning communion, Josephine called to her excitedly, 'Is he here?'

Edith stopped, glanced back. An air of disappointment hung in her voice, as she said, shaking her head in disbelief, 'I'm on duty this morning, need to robe. I'll talk to you after the service; it's awful, truly awful. Sorry, I have to go.' Edith dashed into the church and made her way to the vestry to change.

The parish church of St Mary's, in the village of Pi-Ski, was built in the seventeenth century and is typical of many of the country churches across England, with its declining and ageing congregation. Except for John Moss, a single man in his mid-thirties and nineteen-year-old Tina, who had recently moved in with her Grandmother, Catherine Hepburn, to attend Falmouth

University ten miles away, the remainder of the regular congregation were over fifty-five, most the far side of eighty. Unusually, the St Mary's Parochial Parish Council consisted of the younger churchgoers: John Moss, Edith Kelly who was fifty-eight, Catherine Hepburn at sixty-four and Josephine Carter, a sprightly sixty-five-year-old. With the exception of John Moss, the male gender was not overly well represented; John was the only male who regularly attended the church, the rest being women, all widowed, or divorced.

The village name of Pi-Ski was derived, or so folklore would have it, from the mythical pixies, or little people, who lived in underground dolmens. According to mythology, pixies are fond of dancing and gathering outdoors in huge numbers to dance. On still, balmy spring evenings, locals walking home after closing time at the Little People's Arms, the local pub after having had too many ales, often reported hearing sounds of pixies dancing in the night, though few actually admitted to seeing them. When items go missing in the home, or mischief occurs in the town, the colloquial explanation is always the same; it's those pesky pixies. If evidence is to be gleaned from the St Mary's church sign, a message board out-front, on display to all those passing, and on which the Vicar, or Parish Council members put up spiritual messages, Pi-Ski has a prankster in its midst. The previous Easter, following its Good Friday Service, the sign was set to read: Hope is the power of the present.

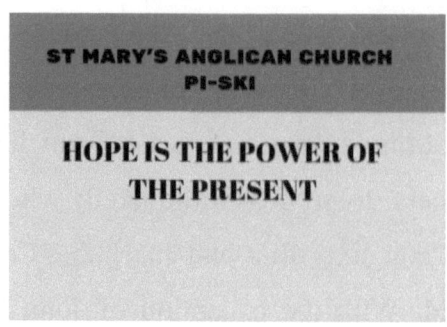

When churchgoers arrived for the Sunday morning Easter service, they were greeted by a different message. It read: Little Hope. An arrow pointed towards the church.

For the Christmas message that same year, the Parish Council settled on: I love this Church, God.

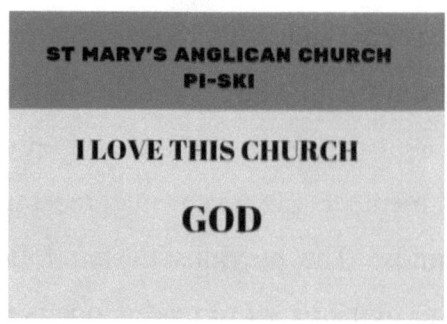

Only to find it changed to: I hate this Church, God.

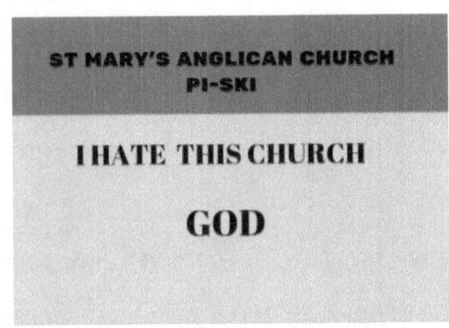

A quick-thinking parishioner however, added SATAN to the end of the words, so the sign now read: I hate this church, Satan.

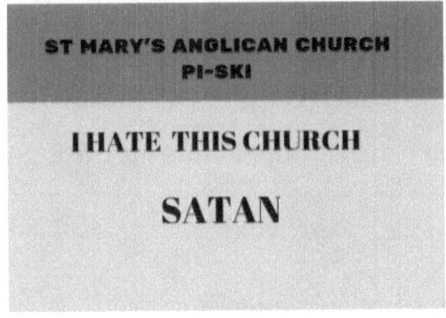

Not to be outdone, the church's inventive pixie retaliated on New Year's Eve, but this time in Latin from Dante's *Divine Comedy*, revealing much about the prankster.

> "Lasciate ogni speranza, voi ch'entrate", which is most frequently translated as, "Abandon all hope, ye who enter here," the inscription at the entrance to hell.

In some towns, gnomes are routinely stolen from people's gardens and it's not uncommon for the owner to be sent photographs from exotic locations around the world, featuring their missing garden ornament. The gnomes, after an extended holiday, magically reappear, wearing a suntan. Sometimes, instead of vacation snaps, the owner receives a ransom demand for the safe return of their missing gnome. That's not what happens in Pi-Ski. Here, you wake up one morning and find your garden invaded by an army of gnomes. Woe betide the grumpy recipient who is unwelcoming to their new arrivals for the gnomes will breed, multiplying like rabbits. Overnight, two unwelcome guests become twenty-two, which is unsettling, unless they like gnomes, of course.

**

The number of people attending that day's church service at St Mary's was unusual. Thirty-five people occupied the hard and uncomfortable wooden pews. While the regulars accept the haemorrhoids and sore rears caused by the cold unforgiving wood, seeing it as part of their weekly ritual of self-flagellation, the visitors desire softer seating for worship. As the sermon drags on, they fidget, wiggling their bottoms in discomfort, the benches creaking. Because this was the Reverend Charlotte Foster's first service as the new Vicar, attendance had doubled. Undoubtedly, normality would return the following Sunday.

St Mary's had been without a minister for ten months, until Vicar Charlotte Foster, accepted the invitation to be the priest in charge of Pi-Ski, her first parish as a fully-fledged minister. At fifty-two, Charlotte was not naïve in the ways of the church, having been a congregational member for most of her life, a Lay reader and Vicar's warden. Throughout her successful career as an accountant, Charlotte harboured a desire to become a Priest. After her divorce from Peter, husband of twenty years, she could resist the calling no longer.

Like most dying churches, the St Mary's Vicars appointments panel, consisting of John Moss, Catherine Hepburn, Edith Kelly and Josephine Carter, which by no strange coincidence, was also the entire parish council, had wanted a Priest with a young family, especially children. Children were the holy grail, the salvation of declining congregations, or so the perceived wisdom would have it. That is, of course, only if the children behaved like sixty-year olds and sit quietly in the pews, not disturbing the status quo. St Mary's knew it needed to change, but the consensus was 'not on my watch'. Children needed more than what the church was offering, yet evolution was being resisted, leaving an uninviting prospect for any youngster.

After an eternity of fruitless searching, the appointments panel heard of Vicar Charlotte Foster, a Curate in London, seeking an 'Escape to the Country'. Although not their ideal candidate, on many levels, Charlotte met the compromised selection criteria: she was warm, standing and could smile pleasantly. She had a pulse.

'I hope the new Vicar doesn't repeat this every Sunday,' whispered Catherine Hepburn to Josephine Carter, who was seated next to her, in the third pew from the front on the left-hand side of the aisle. This is where Catherine and Josephine habitually placed themselves, unless on church duty at the front. When on duty, their regular seats were left vacant. If, by some strange turn of events, perhaps a visiting person on holiday attended a service and inadvertently took their place, Catherine would pointedly ask them to move. On those Sundays when Tina, Catherine's granddaughter, was in Pi-Ski, she would occupy a place next to Catherine, away from the aisle, although this was not one of the covertly reserved spots.

'Repeat what?' Josephine whispered.

Lifting her arm in order to show Josephine the face of the watch she was wearing, Charlotte said, 'The sermon has been going for fourteen minutes. That's too long! A sermon should be no more than ten. At this rate we will be here until half-past eleven. St Mary's is not one of those city Pentecostal, happy clappy type churches, where a service lasts for two hours. One hour ten, that's the maximum time for us country Anglicans. As the Vicar's Warden, I will speak to her after the service. We wouldn't want this to happen again next week!'

'It is her first Sunday Catherine, and the sermon is rather good. Why not wait until after next week? This might be a once off?'

'No Josephine! Vicar's are like small children; they need to know who's boss from day one.'

Josephine whispered, 'Who's on welcoming duties after the service?'

'We are, you and me. If our new Vicar preaches for much longer however, everybody will rush off the moment the service is over.'

'Amen,' Catherine and Josephine heard the Vicar say, signalling the end of the sermon. 'Sixteen minutes,' Catherine muttered aloud to herself, 'that just won't do, it won't do at all.'

'Shush,' Tina whispered, giving her grandmother a gentle poke in the ribs with her elbow, a faint smile adorning her face.

'Vicar! Oh Vicar,' Catherine called out to Charlotte Foster. The service had finished and the congregation was gathered in the church hall to share a cup of tea and a sandwich. There was always a gathering after the Sunday service for tea and biscuits, but this day was special. To welcome the new Vicar, the St Mary's Ladies Guild, John Moss, Catherine Hepburn, Edith Kelly, Josephine Carter and Tina, the co-opted member, had put on a super spread to complement the tea and coffee – sandwiches and cake.

Historically, the Ladies Guild would top up the church coffers with the monies it earned catering for weddings and funerals in the parish hall. In more recent times, the last ten years or so, the number of weddings held in the church could be counted on one hand. Funerals were more plentiful, but as they were all ex-parishioners, the Ladies Guild couldn't proffer a charge. While the St Mary's church hall also doubled as the Pi-Ski community hall, most of those functions were "community activities", for which the church would receive a nominal fee, insufficient to cover the utility costs. Like catering, there was no income to be found from renting out the hall.

John Moss was a member of the Ladies Guild, an ancient title. Gender had long since become irrelevant to membership, though the Guild's name persisted.

'Vicar!' Catherine called again, this time louder, accompanied by vigorous waving of her arms. Charlotte looked at Catherine and raised a finger in acknowledgement before mouthing, 'one minute.' Tina, who was standing next to her grandmother, rolled her eyes and sighed, 'Gran...!' knowing what was to follow.

'Vicar, I wanted a quick word about this morning's sermon,' Catherine said when Charlotte joined them.

'Of course Catherine, but please do call me Charlotte.'

'Thank you, Vicar.' Catherine paused for a moment before saying, 'Far be it from me to criticise you Vicar... and I'm not, you understand. After all, this is your first Sunday, and, as a friend, I want to say that here at St Mary's, as a rule, sermons do not last more than ten minutes. We wouldn't want to become like one of those...' Before Catherine could finish her sentence, the Vicar said disarmingly.

'You didn't like my sermon?'

This line caught Catherine off guard. She stumbled for a moment with her reply, saying, 'No... no Vicar - not at all. It was very moving.'

'Catherine, Ephesians 4:2 is one of my favourite biblical passages. "With all humility and gentleness, with patience, bearing with one another in love". A worthy message for such a wonderful and friendly church. I'm looking forward to my first parish council meeting on Tuesday night and seeing you there. Thank you for making me so welcome. I can see that you and I are going to be good friends. Now if you will excuse me, I will mingle, it is my function after all. I must work the room, as the politicians like to say. Can I tell you a secret, Catherine?'

Catherine nodded.

'Not really my cup of tea, all this mixing, but we each have our own crosses to bear.' After giving Catherine a big smile and a gentle touch on the arm, the new Vicar dashed away.

Catherine was left standing with Tina, trying to comprehend what had just happened. Not offended exactly, more embraced by the new Vicar. Yet her words of wisdom had been unceremoniously dismissed. Or had they? Now, Catherine wasn't sure. One thing however was certain. Catherine knew that she would have to be alert chairing the forthcoming parish council meeting. She started to laugh, stopping herself before the chuckling slipped from her lips. *The last Vicar tried this*, she mused, *thinking he could overturn decades of tradition. We soon put a stop to that; this one will be no different. As long as I have breath left in my body, normality will return after a couple of months. Always has and always will.*

It was a little before one in the afternoon when the congregational gathering began to disperse. The bun fight, as it's colloquially known, is usually over by midday but, being the first service of the new Vicar, a mix of excitement tinged with polite obligation kept people lingering a little longer.

***

At the shindig, there hadn't been an opportunity for Josephine Carter to ask Edith what she had meant, when she'd said on the church steps, "awful, truly awful". The statement had piqued her curiosity, tinged with concern, knowing that she was the only

18

person Edith had confided in - about the online romance. Josephine desperately wanted to speak privately with her friend.

It was a month previously, with a proposal of marriage on offer, that Edith told Josephine about Paul, the fifty-three-year-old ex-USA military officer, who was her cyber lover, or whatever he was. 'We met in one of those internet chat rooms,' Edith had said. 'I felt so sorry for him because, six years ago, his wife died of cancer. He needed to talk to someone. In the beginning, we were just friends. He told me how much my listening and genuine concern had helped. Quickly, we went from talking once a week to everyday. Neither of us had expected it. Soon, our relationship changed, we began falling in love.' Edith had taken a photograph of Paul from her drawer and shown it to Josephine saying. 'He's handsome, so very handsome, not that looks are important, but they do help,' she giggled. 'What's more, he doesn't mind that I'm a few years older than him. That makes me a cougar, doesn't it? If only there were more men like Paul. I'm such a lucky girl!' Alarm bells were ringing and Josephine had tried to caution Edith without causing a rift in their friendship.

Edith was preparing to leave, waving goodbye to people remaining in the hall, so Josephine strode over to her asking, 'Would you like a coffee, dear?'

Edith let out a deep breath, her shoulders slumped and, for a moment, the comforting mask she was wearing, that all was well with the world, slipped. 'Why don't you come over for dinner?' she whispered. Conscious that others may be watching, she pulled up her defences and smiled.

'That would be lovely. Would you like me to bring anything?'

'Just a dunce's hat.'

'Not good?'

Looking from side to side, checking that no one else was within earshot, Edith said, 'Worse than that. I've been such a fool. I'll tell you about it when you come over, say 6 pm?

'That would be perfect. I'll bring a bottle of wine.'

'Better make it two!'

CHAPTER 2

Internet Bride

Josephine was punctual, arriving at precisely six o'clock at Edith's cottage, a habit born from a lifetime of deadlines, thirty years as a fashion magazine editor. Josephine retired five years previously, aged sixty. Husband Harry, who was one year older, retired at the same time. With their two children having flown the coop and with no grandchildren on the horizon, they planned to travel. Both Josephine and Harry were in excellent health and intended to conquer some of the shorter iconic walking trails of Europe and the UK in preparation for tackling the famous Camino de Santiago (the Way of St James). The Camino is made up of ancient pilgrim routes from across Europe that culminate at the tomb of St James in Santiago de Compostela, northwest Spain. They intended to walk the most popular route, almost five hundred miles (780 km) along the French Way from St Jean-Pied-du-Port in the French Pyrenees to Santiago de Compostela. Josephine and

Harry training for the marathon trek started with the Cinque Terre Coastal Trail, an eleven-kilometre coastal route linking the five picturesque Italian towns of Riomaggiore, Manarola, Corniglia, Vernazza and Monterosso. An easy walk that could have been done in six or seven hours, took them two days. They enjoyed lingering moments in each town, marvelling at the views of the Mediterranean and the whitewashed housing glistening in the sun like diamonds. Besides, the food and wine justified their pace. From Cinque Terre they travelled to Florence, the capital of the Tuscany region, for a three-day stopover to visit the ancient city and wonder at its many masterpieces of Renaissance art and architecture before heading to the medieval hill town of Montepulciano, the start of an eight-day walking tour across the undulating Tuscany Hills. The trek was organised, luggage transported between overnight stays, meaning that they could walk with day-packs alone. Harry told Josephine that this, having your luggage transported, was a must for a modern-day walker, something they would repeat for the Camino.

It was on their second day in Florence, Josephine later told the police, that she first sensed that they were being followed, although she failed to comprehend why anyone would want to pursue them.

'My sweet, don't turn around, and I know I may sound paranoid,' Josephine whispered to her husband. 'There is a lady two tables back behind you. She has been following us all day.'

Harry, resisting the instinct to glance over his shoulder, instead smiling said calmly, 'What makes you say that?'

'I saw her yesterday and then again this morning, and now she's seated a little way behind us. My curiosity was sparked this morning. Now I'm concerned.'

'My honey, how can you be sure that it's the same woman?'

'She's wearing a Dolce & Gabbana dress; I notice these things. Not the same one as yesterday, mind you. It isn't only the Dolce & Gabbana dresses, she's also carrying a Louis Vuitton handbag, the same one as yesterday, of that I'm certain.'

'There you go. If she were following us, and why would she be, aren't you meant to blend in? Wearing designer clothes would make her conspicuous; a coincidence, that's all it is, my love.'

'We are in Italy, my dear, Florence no less. Designer clothes are everywhere, exactly what you would wear to blend in. You probably wouldn't notice her, but after thirty years as a fashion editor, she caught my attention. Harry, it's not just the Dolce & Gabbana, it's her poise, hair and hands. Don't forget the handbag, definitely the same woman, unquestionably.'

'What would you like to do? Call the police, or do you want me to talk to her?' Harry asked, hoping his wife's answer was going to be leave it be, but knowing it may be otherwise.

'We can't go to the police,' Josephine answered. 'They'll think that me spotting the petite Louis Vuitton is a poor basis for suspicion. Besides, she hasn't done anything yet.'

Harry considered for a moment before suggesting, 'Let's both stare at her at the same time, to make it clear that we've seen her. And then if she is following us, well, she'll know that we know...' Josephine's mind was elsewhere, vaguely hearing Harry talk, so her response surprised him. 'Why would anyone want to follow us?'

'I've read about this type of thing. There are well-organised crime gangs that prey on tourists,' Harry said. 'She might be working in consort with them and, at some point, will act as the decoy while a pickpocket relieves us of our valuables. What we should be doing is looking for her accomplices. Have you noticed anyone else?'

'If that's the case my sweet, she wants to be noticed. If we were to peer at her, as you suggest, we might be playing into their trap. Could we try to lose her?'

'We could, but if, as you say, she has been following us since yesterday, they already know where we are staying. Let's keep a tight grip on our wallet and purse and head back to our hotel. We can secure our credit cards, money and passports once we're in familiar territory. Hang onto everything and no matter what, even if someone thrusts a baby into your arms, don't respond. Whatever happens, don't let go of your purse.'

What surprised her, or so Josephine told the police later, was that when they got back to the hotel, Harry went straight to the reception desk, telling them they had decided to book out a day early.

'Are we leaving?' Josephine asked.

'I didn't say so at the café in case whoever was following us was listening. I don't want anything spoiling our holiday. It's easier to change our routine, leave early and fool our pursuers. An extra day in Montepulciano will be delightful. No pickpocket gang is going to follow us there.'

They caught the train from Florence to Chiusi and then a local bus to Montepulciano, arriving a day before the walking tour was due to begin. After twenty-four hours spent enjoying their own company, the trek started at the San Biagio church and followed the path to Monticchiello before continuing on to Pienza. Distracted by the scenic countryside and the company of the other members of the tour group, the memory of being followed faded. Tragedy struck on day six of the trek. It was an early start, so the walkers could visit the Benedictine monastery at Monte Oliveto Maggiore, before crowds of tourists arrived.

When a person dies under suspicious circumstances, the spouse is the prime suspect. Despite portrayals on TV or in books, random killings by assailants unknown to the deceased are rare.

As Josephine later told the investigators, now retired, she and her husband both had mundane well-paid jobs. Harry, as a public servant in the London foreign office, she a fashion editor. Yes, she conceded to the police; Harry stayed in London most weeks and she didn't always know what he was doing. She explained that when the children left home, the last one leaving six years before their retirement, she tended to stay with Harry during the week at their London flat, returning together to Pi-Ski at weekends. Josephine knew the police were intent on finding a motive, for they wanted her to admit to killing Harry. 'A secret life would have been difficult to conceal from me,' she told the lead investigator, knowing they were asking if Harry could have had an affair.

'Indeed, and you travelled a lot,' the inquisitor said, a statement of fact rather than a question.

'Of course, I was the fashion editor for an international magazine and often abroad. It was the nature of the job. Are you asking if I was having an affair? The answer is NO! Harry and I were happily married, extremely content.'

Josephine struggled to comprehend how the police reached their conclusion that Harry was pushed from the monastery at Monte Oliveto Maggiore and didn't accidentally fall to his death. Either it was a targeted killing or she was the prime suspect. Despite her apprehensions, Josephine couldn't fault the rigorous manner of the investigation. Scotland Yard had sent detectives to Italy to assist with the inquiry. Josephine was asked if she'd noticed anything suspicious in the lead up to Harry's death and the police had gone to considerable lengths to find CCTV footage, in the hope Josephine could identify the mystery woman in the designer clothes. No CCTV recording was found.

The murder investigation ceased abruptly when the investigators were unable to determine a motive or suspects for the crime. The coronial inquest recorded that there was nothing suspicious with the couple's finances, no secret bank accounts or unusual transactions, no life insurance policy worth millions of pounds, mobile phone records were benign, no reports of domestic violence, no known connections with the underworld, no disputes with family, friends, or at work, and nothing in either of their work histories that would suggest that either Harry or Josephine would be a target. The police were convinced that Harry had been murdered, possibly a case of mistaken identity. The coronial inquest found that Harry's death was not an accident, but that he was pushed to his death by a person or persons unknown.

***

Edith knew the doorbell would ring exactly as the clock struck six. Josephine was nothing if not a punctual woman; so exact that Edith wondered if Josephine paced outside waiting for the precise second to allow her to arrive on time. As the chime made its own idiosyncratic "Ding Dong", Edith shouted, 'Come in

Josephine, I'm in here.' Armed with two bottles of wine, Josephine appeared at the dining-room door. Edith stood and greeted her friend before they settled into the comfortable chairs near the dining table.

Fifty-eight-year-old Edith lived alone in a semi-detached cottage, a gentle stroll away from the church. Everything in Pi-Ski was a short walk from the church. She had been a single woman for the last four years after her husband Felix, of twenty years, traded her in for a younger model, his thirty-something secretary and then, with his new lover and child, had moved to Ireland. Why a fifty-two-year-old would want a baby was beyond her, although, if Felix's secretary hadn't fallen pregnant, she may never have learned about the affair.

For the first few years, the bitter taste of his infidelity tarnished all men, yet, with the passing of time, the pain diminished. With the days long and nights cold, she found herself relishing the idea of a relationship. It was on one of those dark, lonely, cold evenings, having explored many internet dating sites, she stumbled upon an internet romance chat room, vulnerable and ripe for the plucking, not that she knew it.

Romance scams prey on those with a broken heart, emotionally isolated, lonely following the death of a partner or divorce, or people in unsatisfactory marriages, and those who have never married. Traditionally, these tricks were found in the back pages of magazines and newspapers, but the digital time is proving to be a golden age for those selecting, and then grooming their victims. The internet has also heralded the arrival of a plethora of professional, arguably legitimate, dating romance sites and forums. Many people indeed have found their true love on the net, swiping left or right during their search. However, with millions around the world looking for that special person, the internet has created an ocean of opportunity for criminals, an opportunity they have become expert in exploiting.

The romance scam starts with the criminal creating a fake profile, the personal details of someone seeking a romantic attachment. For Edith, this was Paul Roman, a fifty-three-year-old ex-USA military officer whose wife had died of cancer. The first indicator that flagged her for manipulation in the scam was when Edith shared on a dating forum the story of her divorce and how, with the passage of time, anger had become loneliness. The deception started when the fake "Paul Roman" shared his bogus story in the chat room Edith was using, of the emptiness he felt after his wife of twenty-eight years had passed away. He wrote, 'I hope that, out there somewhere, is a woman with whom I can share the remainder of my life.' The trap was set.

***

Taking a gulp of wine, rather than a delicate sip, steadying her nerves before telling the story, Edith said, 'I didn't think I was naïve in the way of romance scams; I'd read articles about how they operate in the newspapers. I just chose not to see, blinded by his story. That's how they deceive you. I was convinced Paul Roman was legitimate.'

Josephine fought back the urge to say, *I did try to warn you.*

'I thought I knew what to look out for - really I did! I knew I had to be wary of unsolicited contact by someone who professes their undying love and affection, especially if it happens quickly. At the time, I didn't suspect that Paul, or whoever he really is, was a fraudster.' Edith took another large gulp of wine.

'You see Josephine, it was actually me who initiated the contact, not him. After reading his post about his wife dying of cancer, well, I commented on it. The truth is always clearer in hindsight. When I think about it now, he had responded to a post I made about being divorced, nothing substantial, it was only a couple of words, and with nothing inviting me to reply. Subtly drawing me in. He was just one of many, lost in the crowd. When he wrote about his wife, and I know this will sound bizarre, I felt like we'd already met. I gave him the same sympathy he had shown me, writing a few words. When he didn't respond to my comment, I feared he might think of me as a scammer. It was a week later before he thanked me for my thoughts. I still remember how excited I felt when he replied, and then, lying awake that night contemplating whether I should respond. I wanted to, mind you, but was nervous. If I wrote back too soon, would he be frightened away? With what happened, of course, it's clear that I was being baited and I swallowed it, hook line and sinker.' Edith went silent. After thirty seconds that seemed much longer, Josephine asked,

'What happened next?'

'Are you sure you want to know?'

'Only if you want to tell me. It isn't like me to pry, although I am both concerned and interested; not nosy. Please Edith, share only with me what you want me to know.'

'Oh Josephine, it's so embarrassing, being the victim of a scam, especially a bleeding heart one. You feel... pathetic and stupid.'

Josephine didn't respond. In the silence Edith's words hung in the air until she sighed, a deep audible breath, before continuing. 'I wrote back to him, saying something like–"it's a difficult journey when someone you have loved is no longer there." His response came as an inspiration to me in the struggle to move on from Felix. I've read it so often that I can recite it to you. *"Thank you so much for your condolence! Life is full of miseries and ironies; the most important thing is our willingness to stand up to our challenges and wanting to move on with life once again. As it is said, winners never quit, and quitters never win; I know we are winners"*. That really was the start of the online romance and, a short time later, he asked

32

if we could correspond by email, rather than in a public chat room. It was a relief for me and we started to write to each other each day. After a week, he asked if I had a profile, you know, like you post on one of those dating sites.'

Josephine wondered if she should admit to once having joined an internet dating site and written a profile. She thought to herself, perhaps I will, when the time is right... it wasn't now. Josephine asked, 'A profile? Did you send one?'

'I did, but without attaching a photograph of myself; I wasn't being cautious, I just didn't think anyone would find me physically attractive. Promise me you won't laugh when I tell you what he said?' Josephine nodded.

Edith sighed. 'I read it again this morning before church. It sounds so corny now, obviously a con. At the time it seemed... well, beautiful. I'm making excuses, aren't I? For my stupidity?'

Josephine smiled. 'How about I top up your glass?' Without waiting for an answer, she picked up the bottle, filling Edith's near-empty glass, before doing the same to her own, then raising it she said, 'Be brave.' They both took a sip. Edith continued her story.

'He said...' Edith paused before saying. 'Oh heck, what does it matter. He told me, "*Honestly, you have a very lovely profile and I wish I could just see your picture. There is this feeling that tells me you are as beautiful as your profile. Though what matters is the internal beauty, which I can see already. But nevertheless, I would still like to see your picture.*" He attached a picture of himself to the email. He was to die for, drop dead gorgeous. I almost ran a mile at his response, because I feared rejection were I to send a photograph of myself. Now of course, I wish I had jogged a marathon to be away from him. At the time, I remember thinking, look at me, he's so amazing, there is no way a good-looking man like that, is going to find me attractive, let alone sexy. I waited a couple of days, unsure what to do, but in the end, I sent a picture. When I rose the next morning, he'd replied with. *"I received your photograph and I am glad you sent it. Your picture means a lot to me."* What he said next, should have been a huge red flag, somehow it wasn't. *"It shows how real and ready you are."* Rather than seeing the con, my heart fluttered; he wasn't rejecting me because of my picture.' Edith went quiet for a moment. Then she said forlornly, 'Someone found me attractive, or so I thought. It was mesmerising.'

'I'm so pleased it isn't just me,' confessed Josephine. 'When I was with Harry, I felt beautiful, an attractive woman. After his death, maybe because of my age, I doubted that anyone else would see me that way; it changed the way I saw myself. Between you and me, I once signed up to one of those dating sites but couldn't go through with it. It's strange, when you know someone, you don't see their age. On those dating sites, when you look at photos of the over 60s, men and women, they look old. You then understand, that's how you must seem to others. I couldn't put my photo on the site. Besides, most men over sixty were after women in their forties.' Realising what she'd said, Edith's husband, having left her for a younger woman, Josephine apologised. 'I'm so sorry.'

'There's no need to apologise. That was all a long time ago now.'

Josephine smiled, saying, 'Sorry Edith, I've interrupted your story with my own musings.'

'That's alright Josephine. I've told you some of this tale before, when I thought Paul was the real deal. He seemed such a romantic, and at the time, I understood why he had such a wonderful and loving relationship with his wife, and how devastating it was for him when she died.' Edith fetched her laptop, which was resting on a small table next to her seat. 'This is one of the emails he wrote to me about Mary, his wife.'

"I lived happily with Mary for twenty-eight years, a wonderful angel; a wife any man would pray for. It is so sad to say that she is no more. When I lost her to cancer my life suddenly turned my table of great joy into a terrible agony. Such is life. Sometimes we pass through situations we do not have control of, and we only do nothing but bear whatever it is. I want a woman who would be my best friend and everything. You know someone whom we would still love each other more as

35

the days pass by, even when we can't make love anymore and all we could do is play bingo."

'Now when I read this aloud, I see that it's obviously a trap. Don't you think?'

Josephine was wary of answering and instead asked a question. 'Which came first, the email about Mary or the one seeking your profile and picture?'

'Sorry, I'm jumping all over the place. It was the one about Mary, which led me to tell him about Felix and to add that his suggestion of bingo sounded wonderful, hoping that he wouldn't run a mile. After that, he asked for my picture and profile. As silly as this may sound, it all happened really quickly. I was annoyed when he didn't write back almost immediately. We had so much in common, or so it appeared. He told me he was a spiritual man, attending church each Sunday and that he lived in a small country town, and from how he described it, it was similar to here.'

'What about the distance between you?' asked Josephine. 'Wasn't that a barrier?'

'I thought that as well; I raised it with him. Let me see if I can find his reply.' Edith scrolled through her old emails. A minute later she said. 'Here it is. Let me read it to you.'

"My dearest Edith, I understand your concern, part of me feels the same way. I believe however it's too early

to discuss distance because wherever I find my true love, is where I would live for the rest of my life. If you find a wicked love close to you and a true love far away, I bet you would wait for the true love to come rather than go for the close wicked love that will end up hurting your feelings. True love knows no bounds nor distance nor limits. It doesn't need a map either because it will always find a way. There is something in me that wants to continue with you and for your information this was my first time in a romance chat room. We should get to know each other and see where life leads us. I am mature enough, and with the passing of Mary, I know what I want with the remainder of my life. I mean, I am looking for a relationship that would be my last till my dying days."'

Edith looked up from her computer screen. 'How could I have fallen for them? They are so over the top, aren't they?'

'Maybe,' Josephine said, knowing that Edith would keep repeating the statement, experiencing guilt from being conned. 'Though I don't think so. I might have... anyone could have fallen for them, really.'

'Thank you, Josephine, you're being kind. Are you ready for dinner?'

'I'm looking forward to it. Do you need any help?'

'No. Why not take a seat at the dining table? I'll be back shortly.'

Josephine moved from her comfortable chair to the table while Edith went to the kitchen. Waiting for Edith to return, Josephine wondered if the conversation about Paul had ended, or whether there was more to come. Hidden from view, Edith was carving roast lamb onto their plates in the kitchen and contemplating whether to tell Josephine that she had been fleeced of money by the scam, quite a substantial sum.

With the meal served, and the wine helping conversation flow, the dinner table talk moved on from the romance scam to the problems of St Mary's church. The two ladies lamented that, with its ageing and declining congregation, the church was dying. 'Do you know what we should do?' Edith suggested, only half serious. 'Start our own dating website. The St Mary's Dating Agency, although we might need a better name. A legitimate site, moderated, not one that scams you of forty-five thousand pounds, as Paul did to me.' This was the first Josephine had heard of the money, however it wasn't the time she thought to ask questions. Instead she let Edith keep talking.

'We could marry off the singles in our congregation. That would give our numbers a boost. We should start with John Moss, he's thirty-five and single.' Josephine laughed warmly at the suggestion, thinking the idea a bit of fun, not a serious proposition.

'Go on Edith,' Josephine said, still laughing. 'What would we write about John?'

'Oh, I don't know. Maybe something like... *Are you looking for a handsome, lovable, thirty-something male, with witty, schoolboy charm? If you don't mind the occasional odd socks, crooked tie and beige cardigan, and if beautiful weekends skiing the Alps, sailing the seven seas, or fine dining, are not your thing, then here I am. The kind of fellow you'd be embarrassed to take home to your family, where if I was only a rocket scientist, perhaps you could explain away my awkwardness. The beige man; the gentle teddy bear; a faithful Lassie dog.*'

'He is lovely, isn't he?' Josephine said. 'I do sometimes feel just a little sorry for him.'

'Me too. Do you know what he needs?'

'What?'

'A good rogering!'

'You are awful,' giggled Josephine. 'Do you think he is... you know.'

'Gay?' Edith suggested.

'No. He is nice enough to be gay, but I meant - a virgin!'

Edith considered the question, wondering if Josephine was being serious, before saying, 'A thirty-something bloke–I wouldn't think so. It would be sad if he was.' After a brief pause, she announced triumphantly, 'The St Mary's Dating Agency to the rescue.' The two ladies raised their wine glasses and toasted the revelation. A flippant idea was taking form.

'More wine?' Josephine asked, and they filled their glasses.

'Go on, it's your turn,' Edith said. 'What would Catherine's dating profile look like?'

'This is really naughty,' Josephine said as she pondered before saying, 'How about... *I don't like most men, but then again, I'm not interested in an ordinary man. I live for those moments you can't put into words, an affectionate, passionate and mature woman. If you are the one, I will bite and if delicious – yum... Come into my parlour, if you dare. Signed, The Black Widow.*'

'The Black Widow spider! Now, doesn't the female eat its partner after mating?' Edith questioned.

'That's the one with unusually large venom glands and a bite that is deadly. Our gorgeous Catherine to a T - bless her little cotton socks.'

'Do you think she's always been... dominant?' Edith asked.

'I've known her since primary school,' Josephine answered. 'She was always - how would you say - a little snobby, even though she was no better off than any of us. Her parents worked for the local council; I think her father was an accountant there. Even back then, she portrayed an air of superiority, mostly because she was very attractive, and she knew it. At secondary school, the boys would swoon all over her. She treated them badly, playing them off against each other, which only seemed to encourage them more. Catherine exploited her good looks, but I don't think she... you know... put out, to get what she wanted. Unusual girl, she had sexual power without having to have sex, used her allure to dominate. It was when she married Charles that she morphed into what we see now. You know, he was fifteen years older than her, a surgeon from London. You'd call him her "sugar daddy" nowadays, although I doubt he received his conjugal rights in return. That's probably a very wicked thing to say, isn't it? But can you imagine her performing? Of course, they did because they had two children. I wonder if that was their only time?'

'You can't always tell,' Edith commented. 'You know what they say about the quiet ones.'

'Oh, quiet ones I can understand, but she's not quiet, she's...!'

'A bitch?' Edith intimated.

'Sometimes. A lovable bitch in her own way, difficult not to like. I just wish she wasn't always so sure of herself, or do I mean, full of herself? Self-righteous, even.'

'You can't guess what she was really like, she may be an enigma, especially in the bedroom. A real animal, maybe.' Edith spoke in a deep husky voice. 'Charles come here... Now!' Then, gesturing with her arms, stood up and mimed reaching out and grabbing Charles aggressively, giving the imaginary figure, three quick pelvic thrusts. 'Finished,' she exclaimed, before throwing the imaginary Charles away, collapsing back in her seat.

Laughing, Josephine said, 'Perhaps she's a Dominatrix? On our new dating site, her profile photo could be a woman dressed in black, holding a whip... with a title reading: The Black Widow!'

Edith raised her hand to her chin, imitating a woman in deep thought. 'Black lace or leather?' she asked.

'Goodness gracious,' Josephine joked. 'At our age, I think black lace is a scary thought. Leather may hide some of her unsightly parts.'

'Hold in the belly rolls!' replied Edith laughing.

'That too. I was thinking of our saggy breasts.'

The two ladies went silent and finished their dinner, then adjourned, returning to the comfortable chairs. 'Another glass of wine?' Edith proffered.

'Just one more, that would be nice, thank you.' Josephine had pigeon-holed Edith's passing comment of being fleeced forty-five thousand pounds, waiting for the right moment to raise it. Now seemed the right time, so she struck. 'Paul took you for a lot of money,' she said cautiously.

42

Edith sighed. Picking up her laptop, she said in a sad voice, 'He did. There were enough warning signs I was going to be ripped off, but I missed them, or ignored them.'

'We had been writing about the tyranny of distance and romance. This is something else that he wrote:

> *"I believe we both know that Love is not a destination but a journey and this is a journey that takes two to walk."*

'He then asked about my thoughts of true love and life. If you don't mind, I will keep my reply private. There's only so much embarrassment a girl can take, however it's safe to say, his response to my email introduced the prospect of marriage. He signed off his email with, "Your Husband, Paul".

'It hadn't been my suggestion, but I wasn't unhappy that he raised the prospect of marriage.'

Josephine smiled at Edith's comment but remained mute.

'Let me read it to you:'

> *"My love, you have sent me the best message I have ever received in my whole life. How wonderful it is to know our love is reciprocal. You see honey, we will be spending the rest of our lives together in great joy and fulfillment of heart. Will you write more later today? Your Husband, Paul."*

Without thinking, Josephine blurted out, 'They don't muck around do they? More front than Harrods.'

Edith looked at Josephine in a contemplative way, not offended, as she said, 'I now imagine that he had multiple romance scams operating. I was just one of many. My guess was that this was his way of filtering out those who wouldn't fall victim. I suppose it's easy to be bold and brave when he's a con artist, with nothing to lose and no emotional attachment. When I replied, he knew I was hooked because his next message started with the words, "*Oh, my wife!*"

'Over the next few weeks our conversations became, well... intimate. Not that I sent him any compromising pictures, or anything like that, but our messaging was at times... sexy, of a sexual nature.' Edith raised her eyes from the computer screen and looked at Josephine to see her response. Josephine remained expressionless, saying only,

'We might all have done that.'

Returning her concentration to the computer screen, Edith scrolled through her emails saying, 'I'm looking for when he first began springing the trap, asking for money, weaving his web of emotional blackmail. Here it is. I'll read it to you.'

"Please keep my secret to you and you alone because I will never discuss my business with anyone except for

you my love. This is how much I have given my life over to you. I believe that a husband and wife should not keep secrets from each other if truly they are in love. So, I will never keep anything from you my love, I want us to know each other in and out. For you to know me more than I know myself and for me to know you more than you know yourself. Without saying any word, just a sign on the face or body should be able to tell me, or you, what we mean. I want us to be inseparable twins (lol)".

'You can probably guess Josephine, that he told me nothing of his secret, his lie. Instead, stupidly, I asked. I'm so angry with myself.' Edith took a deep breath and shrugged, disappointed at her own gullibility. 'I won't read it word for word, but the gist of it, the emotional entrapment, went something like this. He said things were tougher in America than the UK, which has a National Health Service (NHS), giving free health care if you were sick. His supposed secret was that he sold everything to pay for his wife's cancer treatment, but that it had been a losing battle. Oh, now I do have to read you this bit, it's enough to make you want to vomit... After telling me he had sold and spent everything trying to save his wife, he wrote,'

"Money can buy a good bed, but never will money buy sleep; it can buy the best diamond watch, but can never buy time; it can buy a pile of books, but can't buy

45

knowledge, it can buy food, but not satisfaction. Money can buy sex but can never buy love."

'At the time Josephine, I really did think of him as a remarkable man. Even when he had supposedly lost everything in the fight to save his wife, he told me that he would do it again in a heartbeat if the opportunity arose. He was preparing my subconscious so that, if I didn't give him money when he asked for it, then I wasn't capable of unconditional love. Unlike him, I was being selfish, undeserving of true love. I know because that's how I felt when I refused his request, as I did at first. He covered me in praise when I finally handed over some money and I felt good about myself. Can you stomach me reading another of his sickly messages?'

'If you don't mind sharing it with me'

'I'm so angry, but I need it off my chest. Thank you for being a good friend and listening to me. I'll read you one last one, then I won't bore you with any more.'

'Edith, you're not boring me, I promise.' Churning over in Josephine's mind, was Edith's idea of creating a dating agency, to bring new people into the church. Josephine mused whether Edith's experience might help them to target candidates for the website. Perhaps the format of the emails would provide a script to be adapted. Josephine was keen to understand what Paul could have written that would encourage an otherwise rational and intelligent woman to send, then keep sending, money. St Mary's Church, she considered, could use a technique like this, but for good, not evil.

'I've been looking for this one. Here it is. Paul wrote this before he asked me for more money.' Hearing Edith's voice, Josephine's thoughts returned to her friend.

> *"I want you to know that everything you do for me reassures me that I am appreciated. I want you to know that you mean so much to me. From the first day we found each other, we were determined to get to know one another. From that very moment, I knew it was you and we quickly grew on getting to know each other. I want you to know that every moment since that first day holds a special place in my heart. I was afraid at first that if I let you in, I'd regret it, but I haven't regretted a single moment. I trust you, and I know you'll be there for me no matter what. I trust that you'll be faithful to me and that you won't hurt my heart."*

'It's only when you read those sentences, in the knowledge it's part of a money-making scam, you can see how emotionally manipulative his words are. I went to the airport in absolute faith, expecting him to arrive. It wasn't until he didn't show that the truth hit me like a thunderbolt. I stood there at the arrivals lounge feeling utterly ashamed of my stupidity. I felt so wretched. I'm sorry Josephine; I keep saying that.'

'That's alright, say it as often as you need to.' There was a pause in the conversation while they each took a sip of wine. Josephine wondered if she should ask the question that was on her mind.

'I hope you don't mind me asking, but weren't you–I'm sorry for being so direct - I mean, weren't you ever just a little suspicious? That he was after your money, and not your wonderful body! Sorry, I'm being flippant.'

'Since his cut and run, I've spent time researching the internet for romance scams. I've been luckier than many. At least I can afford to lose forty-five thousand pounds, whereas some people lost their entire life savings, while others have been tricked into becoming drug mules, then caught and imprisoned. I'm able to laugh at my stupidity; that's a good thing and has taught me a lesson.' Edith sighed, then wanting to lighten the conversation, said with a touch of sarcasm, 'Anyway, I thought Paul loved me for my brilliant mind. Until you raised it, I hadn't considered it might have been my fifty-eight-year-old sexy body. Maybe I should have sent him some erotica, my bare breasts with a caption reading, "Swing low sweet Chariot". The shock of seeing them hanging around my navel would surely have given him a heart attack. Then one more bastard would have been banished from the world, and I would have saved forty-five thousand pounds. Maybe the moral of the story is, get your gear off early.'

Josephine thought for a moment before replying. 'There's your problem!'

With confusion written across her face, 'What?' Edith asked.

'A picture of breasts is no longer considered pornography, let alone erotica.'

Edith asked without thinking, 'What is erotica then?'

'It implies showing or describing sexual activity, stimulating sexual arousal. When you sent each other - how did you describe it... intimate, sexy messages, they were probably erotic.'

Smiling, Edith said, 'You seem well-informed in the ways of erotica.'

'Have you forgotten I was in the fashion industry for thirty years? Many of the pictures we used in our magazines implied erotica, but they weren't explicit, so both men and women could enjoy them.' Josephine paused before continuing, 'I have an idea. At the last parish council meeting, we agreed to go away and return with suggestions of how we could raise the thirty thousand pounds still needed to repair the church roof. I've just come up with a sensational one. The parish council could model for one of those nude calendars. Each one of us, month-by-month could bare all, to raise money. A few community groups have done it, even elders like us, exploiting the notoriety of nude seniors for publicity and sales. A church group, a parish council, raising money for the church spire could be unique. I think even the BBC might put that on its news. Charlotte, our new Vicar, could be the June centrefold.'

Edith laughed, 'I think that sounds like a wonderful idea,' though she didn't really think so. Playing along, Edith said, 'There are, however, just a few problems I can foresee.'

'What?'

'First, we don't have a church spire, and second, there's only four of us on the parish council, with the Vicar, five. We are a few months short. Other than that, I'm right behind you... about twenty feet! Thirty, if you've got your clothes off.'

'Fair point. Maybe the Vicar could do a double page spread. I'll suggest it at Tuesday night's parish council meeting, shall I? It shouldn't be too difficult to find a church with a nice sleek, phallic spire, perfect as a backdrop for our photos, reaching to the heavens. Maybe we could ask the Bishop to be December's image? He could be photographed holding a lamb from the nativity scene in front of his holy parts.' Laughing, Josephine continued, 'That would make us five people short of a year and, if they reject my most brilliant fundraising idea, I will suggest yours: "The St Mary's Dating Agency". I promise, not a word about your experience. It will be our secret and you will be our silent expert.'

Mortified that Josephine may have been serious, Edith said, 'You are joking, aren't you?'

'Absolutely not. I'm deadly serious. If fresh blood and money are not injected into this parish, there will be no church. What did they say in that movie, the Blues Brothers wasn't it? The St Mary's Anglican Church is "on a mission from God".'

Edith sighed in disbelief, 'I'm not sure Josephine!'

'It will be fine, Edith. Do you think the Vicar knows the truth, that within a few months, we won't be able to afford her salary and the church is falling down?'

Edith thought for a moment. 'We didn't tell her during the selection process. Unless one of the other panel members has spilled the beans, I imagine the treasurer's report on Tuesday night will be a shock to our dear Vicar.'

'Oh, yes and that will provide us with the perfect opportunity to issue an ultimatum - a choice would be a softer word. Vicar, you can either get your gear off, find a husband, or starve. And by-the-way, welcome to Pi-Ski... What's your preferred poison?'

Edith shook her head, sceptical. 'Do you think the Vicar should be the first client of the St Mary's Dating Agency?'

'Oh no, not at all. John must be the first. Let's use that parish council gender imbalance to our advantage; four against one when it comes to the vote.'

'What happens if he's not interested in joining the St Mary's Dating Agency?'

'I'm sure he will. Besides, we're on a mission from God to save the church. He must play his part and that's exactly what we will tell John. A little emotional blackmail, just like your emails from Paul. You see, there's always a silver lining - we can learn from your misadventure.'

CHAPTER 3

Parish Council

Tuesday, the evening of the parish council meeting, was soon upon them. The members, Catherine Hepburn, Josephine Carter, Edith Kelly and John Moss were seated around a table in the church hall where they met, as was the new Vicar, Charlotte Foster. They were talking amongst themselves, chitchat, waiting for the meeting to begin.

'Welcome everybody,' said the meeting Chair, Catherine Hepburn, hitting the table three times in quick succession with the small wooden gavel that she wielded like Thor's Hammer, bringing the group to order. 'I declare the meeting of St Mary's Parish Council open. We have no apologies. The first order of business is to formally welcome our new Vicar, Charlotte Foster.'

Catherine looked directly at Charlotte. 'Welcome to Pi-Ski and to St Mary's, Vicar.'

The other members followed Catherine's lead. 'Welcome Vicar!'

For a fifty-two-year-old, Vicar Charlotte Foster was an athletic looking woman. She enjoyed bike riding and had tried her hand at triathlons, although, after hurting her knees and back during her last event, she'd decided that there were more sensible ways to stay in shape.

The Vicar was a late starter to the Lycra Brigade, an unflattering term describing middle-aged pseudo-athletes, dressed in colourful tight-fitting outfits, peddling their bikes in a disordered peloton along narrow country lanes, oblivious to other road users. Charlotte turned to physical exercise after her separation and subsequent divorce, finding long bike rides with a group of people with nothing else in common other than a sweaty crutch and the joy of a carbon fibre bar throbbing between their legs very cathartic. A late convert, but now a true believer, like her faith.

'Thank you for making me welcome,' Charlotte said.

'I only started on Sunday so haven't had time to prepare a Vicar's report for tonight's meeting but there is an item I would like to bring to your attention. When I was in the church yesterday, the rain was dripping from the ceiling onto the altar.'

'Ah,' John said, 'That would be the roof. It's been leaking for the last three years, slowly at first, but it's now in need of urgent repair. The recent builder's report said that if restoration work wasn't carried out soon, we will lose the roof; unfortunately, we don't have the funds.'

Charlotte looked at John with an inquisitive stare, wondering why she hadn't been informed of this before accepting the post at St Mary's.

Catherine smiled nervously, 'Vicar, we have a committee that's been working on the problem. However, the restoration fund is a little short.'

'This would only be a guess, mind you,' Vicar Charlotte said. 'Would you,' peering around the table, 'be the fund-raising committee?' They all nodded. 'I see and what does "a little short" look like?'

'That's an item in the treasurer's report,' John said, glancing at Catherine, seeking her permission to continue the matter elsewhere in the agenda.

A stickler for order, Catherine thought for a moment. 'As this is your first meeting, Vicar, on this occasion we will skip the next two items on the agenda and move to the treasurer's report. This surprised John, as it did Edith and Josephine, who looked at each other with raised eyebrows.

'However,' Catherine continued, 'I would not wish for this to become a habit!'

'Ah, right,' John said. 'In that case... to answer your question Vicar, um... we are still... thirty thousand pounds short. Thirty-two to be exact.'

'That sounds rather daunting,' Vicar Charlotte replied. 'How much have you raised so far?'

The parish council members glanced at each other before Josephine spoke on their behalf. 'Well, Vicar, we had a very successful jam, cream and scone morning, didn't we?' The other council members all nodded vigorously.

'Very successful,' Edith added.

Raising her hand to her chin as a sign of frustration, Vicar Charlotte asked, 'Did anyone, other than the parish council members, attend the jam, cream and scone morning?'

'I think so,' Edith said, looking at Catherine. 'Didn't your granddaughter, Tina, also come?'

'That's right, she did,' said the parish council members in unison.

'In the - three years was it - that you have been raising money, how much have you actually made?'

'Ah,' John said, 'I checked that this morning, just in case you asked. A rather splendid five hundred pounds.'

Vicar Charlotte resisted the urge to shake her head in disbelief, and said instead, 'Couldn't you take it from the parish reserves?'

The members looked at each other nervously, their eyes settling on the Parish Council Chair, Catherine, who gave a nervous cough. 'Vicar, unless you want to forgo your salary, without a miracle, or we discover new ways of raising funds, in five months the parish will be broke. Penniless.'

Hiding her rising disquiet and anger, Vicar Charlotte said calmly, 'You didn't think the financial position of the parish was something that should have been disclosed before I left London?'

'Of course, Vicar,' fibbed Catherine, as if affronted. 'It's the Bishop's...'

'You needn't worry, Vicar,' Josephine interrupted. 'At our last meeting, we agreed to go away and come back tonight with new ideas. Nothing was to be out of bounds - innovative ways of making money to save St Mary's. Did anyone bring a plan?' While mumbling to themselves, the parish council members, including Edith, diverted their gaze and looked at the table. 'I will take that as a no,' Josephine continued.

She wouldn't dare, Edith thought.

'Edith and I have a brilliant idea. Don't we Edith?'

Edith opened her mouth and closed it again without saying a word. Josephine launched into her proposal for a Naked Charity Calendar. She spoke of various local community groups, 'Some,' she said, 'feature older ladies who have taken their clothes off, to raise funds for good causes.'

Surprisingly, the Vicar hadn't flinched during Josephine's dissertation. Vicar Charlotte didn't consider herself a prude. She had seen charity calendars and knew that they were tastefully produced, not pornographic. When Josephine had finished speaking, Vicar Charlotte said,

'To make decent money, we will need to market and distribute the calendar; it helps if someone famous appears in the photographs. I can see this being an obstacle to your plan.'

'Not at all,' Josephine said, grinning, 'I spent thirty-years in the magazine game and I'm sure some of my old contacts would assist, help us become infamous, if not famous.'

John, thinking as a man he was safe from stripping naked, played along, even though he considered it an outrageous plan. "Nutty" was the word going around in his head. While keeping a straight face he asked. 'How much would the church earn?' When Josephine proposed a sum of five or six thousand pounds to be an excellent result, Catherine, who under no circumstances had any intention of taking her pantaloons off and revealing her nether regions, protested.

'I would naturally support innovative ways to save the church, and I wouldn't want the council to think of me as stuffy, but it's not five, or thirty-two thousand pounds we need, it's bums on our pews. Even if we stop the roof from collapsing, the congregation is declining....'

Edith, seated next to John, gave him a gentle elbow in the ribs as Catherine was speaking. When he looked at her, she leaned in and whispered. 'We might get a bit more than five thousand if we had a picture of the Vicar on her bike. She's perky for a fifty-two-year-old.' John looked at Edith naively, wondering why a picture of a "cheerful Vicar", naked on a cycle would help with sales.

Working herself into a frenzy, unsettling the others round the table, Catherine continued her rant. 'Unless you're suggesting we do a version of the Naked News; calling our Sunday services something like *The Nude Communion*, or *Songs of the Great Undressed*, in a vain hope that people may pay to see our freak show. Going stark naked is not what I would call a good return on investment. I'd want much more than five-thousand pounds before I'd be seen in my birthday suit. We need more people, not fewer clothes. St Mary's is a church, not some cheap strip joint.'

'I don't disagree with you, Catherine,' said Josephine, pleased with the direction the conversation was taking. 'Where do we find new people?'

'Desperate times require desperate measures,' suggested John, unaware that a trap was being laid for him.

Josephine nodded at John's comment, repeating his words. 'Desperate times.' Laughing, she said, 'I know what we can do, marry John off to a sugar mama!'

John's jaw dropped.

'I don't mean a sugar mama in the traditional sense,' continued Josephine. 'I was thinking of a loving and wonderful wife who also happens to be well endowed.' Cupping her hands under her breasts to emphasise what she was saying. 'Not big breasted, I mean a financial benefactor and a new person for the church.'

The tension in the air, present after Catherine's tirade, eased with the injection of what most in the room thought was humour.

Happy the conversation had moved away from parading about stark naked, Edith chimed in, 'What a great idea.'

Vicar Charlotte questioned, 'Are you suggesting we "Flirt to Convert"?'

Josephine gave a horrified look, speaking in an elevated tone. 'Goodness gracious, no, Vicar, that sounds like something those Catholics or Pentecostals would do. We are English Anglicans, judicious, traditional and prudent. Vicar, think of yourself as being the Parish Matchmaker, like the one in Fiddler on the Roof. What I am suggesting would be classic, not tacky.'

'Excuse me, ladies,' John said, disconcerted by the turn of events. 'While I do appreciate your kind, well-meaning intentions, I'm quite capable of finding my own partner.'

Catherine gave him a sideways glance. 'You're not opposed to being married, is that correct?'

'Of course he's not,' answered Edith for John.

'Hey...' John started to say but, before another word could leave his lips, Josephine cut in. 'We women have been doing this throughout history, lying back and thinking of England. You'll be doing it for God, on a mission to save the church. I vote we form a new committee, the St Mary's Dating Agency. All those in favour?' With the exception of John, they giggled and lifted their hands in the air in a gesture of triumphant support.

Giving him a death stare, Catherine commanded, 'John!' Reluctantly, he raised his hand.

That's how the St Mary's Dating Agency came into existence. An accidental occurrence, everyone thought, except Josephine and Edith, who knew better.

Clapping her hands and grinning, Josephine said, 'It's unanimous. Our inaugural meeting will be 7.30pm, Thursday night. The first order of business, creating a dating profile for John.

In trepidation, John said, 'I'm not sure about this.'

Josephine smiled warmly, barely able to contain her excitement. 'You'll be fine, in total control; we will do everything for you.' A contradiction, of course, but the irony was lost on John, who said, 'I'll do it as long as someone else joins.' John was sure that his condition would bring the ridiculous idea to an end.

Josephine looked at the others as silence filled the room. Everybody waited for her to respond. Excitedly she said, 'That sounds fair. We will choose someone on Thursday night.' She paused, contemplating what to say next and, after ten seconds, she said, 'I know what we can do, draw a name out of a hat. John, you can be the barrel boy.'

CHAPTER 4

A Man of the World

For the next two days, Josephine spent her time researching online romance scams. Their dating agency was not planning to ensnare and fleece an unsuspecting woman but, to manage John's profile and correspondence with potential suitors, they would need all the help they could find. Understanding the addictive quality of the fraudsters' tricks would assist and deliver a result they wanted. Josephine was surprised when she discovered "a cookbook" - a "how to guide" - of romance scams. Its contents contained information about establishing an appealing profile, selecting targets and a daily email script. It gave instructions about what to write when a potential victim asked curious or cautious questions. Josephine was shocked to learn that requesting funds was important to cement a bond between victim and scammer. The more skin the prey had in the game, the more likely they were to continue with the online romance and fall in love. If her fellow dating agency colleagues were squeamish in asking for money, she would have to convince them otherwise. It is one of the key things that makes a scam work. Money was vital in establishing a dependent relationship. The difference she would tell them is that the scammers are about lies, profit and heartbreak, but John was a real person, seeking romance and love. We'll use proven psychological techniques to achieve our goals, legal and aboveboard. What Josephine found most appealing about the dating agency is that it was a win-win. John and council members would find loving partners, which, in turn, would grow the congregation and parish funds, meaning the church roof would also be repaired.

On Thursday evening, the St Mary's Dating Agency committee gathered for the first time. Josephine, the self-appointed chair, shared her discoveries of the previous days, giving them a "how-to" handout, not the full Romance Scammers' Cookbook, which she was saving for later in the meeting.

'As you can see from the material I've prepared, the scammers typically create fake online profiles designed to lure their prey. John, please don't take what I'm about to say the wrong way. Part of the scammer's trap is to use profiles of trusted and interesting people, for example, aid workers or ex-military officers.'

'Are you suggesting,' John smiled, while wiggling his glasses up and down on the end of his nose, 'That my mild-mannered Clark Kent profile would be boring?'

Josephine, wanting to phrase her response carefully, thought for a moment before answering. 'I think we should add a touch of derring-do.'

'We will not lie,' interrupted Vicar Charlotte. 'That would be neither charitable nor Christian.'

'Don't worry Vicar, we won't,' Josephine replied. 'Now, I found this on the internet.' Josephine passed round a copy of what she was calling, "The Romance Scammers' Cookbook". 'When you read it, you will find the romance swindlers express strong emotions for their victim in a relatively short time. They also suggest moving the relationship from the dating site to email or someplace more private where they can communicate one-to-one.

'Once we've listed John on the dating site, myself and Edith will engage the potential partners, by following the scripts you will see laid out in the cookbook.'

'I thought,' John asked hesitantly, 'that I was to be in total control?'

'You will be,' Josephine answered. 'Just think of us as your private executive recruitment team.'

'Romance consultants,' Edith added excitedly.

'That's right,' Josephine continued. 'We will do the shortlisting; the final decision will be yours.'

Vicar Charlotte and Catherine nodded in agreement.

Josephine said, 'Can I take us back to the cookbook? I know it sounds counter-intuitive, but, as I said, you need to profess strong feelings quickly, showering your target with loving words. One of the reasons for doing this is to weed out those who are unlikely to fall for the scam. In our case, fall in love with John. The technique and reason for seeking money is a discussion for another night. The purpose of tonight's meeting is to create an irresistible online profile for John.'

'How do you do that without lying?' Catherine asked, her countenance suspicious.

'Hey... don't forget I'm here,' John grumbled.

Josephine ignored both comments. 'Last week I watched a movie called, "The Secret Life of Walter Mitty". Have any of you seen it?' They all raised their hands.

'My proposal is that we send John on a whistle-stop selfie tour. He comes back with photographs of himself in exotic, maybe rugged places, which will speak volumes about him. What do they say? A picture says a thousand words. It won't be a lie because he will actually go to those places.'

'Like where?' Catherine asked gruffly.

'I don't know,' Josephine shrugged. 'Tower Bridge, the Eiffel Tower, the Colosseum... the Pyramids?'

Vicar Charlotte scoffed. 'Never. That itinerary sounds more like a twenty something Contiki tour. A boozy sex jaunt in the guise of "The Grand Tour".' The council members looked at the Vicar, saying in unison, 'Really?'

'I went after University... for "The Grand Tour" part - those were my observations and not necessarily my experience.'

'Never mind Vicar,' consoled Josephine, giving a humorous, sympathetic smile.

Catherine rolled her eyes. 'Yes, well thank you for sharing that with us, Vicar. What pictures will create the illusion of a worldly, appealing superman?' Then she said, her tone sarcastic, 'John photographing snow leopards, like in the silly film, is that it?'

'I'm still here!' John protested. 'And it wasn't Walter Mitty who was taking the photograph of the snow leopard. That was a metaphor...' His comments were to no avail as the women continued their conversation around him.

Vicar Charlotte, ignoring Catherine's mocking, continued. 'Obviously a place like Saint Moritz... representing the modern jet-setting man. Perhaps St Cyril's monastery in the northern mountains of Greece, the one used in the James Bond film... a man of mystery and intrigue. Then, one of the most picturesque places I can think of, Lake Bled in Slovenia. It's a lake in the Julian Alps of the Upper Carniolan regions of north-western Slovenia... This will be a representation of a man of romance. And finally... Iceland, a man of adventure.'

'A stroke of genius,' congratulated Edith, clapping her hands. 'The discerning woman would definitely want all of those characteristics in her man. There is however, something missing. Something new age and trendy... "The Master Chef". Picture this. John wanders the stalls of a local Slovenian market selecting his fresh ingredients. He then carries them, with an outdoor stove, up into the Carniolan Alps, where he cooks an exotic meal with the beautiful Lake Bled as a romantic backdrop. The only thing missing from the image is a beautiful wife to share his experience. Perfect.'

'Brilliant,' Josephine said. 'The mere thought brings a tear to my eyes.' A look of concern suddenly crossed her face, worried that John had never left Cornwall, let alone England.

'John, you do have a passport?'

'Yes, but..?'

'No buts! It's decided,' declared Josephine. 'When should he leave?'

'I think this is absolutely ridiculous,' grumbled Catherine. 'Who on God's earth finds a partner on "Facegram" or "Tinderbox", or whatever their proper names are?'

'Lots of people do,' Edith said, before abruptly stopping, frightened of letting the cat out of the bag as the image of Paul Roman, her charlatan, suddenly flashed into her mind.

Josephine, noticing her friend's predicament, came to her rescue. 'That's right Edith, you were joining for research purposes. Have you the links to show us?'

'I was,' Edith said tentatively, 'joining for research purposes.' She paused.

'Well?' Josephine prompted.

Edith smiled with enlightenment and in a confident voice said. 'Yes, I've joined a couple of sites.' She lifted the screen on her laptop. 'Here,' she said, signalling to the members of the Dating Agency to gather round. Edith proceeded to provide a guided tour of prominent dating websites, reading aloud some of the male profiles. The women became engrossed and when John tried to remind them, they were intending to find him a female partner, Catherine, their doubting Thomas, dismissed him, saying, 'We're researching what the appealing men write. My, he looks nice.' She pointed to one of the male images on the screen. 'Look at those abs!' The assembled females giggled.

After twenty minutes of exacting research, Josephine repeated her earlier question. 'When should he leave?'

'As soon as possible,' Vicar Charlotte answered. 'We can't start until we have photographs.' The others nodded in agreement.

Giving John her most serious look, Josephine said, 'Well, Mr John Moss, the future of St Mary's Church is resting on your shoulders. When can you leave?'

He sighed as he said, 'Next week. What about the hat? Weren't one of you ladies meant to be joining me on the dating site?'

'I think,' Catherine said indifferently, 'We old boilers, the chewy mutton of St Mary's, except you Vicar, should wait. It is wise to watch how our young rooster fares, honing our skills before pitching ourselves against the young chickens and lambs. What do you say, ladies?'

'Absolutely,' they called. 'One person at a time.'

'John shook his head in defeat as he smiled and said, 'Then you ladies must do the naked calendar.'

CHAPTER 5

Love

The luxury alpine resort of Saint Moritz in Switzerland's Engadin valley was the last location on John's whistle-stop selfie tour. Although he had successfully navigated the airports, trains and buses over his two-week trip, that did not mean John enjoyed the travel experience. The moment he arrived at a location, his mind was awash with anxiety, dreading the next part of the journey. Eating alone in cafes and restaurants was unsettling, feeling like a shag on a rock, alone among intimate couples or raucous groups. Nobody noticed him, of course, but self-consciousness made John feel as though he stood out like a beacon, signalling *look at me, a lonely man with no friends*. Beautiful cuisine in stunning locations, which should have been a highlight of the trip, turned burdensome. Evening meals were particularly bad. With no company they were over in twenty minutes, then rather than exploring the location's after dark activities, he rushed back to the safety of his hotel room to spend the long evenings alone. John missed his own surroundings, the trip reminding him of why he liked holidaying at home in the UK, where things felt familiar. *If I had company*, John thought, *I might feel differently and enjoy the places I visit.* Although he wanted to embrace the travel experience, he found himself unable, his indifference something he would keep secret from the ladies on the Parish Council. To them, he would say it was a wonderful and enjoyable journey; *I had great fun.* His feeling of inadequacy was a private matter.

It was the last full day of John's enforced overseas excursion and just one more sleep for him to survive before returning home to the wonderful UK. Deciding that he needed a final selfie picture with hire skis in hand, John took the cable car to the top of the mountain, safe in the knowledge he would make the same return journey, without having to tackle the slopes. John had never worn skis before, let alone attempted to ski. As he whisked up the mountain in the cable car, John worried he would fall flat on his face as he tried to mount his skis. He imagined the masculine snow moose and attractive ski bunnies giggling as he fell. *Maybe this isn't such a good idea*, he said to himself.

The cable car slowed, then stopped as it reached the summit, causing John to rock on the balls of his feet as it ground to a halt. With the order and discipline of a military parade ground, the passengers disembarked, gear in hand, minds set on the adventure ahead. John waited until last, following the others out of the cable car building. Once outside he paused, spending the next few minutes gazing about, engrossed by the view and his surroundings.

If I could ski, he said to himself, *this would be one heck of a great place.*

It was a magnificent morning, the kind of morning that made life worthwhile. A brilliant clear blue sky, crisp dry air and shimmering pure white snow as far as the eye could see. After John had left on his selfie tour, he discovered that his original English winter gear was not up to the task, forcing him to purchase new gloves, snow jacket, insulated socks and jumper. Multilayering prevented him from shivering. Today, with the sun reflecting back from the snow, he was warm as toast. The feeling came as a surprise. He was actually enjoying himself. *This is such a wonderful place, I'm going to ask someone to take the photo for me*, he said to himself. *Maybe not*, he mumbled in self-doubt. Dismissing his trepidation, he said. *No, I will. Today I'm going to ask someone to take the photograph of me.*

Seizing a deep breath, John reflected on his next task–putting on the skis. Standing, poles in hand, he looked for a flat area to clip in and near the top of the downhill he saw the perfect place. Striding over with confidence, looking as though he was preparing to make a descent, he put the skis on the ground. All poise vanished when he fell over three times whilst trying to secure his skis. A young couple who had been watching John came to his aid. The young woman held John's arms while the partner clipped his boots into the skis for him.

'There you go,' said the man. 'You look like a true professional. Would you like a hand before we leave?'

'That's very kind of you, but I'm fine now,' John said.

The woman looked concerned as she said, 'Are you sure you will be okay?'

John gave her the thumbs up while nodding, then said, 'I'm just getting my sea legs, that's all, it's been a while ...' From the look on their faces John could see that they had missed his self-deprecating British humour.

To preserve his dignity, John waited until his saviours commenced their downhill run and were out of sight before shuffling towards the edge. Spotting another couple taking photos of themselves, he approached them, trying not to fall as he moved forward. Holding out his camera in their direction, he called to them. 'Excuse me - hello. Would you be so kind as to take a photo of me?'

'Sure thing,' the man replied, reaching out and taking John's camera from him.

Had the man taking the photograph not turned to answer a question from his wife or partner, he would have spotted John sliding backwards, then simply reached out and grabbed him.

However, by the time the man turned back, John had disappeared from sight, over the edge. The man missed the look of fear stamped on John's face as he waved his arms frantically. Involuntarily out of control and backwards, John commenced a downhill ski run.

The top of a ski run is crowded, so within a few metres, John had crashed into a group of three preparing for their descent, sending them sprawling to the ground. To John's relief, the impact spun him around. The reprieve was short-lived for as he came about, the front of his skis dropped over a ledge, where the mountain dipped away sharply, the point where people launched themselves for a fast and furious home run.

With his hands flailing about wildly, the ski poles became dangerous weapons, knocking two more skiers to the ground as John picked up speed, screaming as he sped past, 'Watch out!'

Lucy had stopped on the slope, soaking up the vista as she attempted the last run of her stay at Saint Moritz. Failing to see or hear John, her keen senses prickled, alerting her to the approaching danger. Lucy adjusted her stance to avoid the collision, assessing that the man was no threat, just a person out of control. A year ago, watching someone plummet to their death would have tickled her fancy, but she'd mellowed with the help of her fellow spies, Max and Olivia who had become friends. With no time to spare and with John now racing towards a high-speed impact with a tree, she tugged her boots free of the ski clamps and launched herself, tackling him to the ground. The gradient meant that despite both now lying flat on the snow, the momentum of John's cascade continued to carry them downhill. Had it been an ice run, stopping would have been problematic, but a fresh layer of powder snow improved their odds. Wrapping John tightly in her arms, Lucy swivelled her body, using her feet and legs as a brake, digging them deeply into the snow. They began slowing, then halted, a white mist scattering in their wake.

Wiping snow from her face, Lucy gauged her companion; thirty-something male, cheap ski wear, hired equipment and unflattering glasses hanging crookedly across his nose. *He is as green as grass*, she thought. She found the naïve, awkward men sexually attractive, though she wasn't sure why. Perhaps it was because she enjoyed playing "Little Miss Innocent," or the sophisticated worldly woman, whichever was appropriate at the time to lure a man into bed. The unworldly, wholesome girl-next-door look, exuding cuteness and innocence, was Lucy's favourite sexual persona. Something aroused her in the contradiction, what the men were expecting compared with her sexual domination in the bedroom. The girl-next-door gave a man a night he wouldn't soon forget. When they awoke in the morning, she was gone.

Having saved John, adrenaline was pulsing round her body. She could taste it on her lips, heightening her need for raw sex. Her blood was running.

Standing, Lucy brushed a covering of snow from her clothes. John was still lying on the ground. With both hands, she reached out towards him, offering assistance. He grabbed hold, flopping back into the snow when the gloves he was wearing pulled free of his hands. Lucy spotted that he wore no wedding ring.

Sorry,' she said, helping him stand again. *No callouses, smooth skin; accountant or teacher. If I weren't leaving today, he would do nicely for tonight, easy pickings.*

Fumbling to find the right words and unsettled by the beauty who had saved him, John stammered, 'Thank... thank you.'

Two people came skiing to a halt beside them. 'Are you alright?' asked the man who was about to take the photograph of John before his untimely adventure.

'Yes, thank you,' John answered. Lucy said nothing.

He held out John's camera as he said, 'Sorry, but I missed the action shots.'

John shrugged. 'I don't think I'll repeat it!'

The couple continued their descent.

Loosening the cuff of her ski jacket, Lucy glanced at her watch. It was 11.30 am. In two hours, she needed to be at the restaurant in her hotel. Looking up, she watched as John fell backwards into the snow. Fighting the urge to laugh, she helped him stand again. Taking the phone from her ski pants pocket, Lucy asked, 'Is there someone I can call who can come and fetch you?'

'No, sorry, I'm on my own.'

Having someone with me at lunch may prove useful, thought Lucy as she said, 'Okay, how about I help? You can either take off your skis and we will try to walk back up the slope, then catch the cable car down or I assist you to ski to the bottom.'

'I think I should walk.'

'Nonsense! I promise I won't let you go. We can do this together.'

Thinking of the St Mary's Parish Council ladies, John thought, *why is it women offer choices that never really exist?* In trepidation, he breathed out and, using an old English expression, said, 'Lead on Macduff.'

Lucy smiled as she turned to John and said, 'Shakespeare, Macbeth Act 5, Scene 8. The phrase should be "lay on", which means to make a vigorous attack.'

'I see my Shakespeare is as laudable as my downhill skiing.'

Lucy grinned, masking her annoyance for showing off. If she wanted to use this man, being a smart-arse was a poor way to achieve it. *I'll have my hands all over him on the way down, to stop him from falling, and shower him with smiles and praise. Be timid and coy until you decide the right course of action. It's easier to switch up than it is down!*

As they descended, the laughter that accompanied his mishaps made John feel a little sad when finally they reached the bottom. That's when he realised he didn't even know this woman's name. *Should I ask,* he thought to himself, but before he had a chance to, Lucy said shyly,

'I'm not normally this forward. You see...' She stopped speaking, pretending to be the virtuous woman, fumbling for the right words. 'I won my stay at Saint Moritz; it was one of those radio competitions. Today, at half past one I have a free lunch for two. As I'm on my own, I was wondering, if you have no other plans, that is, would you like to join me?' Before John had an opportunity to reply, she dropped her eyes shyly, saying, 'I would understand if you say no.'

John floundered for a second before saying awkwardly, 'No. Well, I mean yes. No, I have no other plans, and yes, that would be lovely.' He held out his hand. 'My name is John, John Moss.'

'It's a pleasure to meet you, John Moss. I'm Lucia, but my friends call me Lucy.'

'Lacy?' he questioned.

'No, Lucy. Sorry John, we don't have long before lunch. I'm staying at the Badrutt's Palace and will meet you at the reception counter desk at twenty past one. Is that okay?'

'Where's the Badrutt's Palace?'

'Where are you staying?'

'The Petit Steffani Hostel.'

Lucy knew the Petit Steffani as one of the more modest places to stay in Saint Moritz. Having given John directions and watched him leave, she made her way back to the hotel. Before leaving for the ski slopes that morning, Lucy had hacked into the hotel's computer system, reserving a table next to her target. As she arrived back at the hotel, Lucy went to the restaurant and changed her booking, now for two people.

Even though she was planning to leave Saint Moritz later that afternoon, Lucy had extended her reservation for an extra day, to give herself the use of the room right up to the moment she left. Removing her ski gear, Lucy went to the wardrobe. Typically, she preferred to be chic and glamorous, but not for John. She decided to maintain her sweet, loyal, wholesome girl-next-door persona, even though she wouldn't be taking him to bed. Swooning him would keep her options open. It always amazed her that by changing the way she dressed and accessorised, her perceived character would alter and, from there, acting the accompanying role became easier. Ignoring the designer clothes, she selected a tasteful, discount department store, red floral dress, ideal for John Moss. Slipping it on, Lucy glanced at the mirror, saying aloud, *Oh, very sweet, but I don't know about that cleavage showing. No. Not for John Moss. He won't know what to do with his eyes.* Lucy selected a white bralette and put it on under the dress. *Almost perfect. Now I'm thinking, a scarf will finish it off.* After a last inspection, she plucked her Louis Vuitton handbag from the bed and strode towards the door before halting. *Silly girl,* she reprimanded herself. *John will not notice, but others might.* Selecting a more suitable accessory, Lucy transferred the contents from the Louis Vuitton and headed to the rendezvous and lunch with Mr John Moss.

As Lucy entered the hotel lobby from the lift, John resisted the urge to wave. Out of the ski suit, her beauty stole his breath away. As she approached, he said, 'Hello again.'

Lucy smiled, her head bowed, eyes up, as she said, sweetly, 'You're here. I was worried that you might not come. I'm a bit peckish.'

'Me too,' was all that John could think of to say. He felt himself blush.

Lucy smiled again and John melted a bit more. He relaxed a little as she said, 'The restaurant is this way.'

'Do you have a reservation Madam, Sir?' asked the well-dressed man at the entrance to the hotel restaurant. It wasn't the same person who had taken her change of booking.

'Yes, it's in the name of Lucy.'

He checked the computer screen. 'Indeed. If Madam and Sir would kindly follow me.' The man showed them to a table in front of a large ornate window with stunning views of the snow-covered mountains, snow lifting like dust rings with each gust of wind. Her target, a fifty-year-old woman, was seated at her table as Lucy and John took theirs. She was accompanied by two male companions; they paid scant regard to Lucy and John. *A couple*, Lucy thought, *are less conspicuous; bringing John was a sound decision*. Lucy took the seat closest to the woman, no more than a metre from her.

'This is lovely, isn't it?' Lucy said.

Before John could answer, a waiter arrived, dressed in the traditional black jacket, white shirt and black bow tie.

'Would Madam and Sir like something to drink?'

'We would,' Lucy responded. 'Do you have a wine list?'

Smiling, the waiter said, 'Of course, Madam,' picking the wine list up from the table and handing it to Lucy. 'Perhaps Madam would like me to come back in a minute?'

'Yes, that would be fine. Thank you.'

'This is so exciting, John. If it wasn't for winning the competition, I wouldn't ordinarily eat at such a wonderful place. I'm so glad you could join me; it's more fun when you can share it with someone.' John nodded, knowing exactly what she meant.

Attempting a sophisticated voice, reasoning that he should pay for the drinks, perhaps buy a bottle for them to share, John said, 'May I?' He indicated the wine list in Lucy's hands and she handed it to him. The prices were even more extravagant than he was expecting, but he wanted to impress, so he said, 'Do you have a preference? Red or white?'

'It's lunchtime, so why don't we have a white?' As she spoke, Lucy spotted a waiter carrying a tray of drinks moving towards the table next to them. Achoo!!, she sneezed and then said, 'Excuse me,' as she rummaged through her handbag. 'Oh, I'm a silly thing. I haven't brought a tissue with me. Would you be a real darling and ask for one at reception?'

Pleased with the task, to rescue his damsel in distress, John beamed and said, as he rose to leave, 'Sure.'

Lucy waited for the perfect moment. 'John!' she called out after him. Turning to the summons, his momentum carried him one more step - he crashed into the waiter holding the tray of drinks. Time passed slowly as the waiter stumbled and the glasses and their contents tumbled to the floor. In the quite elegant restaurant, the sound was calamitous. As Lucy had hoped, the attention of her target was drawn to the disturbance, the whole restaurant seemingly transfixed as the drama unfolded. With the speed and precision of a striking rattlesnake, Lucy slipped her hand into the target's handbag, which was on the floor, removing the car keys and popping them into her own bag. Having given his humble apologies, mildly embarrassed, John returned to the table to see what Lucy wanted. 'Oh, I'm so sorry John,' Lucy said, taking a tissue from her handbag. 'I had one all the time. Are you alright? I hope you weren't hurt.' She gave him her practiced puppy love eyes. 'You poor thing, sit down. I will order us some drinks.' The excitement of the collision was quickly forgotten, and the restaurant settled back into its lunchtime hum.

'Cheers!' Lucy said, clinking glasses with John. 'To the wonderful Saint Moritz.' They sipped their drinks and smiled at each other. 'John, will you excuse me a minute? I need to powder my nose. I won't be long.' A polite way of saying she was going to the toilet.

Lucy clasped her handbag as she left the table but, instead of heading for the washroom, she made a beeline for the hotel's indoor car park. The target's silver AMG Mercedes was still parked where she'd spotted it the night before. With the stolen car remote in her hand, Lucy made a quick assessment of her surroundings. Confident that she was alone, Lucy pressed the button and the indicator lights of the car flashed, signalling that it was unlocked. Following the mission briefing instructions, she opened the glove compartment and spotted the silver pen, where she had been told it would be. Removing it, Lucy unscrewed its two halves, revealing a hidden compartment. Inside, about the size of a microchip, was a cube-shaped, black metallic object. *It was too easy*, she mused. *Is my target an unwitting mule, unaware of the value of what she was carrying?* Screwing the pen back together, Lucy slipped the object into her purse, then glanced at her watch. *Four minutes, John will wonder where I am.* Her thoughts were shattered by the sound of approaching footsteps. Practised, Lucy calmly closed the glove compartment and quietly pushed the car door shut with a soft click. Instinctively, she reached inside her purse for the pistol before remembering she wasn't carrying one. Lucy calculated the position, distance and direction of the approaching person, slipping behind one of the concrete pillars that supported the garage ceiling. A menacing eerie quiet befell the space as whoever had entered halted and waited.

From the opposite direction, Lucy heard the sounds of new footsteps. After a moment, they were accompanied by the voice of a child calling. 'Mummy, mummy?' *A family*, Lucy thought. The child again. 'Where's the car, mummy?'

A woman's voice, the mother, said, 'It's just over there Peter, can't you keep up!'

'Yes,' said a little girl's voice, repeating her mother, 'Peter, can't you keep up!'

Lucy assessed that there were three people, mother and two children and, unlike the other footsteps, not a threat.

The impact of the woman's high heels as they struck the ground echoed loudly around the concrete garage. Seizing the opportunity, Lucy pushed the remote control, locking the car, knowing that the sound would be lost in the midst of the approaching family. As they drew closer to her, Lucy forced her back against the concrete pillar and slid around it to avoid being seen. Her dress caught, tearing, on a piece of protruding rough concrete. Once the family had passed, Lucy, without looking back, strode purposely in the direction from which they had come. Forty seconds later, she was safely out of the car park, making her way back to the restaurant. As she walked, Lucy dropped a hand and felt around her bottom in search of the rip. Finding it, she used her fingers to explore its dimensions. Annoyed, she said to herself. *Small. I don't have the time to change, hopefully no one will notice.*

At the entrance to the restaurant, Lucy sensed John's waiting eyes. She waved at him with a beaming smile and, when she reached their table, Lucy purposely clipped it with her leg, making the cutlery and glasses on it sing. Keeping her hand low, using the noise for cover, Lucy discreetly tossed the car keys back into the target's handbag. Placing her hand over the tear in the dress, Lucy leaned over the table and whispered to John. 'I'm sorry for being so long, I thought I would use the privy in my room, it's further than you think when someone is waiting for you.' She leaned back and sat down.

Secretly, John feared Lucy had done a runner, so was relieved, smiling as he said, 'That's okay.'

Touching his arm lightly, she said, 'You're a kind man.' Her thoughts were different. *Mission complete, it's time to dump this bloke.* Being a consummate professional however, Lucy countered her initial thinking, musing. *It's not wise to burn someone, other than if it's just for sex, because you never know Lucy, you might yet need simple John again and besides, you have plenty of time now.*

They enjoyed a delightful lunch together, Lucy appearing to give John her unwavering attention, seeming to relish, and hang onto every word he spoke. When, with a little persuasion, John told of the St Mary's Dating Agency and his selfie trip, Lucy was surprised by her own feelings, finding the story quaint and amusing.

'Thank you for sharing lunch with me, John. I'm going to be sad leaving Saint Moritz and your wonderful company, although part of me is looking forward to going home to Australia.' Her mobile phone buzzed. 'Excuse me for a second.'

Lucy took the phone from her bag, looking at the screen, it wasn't a number she recognised. *That's unusual.* Ordinarily Lucy would delete such calls, but because she was on a mission, felt it was prudent to check. 'I'm so sorry, John. I'm expecting a call from my travel agent. I need to take this one.' Lucy left the table, pushing the answer button as she walked towards a private area, away from her fellow diners.

'Yes.'

An unfamiliar voice said in a matter-of-fact tone, 'The police and spooks are waiting to search you when you leave the mountain.' The caller hung up. Lucy went through the motions of pretending she was still engaged in a conversation, giving her time to think. *My plans need to change and John may yet have a part to play*, she thought. She waited another minute before returning to the table, a look of sadness on her face.

Noticing her expression and change of mood, John asked, 'Is everything alright?'

'Yes, it's all fine.' Lucy sighed. 'My travel plans are confirmed for tomorrow. It's just, as I was talking on the phone, I realised I didn't feel like leaving yet.'

John's heart gave an involuntary leap.

'It's my uncle's birthday. I'm going to buy him a present this afternoon.' Feigning shyness, Lucy continued, 'Would you? I mean, if you don't have any other plans, would you come shopping with me?'

Trying to hide his excitement, John blurted out, 'Yes, I mean no.'

Lucy, smiling to herself, gave him a concerned look, even though she knew exactly what he meant.

'What I mean is... no, I have nothing else on and yes, I would like to accompany you shopping.'

She reached across and touched him softly on the arm. 'You're such a gentleman. Thank you.' She withdrew her hand. 'It's cold outside. I'll need to change before we go.'

She considered inviting him to her room, but thought better of it. *Too early,* she decided. Besides, Lucy didn't want John to see the tear in her dress. 'Do you mind waiting for me here, or would you prefer that I call by your hotel?'

'I'll wait.' Unconsciously, John moved his hand to the spot where he had been touched. Lucy noticed and smiled. As she left the restaurant, Lucy felt John's eyes following her. She stopped at the cash register. 'Charge the meal to my room. Four two seven.'

***

Leaving the hotel together on their shopping adventure, Lucy slipped her arm under John's and said, 'This is going to be such fun now that you're coming along!'

For most men, the thought of spending an afternoon shopping with a woman is a nightmare, a fate equal to death, unless they are in the courting phase of the relationship. Then it's bearable.

'Do you have any idea what you're looking for?' John asked, hoping Lucy didn't and he would spend the rest of the day with her, searching for an ideal gift.

'I do.'

His heart sank.

'There's a lovely jewellery store near here called Bucherer. I thought a nice pen would make the ideal gift.' She'd spun John the yarn about winning the trip to Saint Moritz, so she would need to tweak her cover story before spending a pretty sum on a present. As they walked in comfortable silence, Lucy formulated a new story. The key elements of what she'd already shared with him over lunch needed to remain, like living in Australia; a substantial change would make him suspicious. She needed him to know that she had considerable financial resources at her disposal, which was at odds with the lie about winning a trip to Saint Moritz.

Lucy stopped abruptly as they approached the jewellery store, glanced at John and said, 'I wasn't going to say anything.' She took a deep breath. 'John, I need to because I have told you a little white lie.' She dropped her head as if in shame, raised it again and peered into his eyes - a sign of honesty. She knew the tricks. 'I didn't win a trip to Saint Moritz. Both of my parents died when I was small. When I turned twenty-one, I inherited the estate. I'm not wealthy, not by any stretch of the imagination, but I'm comfortable. I'm sorry for being untruthful, but I've discovered that nice people,

people like you, are scared away by my independence. They flee, leaving me with wealthy jerks with one thing on their minds. Please forgive me?' She said, staring into John's eyes as she squeezed his arm within hers.

John's emotions were in turmoil, moved by Lucy's honesty mixed with a sensation of dread. Lost, trying to understand his contradicting emotions, he remained silent as Lucy continued to speak.

'After my parents passed away, it was my uncle who looked after me. He's been like a father to me, so I want to buy him an expensive birthday present.'

Wealthy and beautiful, and I think she likes me. No, that can't be. How could a woman like that find me attractive? Maybe Lucy just wants the company. John's mind was racing, filling with different scenarios. Throwing caution to the wind, irrespective of Lucy's motivation, he wished this day would never end. The thought of Lucy leaving filled him with dread. John bit his lip, whispering to himself, *Tomorrow, Lucy will return to Australia and I will never see her again. This is so unfair!*

Noticing John's heavy expression, Lucy said, 'Are you alright?'

'Yes. 'I was just thinking about what you just told me. I forgive you and thank you for telling me the truth,' he said, trying to shed his discomfort.

They started walking and Lucy said, 'Promise me you won't tell anyone about my inheritance, especially those parish councillors. People seem to treat me differently when they know. It has to be our secret, promise.'

'Of course.'

'I knew I could trust you, John,' Lucy said and, as they turned a corner on the pavement, Lucy pointed excitedly, saying. 'There it is. Bucherer!'

Approaching, John read the date emblazoned above the jewellery store's door. Reading aloud, he said, '1888?'

'That's when they started selling luxury jewellery.'

'I see.' *This woman lives in a different world, he thought. I don't have a hope.* 'Have you been here before?'

'No, I asked the concierge at the hotel if she could recommend a jewellery store and here we are.' She squeezed his arm. 'I'm quite excited about having you with me.'

Lucy's enthusiasm suppressed John's pessimistic thoughts.

Once inside, they were greeted by a smartly dressed man who asked in German, 'Darf ich ihnen behilflich?' 'May I help you?'

'Indeed, you may,' Lucy said. 'We are looking for a special gift for a friend. An elegant pen.'

Switching to English, the man said, 'Certainly Madam, if you would kindly follow me.' He escorted them to a serving counter within the store where an assistant was waiting. Introducing John and Lucy to the woman, he said, 'Madam is seeking an elegant pen as a gift.' He turned to face Lucy and John. 'If I may be of any further assistance, please ask.' Bowing his head, first to Lucy and then John, the man left and returned to his post. Lucy and John watched him leave. Meanwhile, the assistant had placed four pen boxes on the glass top. Opening the first box, the sales assistant said,

'Madam, a sterling silver Graft Von Faber-Castell classic ball-point pen. It's three hundred and twenty-two euros. Next we have...' She opened the second box, 'A Conway Stewart Westminster Teal fountain pen. Very elegant and a little more expensive at one thousand six hundred euros. The third one I have selected is the Montblanc solitaire rollerball.' She opened the box revealing the instrument. 'Four hundred and seventy euro.' The assistant reached towards the last box but hesitated when Lucy interrupted.

'I rather like the blue of the solitaire,' Lucy said as she looked at the assistant before reaching towards the box which contained the rollerball pen. 'May I?' The sales assistant nodded.

'Picking up the box from the counter, Lucy took a discreet step back, then to the side, placing John slightly in front of her and to her left. This move slightly impeded the sales assistant's view of her. Using her left hand, Lucy removed the pen from its box and turned towards John, showing him the pen as she said, 'What do you think?'

Not knowing how to contribute, he smiled and nodded.

She held the blue solitaire pen for him to take and said, 'Do you like the weight?'

When John's eyes were drawn to the solitaire pen he was holding, Lucy slipped her hand into her pocket and removed the pen she had taken from the Mercedes.

Acting as if his hands were scales, John felt the weight of the solitaire pen. He then held it as though he was writing, feeling its balance before handing it back, saying, 'Very nice.'

'I agree, this will do nicely.'

Lucy's sleight of hand was worthy of a master magician. As she turned towards the sales assistant, Lucy replaced the blue solitaire pen with the one containing the cube-shaped, black metallic object from the Mercedes, snapping the lid on the box closed. While holding the box in her hand, she said, 'We will take this one, please.' With her other hand, she slipped the solitaire pen into her pocket.

'Certainly Madam. Would you like it gift wrapped?'

Lucy looked at John with a facial expression that asked, what do you think?

In magic, choices are rarely what they seem. Magicians know how to manipulate people into a false sense of free will while really holding the puppet strings. Lucy was an expert. If John answered yes to her question, she would agree, if no, she would say, I think we should. Asking him was part of the entrapment game, knitting him into the process, giving him the impression that she trusted him and that he was part of the decision making.

'Yes,' John said, unaware of the snare around his ankles.

The sales assistant paused, in case Madam had other instructions. She didn't, so the assistant said, 'Certainly Sir.' Meticulously, she placed the other pens in their boxes and back into their display cabinets. Lucy put her purchase on the glass topped counter.

'Please excuse me while I get the wrapping paper,' said the sales assistant.

Positioning her hand on John's arm, Lucy said. 'Do you think my uncle Michael will like it?'

John smiled, trying to appear as thrilled as she was as he replied, 'I'm sure he will.' He knew that his time with Lucy would soon be over. The assistant appeared holding a piece of golden wrapping paper. Lucy removed her hand from John's arm and picked up the pen in its box. The assistant stretched the paper onto the counter and Lucy handed over her purchase. They watched as the assistant wrapped it beautifully, adding, 'A bow, Madam?'

'Yes please, that would be excellent.'

The assistant left again, this time returning with a red bow. The wrapping complete, Lucy handed the sales lady her Platinum Visa card. After the transaction was completed, the sales assistant said, 'Thank you Madam.'

Lucy picked up the gold wrapped gift, perfect with its red bow and gave it to John. 'Would you mind carrying this for me?' As he took it from her, she thought, *My unwitting mule has the goods in his hands for the first time. Now to close the trap.*

As they were leaving the jewellery store, Lucy said, 'My, Mr John Moss, I don't enjoy shopping, but it was nice doing it with you.' She slipped her arm back into his and as they walked arm in arm, Lucy emitted a sigh of contentment for John's benefit.

With an air of finality in his voice, John asked, 'Shall I walk you home?'

'Yes, that would be most kind.'

In silence they walked along the street, stopping occasionally to glance through a shop window, stalling the inevitable end of their day together. *Come on John, hurry up and ask me out to dinner. You know you want to!*

John's mind and heart were racing as the day drew to a close. *Should I ask her out for dinner?*

Lucy didn't want to be the person to make the next move, because she knew that entrapment worked best when the victim believes that they initiated the encounter. John was naïve, his shyness holding him back; time was of the essence, so she took control.

'Oh John, look at that lovely Italian restaurant.' She led him to the window as she said, 'If you're not too tired, would you like to share a farewell dinner? My treat, for being so patient and kind in coming shopping with me.'

It was the kind of establishment John would normally frequent within his price range. 'Lucy, I would love that. Perhaps you would give me the pleasure of taking you out. I would like to pay - shout?' The moment he said it, John realised his offer sounded awkward. If Lucy noticed, she didn't show it.

'You're such a sweet man; our first date.'

'If you would like to wait here a moment, I'll pop in and making the booking. Does six thirty sound good?'

'Wonderful, John.'

The table reservation complete, John walked Lucy back to her hotel. Outside of the front entrance she stopped, took both of John's hands in hers, she squeezed them and said, 'I'll meet you at the restaurant.'

John nodded as Lucy leaned towards him, kissing him on the cheek. 'See you at six thirty.'

'Wait,' John said. 'The pen.'

Lucy took the pen and he watched as she walked the final few steps towards the front door. Before going inside, Lucy paused, turned around, smiled and waved. *This is going to be like stealing candy from a baby*, she thought.

The hotel door closed and Lucy was gone. John lingered on the steps for a moment, lost in his thoughts. *What's happening?* He turned and began a slow walk back to his own dwelling, annoyed at himself for fantasizing of a future with Lucy. *Stop it*, he said to himself, unsure of what was ahead, certain that he would end up disappointed.

CHAPTER 6

The Mule

As Lucy expected, John was seated and waiting for her as she arrived at the Italian restaurant. Lucy had considered being fashionably late but, reflecting on her absence at lunchtime when she was gone for ten minutes, chose to be on time. As the clock struck six thirty, she walked through the door.

While enjoying their "romantic" dinner, Lucy planned to encourage John to talk about himself, leading the conversation back to the St Mary's Dating Agency, the selfie trip he was undertaking, and the photographs he was snapping for the dating site. When the waiter arrived to take their order, she proposed a couple of pasta dishes for them to share. They would share the food served from the same plates. *An intimate way of eating*, she thought.

Tasting her first mouthful of pasta, Lucy said, 'This is really good! I know you may have told me earlier, but is Saint Moritz the last stop on your selfie tour or are you visiting other places?'

Since meeting Lucy, John was feeling embarrassed by the whole selfie affair and had hoped to avoid discussing the St Mary's Dating Agency, so he replied succinctly, 'Yes, I leave for home tomorrow.'

'Are you really on the lookout for a girlfriend, or is this just something you're doing for the church?'

What was the right answer? thought John, as panic surfaced. His response tumbled awkwardly from his mouth. 'No, er... yes. I haven't got one, but if the right one came along, er... and it's for the church.'

'I do think you're blushing,' Lucy teased as she developed a wry smile. 'Let's take a selfie of us together and send it to them.' John attempted an objection but, before he had a chance to respond, Lucy came around to his side of the table and knelt down next to him. 'Your phone? Do you have it?' Taking it from his pocket, John held it at arm's length, ready to take the shot. As his finger hovered over the shutter icon, Lucy puckered her lips against his cheek, kissing him as the *click* of the photograph being taken sounded. Lucy grinned as she said, 'That will get the women gossiping.'

The waiter, noticing the couple trying to take a photograph of themselves, approached the table and, pointing towards John's phone, said, 'May I be of assistance?'

John hesitated and looked at Lucy as she said,

'That would be wonderful.'

John handed the waiter his phone and Lucy put her arm around John, pulling him in closer until their cheeks were touching. John felt the warmth of her soft skin resting against his and Lucy sensed his longing. *This is going well.*

'Thank you,' John said, retrieving his phone.

Lucy leaned intimately into John to examine the pictures. She was so close that he could smell her sweet fragrance, a delight he'd rarely experienced, becoming aware of her breasts innocently pushing against his shoulders. 'I like them,' Lucy said, adding in a teasing way, 'Go on John, send them to the Parish Council.'

Feeling like a naughty schoolboy, he said eagerly, as he lined up the images for transmission, 'Okay... done!'

Going back to her seat, Lucy sighed. 'Today has been so wonderful, I wish we had had longer together.'

'When do you leave?' John asked, his voice tinged with sadness.

'Tomorrow morning, I have to go back to Australia and work.'

Work! You work? John thought.

'I haven't asked what you do.'

Lucy gave him a mock stern look as she said. 'Because of my inheritance - you didn't think I needed to work?'

'No, nothing like that, I...'

Lucy interrupted. 'I'm just teasing you, John! I'm a kindergarten teacher, working with little children before they start primary school.'

'I can see you doing that.'

Lucy thought, *Now is the right time to sow the seed, the possibility of us as an item.* 'While I absolutely love the children, I don't have to work, but the social connections it gives me are good for my well-being. It's not healthy to be constantly on your own. Did you know that?'

'No.'

Lucy looked at John sadly. 'Couples live longer and are happier than those alone. It's a fact.'

John had been avoiding the question, frightened of the answer, but he asked it anyway. 'Do you have someone waiting for you in Australia?'

Perfect, he fell into that one. Now for vulnerability – poor Lucy. 'No,' she said, followed by a long pause. 'I did once. Like my parents, he died.'

'I'm sorry.'

Almost there. 'That's okay. It was over five years ago now.' She said, screwing up her face, giving the impression of fighting back the tears, 'This is the first time I've enjoyed myself–since–well, you know. Sorry John, I'm being a little emotional. I'm a silly girl sometimes.'

'No Lucy, I understand, truly I do.'

'Thank you.' She reached across the table and gave his hand a gentle squeeze. *It's time to go in for the kill.* Letting go of his hand, she said, 'Do you believe in love at first sight?'

'Yes!'

Lucy sighed. 'I'm going to miss you.'

'I will miss you, too.'

She allowed the air to hang heavy in silence before reaching out, this time with both hands. John folded his fingers around them, staring into Lucy's eyes, emotion overwhelming him, unable to prevent a tear forming, rolling freely down his cheek. Lucy's act continued as she smiled warmly at him, moved by his affection, or so he thought.

Breaking the silence, Lucy asked, 'Had I been a girl you met on the dating site, would you have wanted me to come to England?'

'I think so.'

Lucy let go of his hands, pushing back in her chair as her expression changed to one of thoughtfulness. She counted to five to increase the tension, then said, 'Maybe we were meant to meet each other.'

John's mind matched his heart. Both were racing. 'Fate?'

'Yes,' Lucy said, then her pace of speech quickened, as if being overwhelmed by the moment. 'If you wanted me to, I would come to England. Of course, I would have to go home to Australia first, but I would, I'd come. We could just see what happens?'

John was speechless, thoughts suppressed by the thumping of his heart.

When he didn't answer immediately, Lucy shook her head in feigned disbelief as she said, 'You don't believe me?'

'I do,' he whispered.

Ignoring his comment, Lucy said, 'You think that once I get to Australia I'll forget about you? I want to prove myself to you, show you that you can trust me.'

'There's no need,' John said, tenderly.

A look of determination swept across Lucy's face as she said, 'I know what I can do.' Reaching into her handbag, Lucy removed the gold gift-wrapped box concealing the pen containing the cube. 'John, you know how important this is to me. Well, I want you to take it. I will send it to my uncle when I come to you in England. It's a token, you see, to show you I will travel to England.'

'You don't have to do that.'

'I know I don't, John, but all lasting relationships are based on trust and I'm entrusting it to you. Besides, if you think I'm not coming, you might go ahead and put yourself on that dating site and I don't want to lose someone else that I care about.' *QED–slam dunk*, she thought. *Here it comes. He's about to take the bait.*

'It would be my honour to take care of it for you.'

'You're such a wonderful man.' *Now, my Mr John Moss, to seal your fate, it's time to distract your attention away from the box.* 'John, there's one more thing I would like to do, but you must promise me never to tell. It has to be our secret.'

John looked at her confused.

'Do you promise?'

'Yes, absolutely.'

'I'm going to send an anonymous cheque, from a benevolent benefactor to your parish council, for the repair of the church roof.'

'Oh Lucy, please don't do that, there's no need.'

'Promise me it will be our secret.' When John hesitated, she repeated her command more forcefully. 'Promise me!'

'I promise.'

Mimicking new love, Lucy allowed the conversation between them to flow, talking with excitement, ardently listening to John. She spoke of and imagined the first Sunday when she would accompany John to church and what his fellow parish council members would make of her. Lucy told John that it would take three weeks to finalise her affairs in Australia.

'Can you see if there are places for me to rent, John? I will stay at the local pub, or a B&B, until a property comes up,' Lucy said, although she had no intention of staying anywhere other than at his place. She was intending to make love with him on the day she arrived, waking up next to him the following morning. Then, while he was at work, she'd prepare an evening meal, before bedding him again that night. Lucy calculated that she would have to stay with John for two or three days, the time required by her to retrieve and hand over the microchip-sized cube to her contacts.

Staying with John is inconvenient, but a necessary insurance, Lucy thought.

The evening flew and they were surprised when an apologetic restaurant owner asked them to leave.

Hand in hand, they strolled back to Lucy's hotel, where she stopped just short of the front door, turned towards John and gave him a tender peck on the lips. *I will have you*, she said to herself, attempting to hide the lustful intentions from her eyes. Normally, her arousal could be gratified easily. Lucy would visit the hotel bar and find a frustrated married man away from home on business to satisfy her desires. She was a consummate professional however, and this was work, John the target. Her own lust would have to wait, creating his part of the entrapment.

Squeezing John's hands, she whispered. 'Look to my coming on the first light of the third week. At dawn look to the east.'

He smiled. 'Gandalf, Lord of the Rings.'

'I knew you'd recognise it. You're such a clever man.'

'Except it was five days.'

'If only that could come true. I will try to make it before then, but don't hold your breath. Goodnight, my handsome prince.' She sighed, and followed with, 'If I don't go now, I may never leave. I will write to you every day.'

Lucy kissed him tenderly, then stepped back and they stared at each other. Unable to control the hunger, their lips met feverishly. She clawed at him, drawing him hard against her breasts. Once Lucy was confident that John was aroused, his bulge evidence of his longing, she pulled away. 'I must go my love, three weeks at the most.'

'Make it two,' John whispered hopefully.

'Two, maybe,' Lucy repeated before turning away. Without looking back, she walked into the hotel and, when the doors closed behind her, Lucy was gone. John felt alone and stood motionless, wondering if the day had been a dream. Fumbling, seeking the evidence he needed, he found the box in his ski jacket pocket. His heart leapt. Lucy was real and had promised to come to England.

***

After leaving John, her lost puppy, pining at the hotel door, Lucy went straight to her room and packed. Except for an overnight case containing essentials for the next day, she put the rest of the luggage in the Jaguar, ready for an early start.

Next morning, as she pushed the start button, she smiled as the exhaust note from her V8 F-Type echoed around the car park. Taking a deep breath, Lucy took in the smell of the car's new leather, the aroma strangely sensual and erotic, before looking at her watch, which showed precisely six thirty. Selecting first gear with the paddle shift, Lucy began the four-and a-half-hour drive to Munich, wondering where the police would stop her, for she knew they'd try.

Leaving Switzerland, the Jaguar roared into Germany, eating up the kilometres with ease. She loved the new grand tourer, but her passion for driving and fine sports cars didn't distract her from being ever vigilant. Lucy was confident that she hadn't been followed from Saint Moritz, although that didn't preclude someone waiting for her along the route, as her mysterious caller had said. A little over three hours into the journey, entering the German village of Oberau, Lucy thought it was a good time to pull over for a coffee break. The decision to stop was made for her as a police car suddenly darted in front of her from a side road. Moments later, another appeared behind. Lucy indicated and pulled over before the police officer in the vehicle had the opportunity to activate his blue flashing lights. The following car cruised in behind the Jaguar but her sudden stop caught the lead police car unaware and it disappeared up the road. 'Hurry up', she said aloud, waiting impatiently in the driver's seat. Two minutes later, the vehicle raced down the other side of the road, made a U-turn and parked in front of her. In the mirror, Lucy saw a third vehicle approaching, a black BMW SUV. It stopped in front of the lead car. *The Secret Service*, she thought.

Lucy recognised Eric Storch, from the German BND (Bundesnachrichtendienst) the federal intelligence service, the moment he stepped from the BMW; the woman who accompanied him was new to her. Casually, they made their way to the Jaguar's driver's side window and Eric gave it a couple of light taps with his knuckle.

The window wound down to the hum of an electric motor.

'Lucy, it's good to see you again.'

'Likewise, Eric.' She moved her eyes to the companion and then back to his.

'Lucy, this is Carla,' Eric said and Carla nodded.

Lucy reciprocated the greeting with, 'Hello Sweetie.'

'To what do we owe this pleasure?' Eric asked.

'What's with the police cars?' Lucy countered.

'Occupational health and safety, for a roadside intercept.'

Lucy laughed. 'The world's gone mad.'

'Indeed. Now Lucy, I repeat, to what do we owe this pleasure?'

'Holidaying. I've had a lovely week of skiing at Saint Moritz. You should try it sometime.'

'You won't mind then, if we search your car?'

'Is that the way you greet old friends?'

Eric shrugged his shoulders. 'What can I say?'

Lucy laughed, 'I would tell you "no", but I doubt I have a choice. The Jaguar is brand new so wash your hands before touching her.'

Eric opened the car door and Lucy stepped out. He nodded to Carla who, glancing into Lucy's eyes, said, 'Step over here please.'

Lucy was surprised to see that she was holding an electronic device with a digital readout and it was clicking, similar to a Geiger counter. Carla proceeded to methodically scan the device over Lucy's body; as she reached the hands, the clicking tone changed pitch slightly.

'Lift your arms,' Carla said, running the device slowly over Lucy's hands again.

'Well?' Eric asked.

'The reading is too small to be certain.'

'Oh, I am more than certain,' Eric said. Peering towards Lucy he shook his head in disappointment. As he continued, the words spitting from his mouth, 'Search her car, open and test everything, everything. Is that clear?'

Carla nodded and walked over to the Jaguar and began a systematic examination of the car.

'What are you expecting to find?' Lucy said to Eric. 'An atomic bomb?'

'Let's wait and see, shall we.'

When Carla opened the boot and removed the luggage, Lucy felt at ease. *The device she'd taken must leak a radioactive signature*, she thought. Partly because of the tear in her dress, but also because she was careful, she'd disposed of the clothing she'd worn during the retrieval, including the white bralette. With luck, she thought, the rest of my clothing will be clear.

With a look of frustration, Eric glanced at Carla and snapped, 'Well?'

'Nothing. Clean.'

'Lucy, the word is that you have it!'

'Have what?'

'Don't play coy with me, my friend,' he said, but the stress on the last word did not suggest affection. 'If this is one of your freelance jobs, let me give you a word of warning. Keep it sealed in its container; any exposure will be detrimental to your health. You understand, I'm sure.'

Pointing to the instrument in Carla's hand, Lucy said, 'Are you looking for something radioactive?'

'You don't know what it is, do you?' Carla said.

Lucy shrugged her shoulders.

Eric laughed as he said, 'See what happens when you freelance? Now, enjoy your stay in Germany.'

Lucy climbed back into the driver's seat of the Jaguar and closed the door. Eric looked at her through the open driver's window. 'You do understand that other governments and those underworld types that you seem so fond of will try to extract the information from you? They are not as polite as we Germans.'

'Who would want to extract anything from little ole me?' Lucy said, using her stock cute voice.

Eric laughed again. 'Do me a favour. My life would be a whole lot easier if you didn't hang around Germany for too long. Let's go!' he shouted out as he and Carla headed back to the SUV.

'Hey,' Lucy called out after him. 'This thing you're looking for. Who lost it?'

Eric turned, chuckling as he said, 'The Ministry of State Security, the MSS, the intelligence and security agency of the People's Republic of China. That's who.'

Lucy waited for the cars to leave before continuing with her plan to take a coffee break. Turning from the main road, the Jaguar cruised into the town, stopping outside a quaint looking café. Before getting out, Lucy waited for a full five minutes, watching in case the BND were not alone in waiting for her in Oberau. Nothing seemed out of the ordinary and, in any case a team of Chinese agents would be noticeable in a small town like Oberau. Oberau was an unlikely place for the Chinese state to intercept her, Lucy considered, making it an ideal location for a late breakfast. She knew that as the agency of a rising superpower, the MSS might be more brazen than the established intelligence agencies. With that in mind, she positioned herself at a table with an unimpeded view of the street. Eating breakfast, Lucy was surprised; she felt unsettled, nervous. *Where is that coming from?* she said to herself, unaccustomed to experiencing emotion, especially fear.

The remainder of the drive to Munich was uneventful and she made for the Bayerischer Hotel, near the city centre, her usual haunt. She liked the hotel because of its proximity to the park. With a couple of kilometres to go, Lucy let her mind drift, anticipating a pleasant walk along the wide tree lined pathways. The Jaguar was cruising in the centre of a three-lane road. Refocusing her attention, Lucy knew that, after the next crossing, she needed to move to the left, ready to make a turn. The traffic lights at the approaching intersection changed to amber and then red, so Lucy allowed the Jaguar to gently coast up to the car in front. Checking the mirrors, she saw a vehicle behind and the lanes beside her were free. *Once the lights change, it will be clear to move across to the left*, she thought.

Lucy glanced at the Jaguar's side mirrors. Left, right, they were empty. *Wait, what's that?* She saw two indistinct shapes in the distance, then the unmistakable outline of fast approaching cars.

115

Mind racing, she realised she had to take evasive action. *Too late.*
The vehicle in front was in high-speed reverse, stopping as it
nudged the Jaguar's bumper, forcing Lucy to halt. The vehicle
behind pulled up close until she was penned in front and back, no
options open, except to dump the car and make a run for it. Before
Lucy could open the car door, the other vehicle she'd seen pulled
up close beside her, smashing the Jaguar's driver's side mirror. The
only remaining avenue of escape was the passenger door and that
option dissolved as another car stopped alongside. Lucy guessed
she was about to be boarded. A smartly dressed Asian man stepped
from the car and pulled on the Jaguar's passenger door; it was
locked. A person from the car on her left wound down his window
and pointed a gun at her, saying, 'Open up.' He was also Chinese,
and Lucy suspected, from the MSS.

As her escape options had evaporated, Lucy unlocked the
door and with pistol drawn, the MSS agent slid into the Jaguar. As
the Jaguar door closed behind him, the vehicles containing her
drove off, vanishing as expeditiously as they had appeared.

Lucy greeted her unwelcome passenger, a shallow smile
decorating her face as she said, 'Hello Sweetie.'

Outwardly Lucy feigned calm while inside her brain raced,
searching for a means of escape. She was trapped and using the car
as a weapon seemed her only option. Lucy considered accelerating
hard and slamming on the brakes, sending the assailant smashing

into the windscreen; but that was made more difficult the moment he put on the seatbelt.

'Drive,' the MSS man instructed.

'I'm not an Uber driver,' Lucy said and when he didn't reply, she added, 'Where to?'

'Just drive,' the agent snapped.

Using peripheral vision, Lucy gauged her adversary. He was peering out of the windscreen, eyes fixed on the road ahead, while holding a pistol pointed at her. Coldly, she calculated the chances of disarming him without being shot herself. *If I strike quickly.* Lucy allowed the fingers of her right hand to loosen their grip on the steering wheel, a tiny change that even a trained observer may have missed.

Without moving his gaze from the front of the car, her passenger said, 'Keep both hands on the wheel,' adding a moment later, 'Take the next left.'

He's a skilled agent. Extracting myself from this will prove challenging. Checking in the mirror, Lucy spotted the cars that had penned in the Jaguar; they'd reappeared and were patrolling in formation behind them. She suspected that, like the Bundesnachrichtendienst, the MSS intended to interrogate her about the location of the missing object; for the moment at least, they wanted her alive. *It's time to test the boundaries*, she said to herself.

'I told you to turn left,' the man said, as Lucy cruised straight into the intersection without reducing speed. At the last possible moment, she threw the Jaguar to the left, tyres squealing. She stamped on the accelerator and the Jaguar's V8 engine barked into life. In seconds they were roaring down the road at over a hundred kilometres per hour, the following cars left behind.

For the first time, the passenger looked at her, his face unreadable, but he was unmoved by her antics. Lowering the pistol, he pointed it at Lucy's foot and then, with a voice devoid of all emotion, he said, 'I will count to three.'

Lucy applied the brakes before he could say the first number. They wanted her alive, but just alive would be enough. The agent would maim her, with scant regard for his own safety, as she herself had done on many occasions.

'Next right.'

Lucy followed his instructions and, as they drove down the road, old factories, derelict buildings and warehouses came in sight. They entered a deserted industrial estate. *Time is running out.* On a former mission, she'd crashed the passenger side of a car, driving it head on into a solid object, killing her assailant. Her injuries had not been too severe, managing to hobble away. It was different this time. *If I survive the impact*, she thought to herself, *the chances of getting out of the car and running away are zero, given the following armed escort. No, that won't work. I could slide the Jaguar sidewards, smashing the passenger's side door into a pole and kill him. Assuming I can drive afterwards, the car chase might give me time to find his pistol. Armed, and in the right location, I could take them all. Have I disabled the airbags?* From a previous experience, Lucy knew that when the airbags exploded the car's electronics were fried, the vehicle immobilised. She usually pulled the airbag fuses out; not this time, not on the new Jaguar. Reprimanding herself, she thought, *Sloppy Lucy, you're becoming sloppy.*

'Turn right.'

She did as she was told.

'On your left, you will see a cyclone fence. Then, in a hundred metres, a gate. I want you to enter at the gate.'

Lucy slowed the Jaguar as they approached and passing through, she spotted a warehouse with a substantial roller door, now in front.

'Keep driving.'

As they approached the entrance, it rumbled open.

'Drive in.'

The Jaguar left the gravel surface of the car park and drove onto the smooth concrete floor of the building. Glancing at the broken mirrors, Lucy watched the other cars follow her into the building.

'Stop. Now, keep both of your hands on the wheel.'

Lucy saw the roller door close behind them; she was imprisoned. The passenger faced her and raised his pistol so that it pointed at her head as from outside, the driver's door was opened.

'Out!' commanded a male voice from someone Lucy couldn't see.

As she climbed from the car, Lucy scanned her environment, taking stock of the surrounds, assessing her situation and trying to find a means of escape. The man who had opened the car door backed away. Keeping a safe distance, he pointed a pistol at her. Lucy calculated he was standing five metres away. This agent was accompanied by two others, both armed, also five metres away, forming a half-moon arc around her, each outside of her strike range; they were taking no chances. Looking down, Lucy saw the distinctive red dot of a laser sight on her chest. She traced its origins and spied, on the mezzanine floor above, the barrel of a high-powered rifle. Including her passenger, she counted five people and, assuming the three accompanying cars had two people apiece, there were eleven in the team. *This is a big operation*, she thought.

Indicating by waving his pistol in the direction he wanted her to go, the man who had opened the car door said, 'That way.'

As she started walking, Lucy saw another man about twenty-five metres in front of them. *That makes twelve,* she whispered to herself. He was an Asian man, mid-fifties, wearing silver-rimmed spectacles and dressed in a smart charcoal coloured suit. He was standing by a table, a few metres from which was a high-backed chair. Attached to the arms and back of the chair were leather restraining straps.

I'm going to be tortured.

As they walked towards the table, the escort remained at a safe distance, eliminating any opportunity for her to disarm one to use the weapon against the others.

They have done their homework.

'You can stop now,' directed the man with the silver-rimmed glasses. 'Welcome Lucy. My name is Chen Li.'

'I've never heard of you, Sweetie,' Lucy said, but she was lying and he knew it.

Chen Li laughed cynically as he said, 'Western arrogance. Search her!'

This might be my only opportunity, Lucy thought.

The man tasked with the job handed his firearm to a colleague before approaching Lucy and she knew it was pointless subduing him to use as a shield; the others wouldn't hesitate in killing him to retrieve her.

'Arms out.'

Spreading her arms like a scarecrow, the agent patted down her upper body before saying, 'Spread your legs.'

'You cheeky thing. I'm not that kind of girl,' she said.

Ignoring her comments, he pulled her legs apart, searching her lower body. He was quick and efficient, not lingering around her groin. A professional doing a job. 'She's clean.'

'Good,' Chen Li said. 'Now test her.'

From the table, the unarmed man took a device similar to the one used by the BND earlier.

Larger and more sensitive, Lucy thought.

After being searched in Oberau, Lucy had scrubbed her hands vigorously, hoping to remove residual traces of the object they were seeking. This device was different, requiring its operator to use headphones; she detected no clicking but, like the BND, he was meticulous in his scanning, going back and forth several times.

'Nothing,' he said finally.

Chen Li was angry, snapping, 'Check the car. I want it stripped down to nothing.' The man holding the scanning device nodded as he and his device left the vicinity.

Pointing to the vacant chair, Chen Li said, 'If you wouldn't mind, my dear.'

Once seated, another unarmed agent approached. He proceeded to secure her arms with the leather straps to the chair. When the job was done, he rejoined his colleagues and retrieved his pistol. Lucy noticed that despite being fastened to the chair, her sentries weren't dropping their guard, remaining a safe four metres away, positioned so that they could shoot without hitting one another in the crossfire.

'My dear, we haven't done the proper introductions. As I said, my name is Chen Li. I work for the Chinese Ministry of State Security in The People's Republic of China. You people call us the MSS.'

With few escape options at her disposal, Lucy decided antagonising her captives might elicit a mistake. 'I've still never heard of you, Sweetie,' she said, pausing before continuing, 'MSS, doesn't that stand for "Maintenance Solution Systems", a garbage company!'

Chen Li laughed saying, 'How apt for you, my dear. Yes, that is my job, to dispose of rubbish like yourself.'

Lucy responded quickly with, 'Recycling, I trust?'

From the table, Chen Li picked up a dossier and, opening it, he started reading aloud from it.

'The eldest of three children, you were born Lucia Da-dic in the village of Kula Grand, which is near Zvornik, in Bosnia Herzegovina. From your early school reports, you were a socially and academically advanced girl for your age. Aged eight, you were kidnapped by traffickers and sold into child sex slavery. You were subsequently taken to a house in a town called Macinec, Croatia. This is where you remained until being rescued, aged fourteen, by an international team led by British operatives, Max and Olivia. They had been gathering intelligence on Russian Mafia gangs suspected of illegal arms sales in the Middle East when they stumbled on your image on a child pornography site on the dark web. Cooperating with the child exploitation operatives, it took them another two years to trace you and then mount a rescue operation... How touching,' he added sarcastically.

'After being freed, you were reunited with your family; that was at the beginning of the Balkans war.' He stopped reading aloud, skimming the pages, his eyes flicking from side to side. Thirty seconds later he said, 'In summary, it says that you experienced difficulties settling back into family life. You became a bitch and were even suspected of torturing animals. Very nasty.'

'At age seventeen, at the height of the Balkan War, you ran away from home to be with your then boyfriend Ratimir, a commander in one of General Ratko Mladic's paramilitary militia units, "The Yellow Wasps". It was here that you gained your military training, changing your name to Claudia.'

Chen Li paused and looked at Lucy before he continued, 'The name Claudia comes from the rearranging of letters in your birth name. It was Ratimir's suggestion to create a memorable name, one that would strike fear into the hearts of those who heard it. On all accounts, it seems you succeeded.'

Chen Li looked back down at the dossier and started reading again. 'It says that, while it's not known the exact number of killings, murders and executions directly attributed to you during the Balkan War, it is estimated to be over fifty. Prosecutors have prima facie evidence of thirty-two.'

Chen Li paused and looked at Lucy again.

'You were a busy little thing,' he said, chuckling.

'At the end of the war, sought by the International War Crimes Commission, you vanished and we know you fled to the United Kingdom.'

'Now I find this very interesting,' Chen Li said, smiling sarcastically. 'While living in England, you gained a keen interest in Western literature, philosophy and poetry. Eastern culture is by far more enlightening, my dear. Do you know what else it says about you? You do not believe in a God, yet you can quote the Bible, chapter and verse. You're a peculiar mix!' he mocked.

'You return to the spotlight when you meet Monya Mogilevick, a Russian billionaire, property tycoon and head of a Russia Mafia syndicate called "The Brotherhood". Monya is also a close associate of the Russian President, where he is known as the "President's Gardener". He is the Kremlin's go-to person, with his company called Keiser, providing mercenaries to foster the Kremlin's causes in the Ukraine, Syria, Africa or wherever the Russian President directs. When you met Monya, you were working at a London lap dancing club, one that he frequented. Sources say that you saved Monya's life by killing four assassins bent on taking him out, yet you were unarmed. He offered you a job and you become a lieutenant, an enforcer in the Russian Mafia and then later you became his mistress.

'I have a list of fifteen executions that are attributed to you. I could read you their names?' Chen Li looked at Lucy. When she remained silent, he said, 'You don't want me to?'

Chen Li looked at the dossier again. 'When you were with Monya, myth has it that if a person knew they were the target of the infamous "Claudia", they would take their own life, rather than face your wrath. You had a reputation for nastiness, slaying, enjoying your task, rather than simply killing.' Chen Li laughed. 'You were a nasty piece of work! Then it all began to fall apart.

'You were sent by the Russian Mafia to retrieve a device known as the Janus Key. You were not to know that your adversaries were to be Max and Olivia, the very people who liberated you from child sex slavery and now eighty-seven years of age. Not surprisingly, at first, you didn't recognise them. You held Max captive in one of your safe houses in Scotland and were about to terminate him. With the pistol pointed at his head, you realised his identity. Instead of killing him, you take Max with you to Russia and Monya.' Chen Li shook his head. 'This was the beginning of the end of the famous Claudia. Compassion doesn't sit well with Claudia, does it?'

'Our intelligence tells us it was while in Russia that Max realised your true identity, Lucia Da-dic and he commenced a systematic psychological disassembling of you.'

Chen Li stopped speaking and began scanning and missing pages in the file.

'I'm going to skip to the interesting part. You are holding Max and Olivia captive on board Monya's super yacht, the *Lelantos* and under instruction to dispatch both of them forthwith. Thanks to CIA action, the yacht explodes and starts sinking in the Mediterranean. The crew abandoned ship; Max and Olivia would have drowned, but you went back on board, saving them both.'

Chen Li shook his head. 'The famous Claudia defects to MI6, changes her name back to Lucia, abbreviating it to Lucy and you're suddenly a British agent, although nothing like your former self.

'As you would have expected, your ex-lover Monya puts a bounty on your head and now we have a gap in our intelligence. You see, Monya withdrew the kill order and we don't know why that might be. What happened? Did you kiss and make up?' Chen Li said, laughing.

'My dear Lucy, do you know what our "risk assessment" says about you? It advises that you are highly dangerous and to handle you with extreme care and caution. They give you our highest threat level.'

He stared at Lucy for seconds that seemed like minutes.

'My dear, I wouldn't call you hazardous; intelligence reports can be so misleading. Perhaps you were once a foe to be reckoned with, but not anymore. What I find interesting is what it says about the old timers Max and Olivia.'

He started reading again. 'It tells me that extreme care must be taken and they are regarded in the same manner as yourself, high threat. I also find that unbelievable, they must be at least eighty-eight years of age?'

'Back to where we started. As you see, my dear, although you claim never to have heard of us, we know all about you, well, almost. After this encounter, I will update our records to read: Claudia, aka Lucy, is yesterday's woman, a "has-been", as you in the West would say, threat level low, minuscule.'

He stopped speaking and sniffed in the air three times as he said, 'I can smell the fear on you. I'll write, emotionally vulnerable and weak. What do you think?'

'If I'm so ineffectual, why not untie me?'

'Come now, Lucy. Unlike you, I'm not stupid.'

Lucy ignored the remarks of Chen Li because her eyes were drawn to the sound of activity coming from the direction of the Jaguar. A team of five people had arrived and were beginning to disassemble the car. Seventeen of them, she counted to herself while thinking. *This isn't just big, it's a major overseas intelligence operation, something on this scale, I'll be lucky if I live. How are you going to escape this, girlie?* Even if she could free herself, Lucy knew that she'd be shot before she reached any of the guards. Even though she was tied to the chair, the sniper remained vigilant, a red dot trained on her chest. They were taking no chances. The noises from the Jaguar, hammering, air and rattle guns became Lucy's companion as she waited, her guards mute, watching her. Lucy watched as the engine and transmission were removed from her beloved car and then stripped down. Next, the interior was ripped out; everything inspected with their scanner.

Then the warehouse was quiet. They'd finished.

The man and his scanning device returned and said, 'It's clean.'

Chen Li said nothing. Instead he strolled over to a table and opened what appeared to Lucy to be a medicine bag. When he removed dental equipment, Lucy knew what was coming; agony.

'My dear Lucy,' said Chen Li, 'An item of great value has been stolen from the People's Republic of China. You took it and know where it is. If you return it, you'll be free to leave. A simple choice.'

Lucy knew the risks she took. Pain went with the territory. She could tell them about John, but that would put his life at risk, with little guarantee that she'd be released.

'Sweetie, some would consider stealing from China fair recompense, particularly when your economic rise has been built on stealing others' secrets. If my history serves me correctly, when left to your own devices, the Chinese couldn't produce optical-quality glass, though you were masters of paper folding.'

Chen Li smiled. 'You are trying to insult me, Lucy. Most believe origami was invented in Japan, but paper manufacture and paper folding were perfected in China in A.D. 105, long before the Japanese.'

Lucy smiled back at Chen Li as she said, 'You had glass in B.C, 475 but, without stealing other countries' technology, you couldn't make the jump to optics. Nothing has changed much over the centuries, has it?'

Inside Chen Li felt rage grow. Suppressing it before it took hold, he said, 'For a woman in your situation, I find your provocative behaviour strange. Why would you antagonise your captor? Is it a demonstration of your Western arrogance? Nevertheless, that is a philosophical debate for another time. Now Lucy, I will ask you once more, where is it?'

'The plans for the Dongfeng - 41 or the DF-17?'

'Amusing, but you try my patience,' Chen Li said, laughing as he continued, 'Pure fantasy Lucy. How you in the West wish you had the plans for the world's longest-range Intercontinental Missile or our new hypersonic glider missiles, but you don't. Your anti-missile shields are useless; the balance of strategic power is shifting in our favour. Enough of your petty procrastination. Now where is it?'

'I don't know who's spreading these false rumours about me. Perhaps they are intended to put you off the scent? If so, they're working. The German security services searched me this morning and now, so have you. Can't you see? It's obvious I don't have it, and nor have I had contact with it. Now, if you would put my car back together, I will be on my way.'

Chen Li gave Lucy a look of derision as he held aloft a stainless-steel dental pick and said, 'Toothache is described as the most intense and agonising of pains. Mr Yáyī finds it surprisingly satisfying, digging around in someone's cavities.'

He pointed to one of the armed agents standing on Lucy's left.

Watching the tooth pick, Lucy said calmly, 'There's little point in torturing me. The prisoner will say whatever it is they think you want to hear. You know this. Anything to stop the pain. Torture is a most unreliable way of collecting information.'

'We shall see, my dear, we shall see,' Chen Li said as he took dental extraction pliers from the bag and held them for Lucy to see. 'When you were working for the Russian Mafia, how many fingers did you cut off?'

Lucy didn't answer.

'I find such acts barbaric, a primitive way of sending a message. When we've finished probing your fillings, Mr Yáyī, is going to remove some of your teeth. He's rather good at it, which is why we call him "The Dentist". Despite the agony, I can promise Mr Yáyī will not damage either your gums or jaw. In six months' time with a good set of prosthetics, personally I would recommend dental implants, no one will ever know your teeth were removed and your beauty will be restored, almost. You on the other hand will understand our generosity, while having a permanent reminder of what we might have done. A souvenir, if you will, of what occurs when you cross the People's Republic of China. Torture may be unreliable, Lucy, but it is pleasurable, isn't it Mr Yáyī?'

Mr Yáyī, nodded and smiled.

'Now Mr Yáyī,' Chen Li said, 'if you're ready.'

Like the others had done before approaching Lucy, he gave his firearm to another guard. Stepping behind the chair, he fastened one of the leather straps across her chest, then secured her legs so that Lucy couldn't move. Mr Yáyī joined Chen Li at the table placed in front of Lucy.

'My lower right third molar, my wisdom tooth, has been playing up. While you're in there, could you sort it out?'

Ignoring Lucy, Chen Li picked up a digital camera and said, 'Before I allow Mr Yáyī to ply his craft, I'm going to take some happy snaps of you–is that what you Westerners say? We in China prefer to call it biometric photography for our facial recognition system. You, my dear Lucy, will be blacklisted, banned from entering China. If you were ever to find your way past our border controls, our vast network of surveillance cameras would soon flag you and, of course, you would find that travel on trains or buses would be impossible. Our police have AI technology glasses that can facilitate facial recognition in seconds. Impressive, no?'

'Sweetie, that's very Orwellian of you, just the kind of overreach the world is coming to expect from your nasty autocratic regime.'

'That's hypocritical coming from a Russian spy. Oh wait, you work for the British and Americans now; Loyalty is a problem for you, is it? Did you know that there are over six million surveillance cameras in the UK, more per head than in any other country?'

Lucy smiled as she said, 'Other than China.'

Chen Li nodded, 'Other than China. You see, our countries are not so different.'

'Except the West is using the technology to monitor criminals, not for the social control of its citizens. The world has seen your style of "Re-education camps" before; they were dark times.'

'You should be careful before drawing historic parallels,' snapped Chen Li. 'Ours are vocational training centres, intended to combat extremism. Demonising China is xenophobic prejudice, your Cold War rhetoric. Our aim is to preserve social harmony for the betterment of the Chinese people. Enough of this! Now, you can look at the camera or Mr Yáyī will hold your head, your choice– democracy, if you like. It may be wise to remember that he's about to provide your dental treatment.'

While Chen Li took his facial photographs, Lucy held her head motionless.

'Excellent. Mr Yáyī, she's all yours.'

Opening her mouth partially in defiance, Lucy ran her tongue provocatively over her teeth and then said, 'Is this an extension to your involuntary organ harvesting program? You need free teeth now? Is murdering members of the Falun Gong spiritual group and taking their organs for transplant and forcibly taking the organs from ethnic minorities, detainees, and prisoners, not enough? History has seen these crimes against humanity before. I find it sad that you can't come up with anything original. What was it the China tribunal said? "Victim for victim and death for death, cutting out the hearts and other organs from the living, blameless, harmless, peaceable people constitutes one of the worst mass atrocities of this century." I think I might have been mistaken. You're not repeating history, you're creating it.'

Chen Li felt the rage build again and he wanted to lash out at Lucy, striking her as hard as he could. He took two steps towards her before regaining control. He laughed and then said, 'You're a nasty piece of work, a real turd.'

He looked at Mr Yáyī, telling him to ensure that she was secure.

Mr Yáyī nodded before fastening a further strap around Lucy, across her forehead, tightening it as he said, 'When the pain becomes insufferable, this will stop your head from moving.' He smiled menacingly. 'I wouldn't want to slip with the pliers.'

He walked from behind the chair and moved close, digging his fingers into Lucy's jaw, forcing her mouth open. Mr Yáyī rammed something into her mouth to prevent it from closing. Returning to the table, he turned and held up the dental pick so that she could see it and gave her a sadistic grin.

'My dear Lucy,' Chen Li said. 'This is your last chance. What have you done with our property?'

He approached and removed the object holding her mouth open so that she could speak, but Lucy remained mute, her mouth open, as if visiting a family dentist. However, her outside calm was an illusion, fear rippled through her body. Normally in these situations, Lucy was emotionally numb, but unusually, for the second time that day, she disappointed herself.

Wiping a bead of sweat away from Lucy's forehead, Chen Li said, 'You're getting soft. Mr Yáyī. You won't be needing the mouth wedge, our guest has something to prove.'

Looking at Lucy, Chen Li said, 'My dear, I've always found the macabre art of torture quite satisfying, as I'm sure you have too.'

'If you love it so much, I'm happy to swap positions with you.'

'I'm looking forward to seeing you suffer. The famous Claudia.' Chen Li chortled, a low raucous sound from deep within his chest. 'Oh, I am sorry, it's Lucy now isn't it? You haven't lived up to Claudia's mythical reputation. You've proven yourself to be a disappointment. Mr Yáyī, let the fun begin.'

Mr Yáyī, went to the table, put on a face mask and a white apron over his suit.

'In case you bleed,' he said, while smiling to himself.

Picking up his first weapon, the dental pick, he walked towards her saying,

'Open wide, please.'

Lucy did as she was told and, when he reached her, he leaned in and gazed inside her mouth. Lucy felt the sharp point of the probe enter and start moving about, prodding, poking, exploring her teeth.

'It's a shame,' he said. 'You've taken such good care of them. I will have to do a little drilling to expose a nice, juicy, fresh nerve.'

Chen Li's mobile phone rang and the caller ID display read Eric Storch, his German counterpart from the German BND.

'Wait,' he said softly to Mr Yáyī.

'Good afternoon, Mr Storch. To what do I owe this pleasure?'

137

'Please Chen, call me Eric. I would like to speak with Lucy. I know she is with you.'

'What makes you think that?'

'I'm outside!'

'Outside,' Chen Li repeated loudly. He dropped the phone away from his mouth, so Eric Storch couldn't hear what he was saying.

'Check,' he gestured to his men, while waving his arms toward the front and back of the building. Lifting the phone to his mouth,

'What are you doing out there?'

'Oh, we like to keep an eye on our foreign visitors, to ensure they enjoy their stay in our beautiful country. Lucy, if I may!'

'Just a minute, please.' Chen Li looked at the agents who were checking the perimeter. *We have company*, came the call.

'Untie her,' Chen Li snapped.

Mr Yáyī removed Lucy's straps, and Chen Li placed his phone in her hands. Lucy was tempted to place a sharp kick aimed at the testicles of the dentist.

Now is not the time, she said to herself.

Instead, she gave a polite thank you.

'Hello Eric,' a relieved Lucy said. 'It's not often I can say that I'm pleased you're keeping track of me.'

'Are you okay?'

'I've been a little tied up, if you know what I mean. You wouldn't happen to have a spare set of wheels that I could borrow? Mine has gone to pieces. They don't make Jaguars like they used to.'

'I see you haven't lost your sense of humour. Hand me back to Chen Li. Let's see if we can't get you out of there.'

CHAPTER 7

Penny

German BND (Bundesnachrichtendienst) headquarters Munich

'Am I under arrest?' Lucy asked.

Eric Storch shook his head. 'No, you're a voluntary guest. After we saved your arse, I thought you would be grateful.'

'I am grateful, Eric, yet I find myself seated in one of your interview rooms answering questions while drinking cheap instant coffee from a Styrofoam cup. You must excuse me for thinking that I'm being interrogated. How silly of me. So, I take it, I'm free to leave?'

'Can I be frank with you, Lucy?'

'Of course, Eric.'

'Lucy, you've had a difficult day and considering your reputation the German Government is ...' Eric paused, searching for the right word in English, '... apprehensive that you may seek retribution against the MSS for the loss of your Jaguar and their treatment of you. Acts of aggression by foreign agents on our soil are an affront to our sovereignty. We are expressing this view in the strongest possible terms to the People's Republic of China's State Security Service, and now to you. Lucy. When you depart, I want to be certain that you leave Germany immediately. Am I clear?'

Lucy raised an eyebrow as she said, pretending to be surprised, 'Perfectly. Are you banning me from visiting your wonderful country, Eric?'

'Not at all. I would prefer to describe it as a period of time out, to let everything calm down while you cool off.'

'Who me?'

'I've spoken to London and they tell me that you're not freelancing, which is what I first thought. MI6 is grateful for our intervention. They agree that a break from Germany is wise, under the circumstances. Do we understand each other, Lucy?'

'Yes, we do.'

'Tell me your travel plans?'

'I was planning on staying in Munich for a week before going to Australia. I could bring those travel plans forward?'

'What business do you have in Australia?'

'I'm staying with Penny, Max, and Olivia's granddaughter.'

'The girl who was kidnapped by your ex-lover, Monya Mogilevick, and taken to New Zealand?'

'Yes, that's the one.'

'How is she after her ordeal?'

'She has Max and Olivia's genes, so resilient.'

'After your run-in with the MSS and our timely rescue, I consider you owe us a favour Lucy.'

'Indeed, which is why I will go to Australia.'

'I see. Well, two favours. Why did Monya kidnap Penny? Presumably he wanted something from Max and Olivia in return for her release? The conundrum, however, is why, after you freed her, he removed the bounty from your head. Isn't that out of character?'

'Eric, I am indebted, but I'm sure you will appreciate I'm unable to share operational details. Should I ever work for the BND you would expect my silence too; a guarantee of propriety, if you will.'

Eric admired Lucy's professionalism, but with his curiosity roused, he kept on probing.

'I understand. Confidentiality is essential in covert missions. We know the Bundesministerium für Inneres (BMI), the Austrian

Federal Ministry of Interior, were displeased that British Intelligence meddled in Melk, Austria, as we were when, a couple of days later, Max and Olivia were arrested in Regensburg, Germany, after causing chaos and millions of Euros of damage. They should have been locked up and the key thrown away, but what happens instead? The CIA intervenes and they are released. Without betraying confidences, Lucy, could you at least confirm something that we suspect?' He looked at Lucy, who remained expressionless.

'You stole something from the Melk Monastery?'

Lucy thought for a moment before answering, 'I was at the Monastery.'

'That we already know,' Eric said.

'Did they report something was missing?'

'No.'

'There's your answer, Eric.'

'I'll take that as an affirmative.'

Lucy shrugged. 'Take it any way you wish.'

'Back to the matter at hand. If I were to contact Penny, would she confirm your story about going to Australia?'

Lucy adopted a tone suggesting offence as she said, 'Eric, you don't think I would lie to you?'

'Not at all Lucy, it's just that I like to consider myself thorough, so do you have her number?' Without waiting for an answer, Eric pushed a pen and piece of paper across the table. 'If you would be so kind?'

'It would be my pleasure, Eric,' Lucy said, sarcasm oozing as the words spun from her lips. She wrote down the number and pushed the paper back across the table.

'I'll be back.'

'Isn't that a line out of one of the Terminator movies?' Imitating Arnold Schwarzenegger, Lucy repeated, 'I'll be back.'

Eric shook his head in disbelief before standing and leaving the interview room.

Twenty minutes later he returned.

'Did you speak to Penny?' Lucy asked.

Eric nodded. 'She's smooth. If I didn't know better, I'd say that you've been training her. Have you?'

'Little ole me?'

'Yes, you!' Eric sighed. 'Penny confirmed your plans and will be pleased to see you tomorrow.'

'Tomorrow?' Lucy said, her eyes opening widely.

'Yes. Tonight, you're booked on a flight to Australia...'

'Business class, I hope?' Lucy interrupted.

Eric shook his head in exasperation. 'Yes, and at the German taxpayers' expense. We will see you safely on the plane, for your own protection.'

This will work well, thought Lucy. *I can skype and send photos of myself to John with Australian icons in the background. It builds the credibility of my cover.*

'Can I collect my clothes?'

'From where Lucy? They went the way of the Jaguar.'

'You could lend me your credit card?'

Eric took his mobile phone from his pocket and started to dial.

'Who are you ringing?' Lucy asked.

'The airport, to see if there's an earlier flight.'

Lucy laughed. 'Touché, Eric. To even us up, let me tell you this: we stole a Bible from the monastery at Melk, something Monya desperately wanted and that didn't exist, or so everyone thought. You can't lose what you don't have. Shall we call it a draw?'

Eric nodded.

'You wouldn't happen to have my purse and passport?'

Eric smiled as he said, 'We did pick those up for you.'

***

Melbourne, Australia

Having been asked to leave Germany, Lucy touched down in Melbourne after a long flight. She was feeling particularly cantankerous after twenty-three hours on the plane, the run-in with the Chinese and knowing that the item that she had been sent to retrieve was in the hands of a man she barely knew.

Picking a fight with Immigration or Border Force, as it was known in Australia, is never wise, but can be amusing if skillfully done.

'Good morning, Madam,' said the Airport Border Force Security officer while checking Lucy's Passport. 'How long do you intend staying in Australia?'

'I'll be gone in three weeks minus two days.'

The man looked up from her passport, surprised by the tone of her answer.

'Sorry,' Lucy said. 'Let me help you. That's nineteen days.'

Ignoring her sarcasm, the officer asked, 'You don't have a return ticket, Madam?'

Lucy scoffed, 'That's a bit harsh isn't it? I've only just got off the plane! Are you offering to sell me one?'

'Before letting you into Australia, we need to be sure that you won't overstay your visa.'

'Stay in Australia? Why would anyone in their right mind want to do that when "g'day mate" and "Aussie Aussie Aussie, Oi Oi Oi" is the extent of the manifestation of Australian intellectual achievement,' Lucy said, juxtaposing a broad Australian accent and then what the British call perceived pronunciation or BBC English.

The Border Force officer raised his eyebrows. 'Are you intending to work during your stay?'

'Work in Australia,' Lucy said in mock exasperation. 'You must be joking. I've read how Australia treats its foreign workers. Those in the hospitality industry are underpaid and fruit pickers, if not imprisoned as slave labour, pay more for their accommodation than they earn. According to the Deputy Prime Minister of Australia, your Pacific island neighbours affected by climate change will continue to survive "because many of their workers come here to pick our fruit". As I see it, Australia is intent on sinking their islands with its carbon emissions for the free labour it will get from the climate change refugees. I wouldn't work in Australia if you paid me. Which, as it turns out, you won't.'

The officer suspected by now that Lucy was going to be one of those irritating customers. Keeping his cool, he asked the next question. 'Madam is travelling without luggage, not even hand luggage? Can you tell me why?'

'I've got all a woman needs.' Lucy held up her small handbag. 'Louis Vuitton.'

'If Madam would kindly answer the question!'

'Certainly.' Lucy tilted her head to one side as if in deep reflection. 'What was it again, the question?'

Unfazed, the officer repeated, 'Can you tell me why you are travelling without luggage?'

'That's obvious, isn't it?' Lucy said.

'Not to me,' answered the Border Force officer.

'Clearly, if Australia can't afford to pay its workers, you need visitors like me to spend my money while I'm here. As soon as I leave the airport, I will purchase the items needed for my stay. As Australia hasn't increased the payment it makes to its welfare recipients for fifteen years, I will donate all of my purchases to charity shops the day I leave. Consider my lack of luggage as foreign aid from Britain.'

The officer, finding Lucy's answers increasingly annoying, asked, 'If Madam believes Australia to be so unpleasant, why come here?'

'Most inconvenient, but my friend was born, lives and works here. I did suggest that she sue her parents for their tragic misdemeanour. Bloody genetics, that's why I am here.'

The officer stamped Lucy's passport. 'Welcome to Australia Madam. I hope you enjoy your stay.'

To confuse the officer further, Lucy changed her demeanour from an antagonist, to a sweet, grateful tourist. Giving an apparently sincere smile, Lucy said, 'Thank you. I'm looking forward to my stay in your wonderful country. I hope the rest of your day will be as pleasant as mine.'

***

Lucy didn't expect to be followed, but habit stopped her heading directly for Penny's flat. From the airport, she took a taxi to Southern Cross station, where she used cash to purchase a Myki, the travel card for Melbourne's public transport system. Leaving the station, Lucy zig-zagged her way through the city streets before doubling back and catching a train to Hawthorn. From there, it was a ten-minute tram ride, followed by a two-kilometre walk. Arriving at Penny's flat, Lucy was confident she hadn't been followed, but if they were tracking her mobile phone, they knew exactly where she was staying. She knocked on the door.

'Lucy, it's wonderful to see you,' Penny said, giving her a hug. They'd only known each other for a year, yet it felt like a lifetime; friendship born from adversity. Penny's grandparents, Max and Olivia, had sent Lucy to see her safely from Monya's captivity. Max had told Penny that both he and her grandmother had trusted Lucy with their lives and so must she. After the rescue,

Penny suggested Lucy teach her the "tradecraft", espionage tactics, and Lucy had agreed. In her line of work, friends that could be trusted were a rare commodity. Penny was a friend.

Releasing the embrace, Lucy said, 'I'm pleased to be here.'

'Come in. So what happened? You weren't due for another week.'

'Change of plans, fortuitous, as it turns out. I'll tell you about it when I've freshened up. After twenty-three hours on a plane, even I can smell myself.'

'Your things are in the spare room,' Penny said as she glanced at Lucy's empty hands. 'I see you're travelling light. Is that why you left a suitcase of clothes and a lap-top here?'

'Indeed it is Penny, although this isn't what I had planned. Nevertheless, consider it another lesson in your training. Speaking of which, have you been following the routine we set last time I was here?'

Penny nodded.

'Did you purchase the items I requested?'

'Yes. I used a library computer to order the overseas items and the credit card you sent me. For the local things, cash. Precisely as you directed.'

'Good. I'll go and clean up.'

Penny was waiting in the kitchen when Lucy returned half an hour later, showered and wearing clean clothes.

'You look better,' Penny said.

'Who would have thought clean underwear could feel so good.'

'Cup of tea?'

'Yes please,' Lucy said and looked Penny up and down. 'Your physical training is going well. You look trim, taut and terrific.'

'As instructed, I run every other day and go to the gym four times a week for weights.'

'Martial arts?'

'That too, and with the woman you recommended.'

'The meditation?'

'I practice every night.'

Lucy thought for a moment before saying, 'How old are you now?'

'Twenty-nine.'

'You're closing in on me.'

'It happens,' Penny said, a grin spreading across her face as she continued. 'What brings you here early?'

'Remember, I think it was a topic in your first lesson. Spies need to be discreet and unobtrusive in their ways, neither flamboyant nor loud. My early arrival is the consequence of disobeying that rule. The German secret service suggested I take a short holiday. They wanted me out of Europe.'

'What did you do?'

'A preventative measure, not so much what I did, more a fear of what I might do.'

'Someone pissed you off?'

'The Germans thought so, but no, it was all in a day's work and the topic for your training on this visit. Staying calm and detached, even in the most terrible and high-pressured situations. Carry no anger, it muddles the mind.'

'Is that where my meditation training helps?'

Lucy nodded.

'I'm looking forward to what you have planned. You mentioned that coming here early was fortuitous. What did you mean?'

'Penny, this is lesson number two, the art of building relationships. My last assignment was to intercept an item in Europe and take it to Britain. Unfortunately, I was compromised so enlisted an unsuspecting person to carry it to England, a mule as they're called. Fortuitous, because I told him that I lived in Australia and had to return home before meeting him again. It's lesson number two because in the space of one day he believed we were romantically attached, in love even. Now that I'm in Australia, I can skype him with iconic Melbourne landmarks in the background. He'll never suspect. Authenticity helps build trust, Penny. It always pays to stay as close to the truth as possible because it makes for a more convincing lie.'

'Did you sleep with him?'

Lucy laughed. 'I see you want to skip lesson two and go straight to three. In our game, sex and sexuality are purely assets to be deployed or withheld, depending upon the situation. This time, no, I didn't. When I go to England in three weeks' time as his girlfriend, yes, I will sleep with him and the role will require more than that simple act. Our love making needs to be passionate, intimate, caring and sincere. It requires more effort than faking an orgasm. I will be dispassionate and detached inside but outwardly however, he must not sense that. The art of relationships is the ability to manipulate a target to achieve the desired outcome. Trust is essential. You build a mental profile of the person you're influencing and change your approach to maximise success. Be agile yet persuasive. You see, sleeping with John on the first day would have been counterproductive. He needs to anticipate more.

My task is to build on the relationship he thinks we've established, making him feel secure and comfortable, so vulnerable. Understand?'

'You make it all sound rather clinical.'

Lucy shrugged as she said, 'Fabricating relationships of hope and trust is what we do. I call it the craft of spying. Think of yourself as a thespian and learn how to live "in character". We are actors playing in a dangerous theatre. What we achieve is a stage performance and nothing else. A word of warning; sometimes, when you sleep with someone it is enjoyable, but be wary of the dark side.'

'What's that?' Penny asked, her eyebrows rising.

'When operatives are locked into their character and boundaries blur, they risk being trapped in their role. For example, falling in love with the person you were sent to seduce in order to gather intelligence is possible. Remaining detached is essential. I think of it as the art of being a caring psychopath. Invent cues that act as triggers to help you move seamlessly between you and the role you're playing. My trigger word is "Sweetie".'

'What happens if you ever call me Sweetie?'

'Run!' Lucy said and smiled reassuringly.

Penny wanted to lighten the conversation, so asked in a humorous tone, 'Are you suggesting it's not wise to enjoy the sex?'

'I think I am.'

Penny smiled. 'Does that take practice?'

'Ha, I wish it did. I can assure you, on most occasions, it's not a problem.'

'My lesson,' Penny said, 'To see if I can stay calm under pressure. You've piqued my curiosity. What do you have planned?'

'Remember what I said about not being flamboyant?'

'Yes.'

'Standing out attracts attention, mostly unwanted attention. In testing your nerve however, what better than performing tasks that are sure to be noticed and if you're caught would have catastrophic consequences? Forty years behind bars, as an example. Penny, that would be all the good years you have to look forward to.'

Lucy paused to allow the enormity of what she was suggesting to sink in.

'This is the mission, if you're willing to accept it?'

'Of course,' Penny said, dismissively.

Lucy was surprised but pleased that Penny hadn't asked for clarification before agreeing to the operation. With a serious expression on her face, she said, 'I will ask you again tomorrow, when you've had time to sleep on it.'

'No need, I'm in.'

Lucy nodded.

Penny asked, 'Will we be using the disguises I bought?'

'Testing your nerve will bring together a number of the techniques we've used in training: concealment, surveillance, disguises, ingenious ways of communicating. How's your Russian coming along?'

'Good. Is that why you procured the false driver's licence and credit cards that arrived in the mail?'

'Yes, they came from my old Russian Mafia friends.'

'Excuse me for asking, but why would your Mafia contacts help?'

'Economics, Penny, simple economics.'

'You paid?'

'Not exactly, but if we fulfil our part of the bargain, the Australian Stock market will fall, as it always does after a terrorist attack and my old associates will make a substantial windfall, having short-sold beforehand. You see, besides your training, we are buying you access to my old networks, something you will need when there is no state sponsor to assist you. The Russian Mafia can provide you with everything; connections, fake passports, weapons, hacking services, electronic surveillance, money and even intelligence. Access to that comes at a price, which is why what's being proposed is more than a test of your fortitude.'

With an element of surprise in her voice, Penny said, 'Did you just say terrorist attack?

'Yes, I did.'

Penny considered a moment before saying, 'I see you're planning a noteworthy lesson for me.'

'We shall see.' Wanting to change the topic, Lucy glanced at Penny as she said, 'Don't worry about making tea. I'll take you out for coffee and a bite to eat instead.'

CHAPTER 8

Home Coming

He'd only been away two weeks yet, on his way back from Saint Moritz, all that was in John's mind, other than Lucy, was being home and sleeping in his own bed.

The drive from the airport to Pi-Ski dragged, but with every passing mile, his excitement at being back grew. It was seven minutes past three in the afternoon when the car rolled to a halt in front of his home. John sighed in relief, before calling out aloud and triumphantly, 'Made it–I've made it!'

He opened the car door, jumping out with a spring in his step before grabbing the luggage from the boot. John raced to the front door, touching it with unconscious affection as he burst inside, yelling to the empty house, 'I'm home!'

Feeling energised by the inexplicable euphoria accompanying his homecoming, John consumed the first two hours by unpacking, checking emails, expecting one from Lucy, but finding nothing, and completing routine domestic duties, neglected while he was away. Afterwards, with a cup of tea, he slumped into his favourite winged leather armchair in front of the TV. 'I'm home,' he called out again. This time however, John was aware of the eerie silence that followed his greeting. The jubilation of his homecoming was receding, replaced by loneliness. Seventeen years previously, John moved from his parents' house to live alone, preferring his own space, something he had cherished, but now a subtle change had occurred. Today he felt alone and his house empty. Despondent, John walked up the stairs to his bedroom where he'd left the parcel, still wrapped in its golden foil on the table beside the bed. He plucked it from its resting place, examined the delicate wrapping and carried it back to the living room. Slumping down into the chair and closing his eyes, he gently caressed the package and conjured up an image of Lucy.

His eyes popped open, a new dawn arising in his mind; he wanted to be with someone. The chance meeting with Lucy in Saint Moritz had changed everything and he knew life would never again be quite the same. No matter what was to happen, whether Lucy materialised or they parted company, he recognised that time was meant to be shared. Living alone was a false paradise. His St Mary's Parish colleagues had been right. He needed someone to share his life and John was grateful that they'd persuaded, cajoled and bullied him into taking the trip. Closing his eyes again, he settled his head into the high back of the chair, letting his thoughts wander aimlessly until they drifted towards the Parish Council meeting in five days time. He smiled, wondering how they'd react when he told them of his travels and Lucy, his hopes for Lucy and their imagined future together. The fog of melancholy enveloping him lifted and he drifted into a blissful sleep, dreaming of Lucy's beautiful lips softly touching against his own.

Lucy had goaded John into sending the selfies of them to the St Mary's Dating Agency, two pictures of him with a mysterious, beautiful lady. He'd expected a delegation of inquisitive women to descend on his house the moment he arrived home. When nobody arrived, he was surprised by his disappointment. Part of him wanted to shout "Lucy and John" from the highest mountain top. The flip side was that he could keep Lucy's coming to England a revelation until Tuesday. By the time the evening of the next parish council meeting arrived, he was champing at the bit, wanting to tell all about his new love. Before the meeting, every time he imagined revealing that Lucy was moving to Pi Ski to be with him, he couldn't stop smiling. *They just won't believe me*, he said over and over again. *They just won't believe me.*

John missed the pre-meeting chatter deliberately; he wanted to reveal his news about Lucy while seated, not standing and gossiping. The Parish Council meeting was underway as he rushed into the church hall, feigning puffing as if he'd been running.

'Sorry I'm late everyone,' he said.

'Hi, hello, welcome home,' came a chorus of greetings from his Parish Council friends.

'Order, order, order' called Catherine, hitting the gavel three times on the table to gain their attention. 'There will be plenty of time for congeniality after the meeting, as there would have been beforehand had Mr Moss chosen to be punctual.'

Emphasising the word "chosen", she gave John a disapproving glare.

'Did you miss us?' mouthed Edith warmly to John, while rolling her eyes at Catherine's comments. He smiled.

Ignoring Catherine's desire to focus on the business at hand, Vicar Charlotte blurted out, 'We all want to know about the trip John, and those photographs with the woman kissing you on the cheek.'

'Yes, yes,' the other members mumbled in unison.

Edith called out, her voice rising above the excited collective chatter, 'Who is she? Do tell.'

Catherine hit the table again and speaking loudly, she said, 'Edith, and fellow members, I must have order.'

They were each silent for a moment, before the Vicar pleaded with Catherine, saying, 'Please, let John answer. We are all dying to know.'

Displeased, Catherine shuffled the meeting papers in front of her and groaned loudly; inside however, she was as keen as the others to discover who John's admirer was.

'Very well, but we will complete the current agenda item, then adjourn the Parish Council business and open a meeting of the St Mary's Dating Agency. Those in favour?'

Their hands reached for the sky with a speed and enthusiasm rarely seen at the table.

'Right then, where were we? Ah yes. An anonymous cheque has been received for thirty thousand pounds with a note saying that it's for the Church roof restoration fund. Does anyone know who may have sent it?'

John's heart leapt, as he whispered to himself, *She loves me*. If he had doubts, they were now gone.

Edith heard John muttering, but not the content of his discourse. She glanced at him inquisitively, paused, and then said, 'Has this something to do with the woman in the photograph?'

The other members of the meeting looked at him expectantly.

John had promised Lucy that the donation would be confidential so he shrugged his shoulders as he said, 'No, nothing to do with me, but isn't it wonderful now we can fix the roof!' Searching for a distraction to move the focus from Lucy, he said, 'No more Sundays where we're...' John started singing the words from a 1952 American musical. 'singin' in the rain, Just singin' in the rain. What a glorious feeling...'

Most laughed, but Josephine Carter stared at him suspiciously as she said, 'A coincidence?'

When John didn't reply, an awkward silence engulfed the room as they waited for his reply, which didn't materialise.

'Yes, well,' said Vicar Charlotte, who hated uncomfortable silences. 'Where the money came from isn't important, let's just say God has answered our prayers.'

Edith looked at John excitedly and giggled. 'From the pictures you sent, it looks like God has answered *your* prayers too.'

John, unsure how to answer, shrugged his shoulders and smiled, playing coy, the unspoken message clear, ask me more questions.

'Yes, John, tell us about your trip and the mysterious woman in the photographs. Despite my initial scepticism,' Catherine said, 'Has the St Mary's Dating Agency had its first success before it has even started?' Her objections to John's interruption of the meeting were behind her now.

He tried to conceal his emotions, but John couldn't prevent a beaming smile from creeping across his face as he said, 'I hope so.'

'Ooh,' the women said in excited unison.

John went silent.

'Go on,' prompted Vicar Charlotte awkwardly, then in a rambling voice, added, 'You have us all hanging in suspense. Don't leave a single detail out, well, obviously not the intimate bits, not that there were any and if there were, just because you go to church, doesn't mean you can't. Oh, my goodness.' She blushed. 'You know what I'm trying to say. Tell us the story of your trip.'

'Yes, all of it,' said a chorus of voices.

Despite the committee saying that they wanted to know about his entire trip, they were only interested in Saint Moritz and the beautiful woman from the pictures. Little else mattered to them.

A cacophony of laughter erupted as he described careering backwards, out of control, down the ski slope, and Edith clapped expectantly when he said, 'I was only saved, probably from certain death, when a beautiful woman rugby-tackled me to the ground. She was wonderful and patient, helping me down the mountain, returning me to safety.'

'She?' questioned Edith, quickly adding, 'Does she not have a name?'

'Haven't I told you?' John teased.

'No, you haven't,' they said in unison.

'Lucia, but everyone calls her Lucy.'

'What happened next?' Edith asked impatiently.

John told a little white lie. 'I invited her out for lunch and she accepted.'

The truth was different. Lucy had invited him.

'We hit it off right away, talking as if we had always known each other. When lunch was over, Lucy asked if I wanted to go shopping and it was my turn to agree.'

Because of Lucy's wish to keep her wealth secret, John left out their visit to the jewellery store to buy the expensive gift. As the description of the encounter continued, Josephine Carter became increasingly concerned, and when John told the committee that he had an announcement to make, telling them that Lucy was leaving Australia and coming to Pi-Ski to live, she scowled with worry. Her worst fears about the encounter were realised, the similarities between Edith's romance scam and what was playing out for John were too obvious to ignore. What surprised Josephine however, was Edith's reaction to John's tale. Having recently been burnt, she expected that Edith, of all the people at the table, would be wary and suspicious. Instead, she clapped her hands excitedly as John's story unfolded. At the promise of Lucy coming to England, Edith had cheered, then said, 'I think John has found true love.'

When Parish Council finished their chitchat about John's romance, the discussion turned, focusing on who should be the next client of the apparently successful St Mary's Dating Agency. Josephine however, lost in her own thoughts, mused on John's gullibility.

He's been taken in. I doubt Lucy is her real name. For some reason even the photographs he sent make me uneasy. I can't dismiss a nagging feeling I've seen her before. This is a more sophisticated scam than Edith's, but it's a swindle none-the-less. The idea of love at first sight is wonderful and I wish for John it was true. This woman is after something and it's my task to find out what.

'Is anything wrong?' Josephine heard Catherine ask, and the question brought her attention back to those in the room.

'No,' she said, trying to hide her concerns, glancing at John as she continued, 'I was wondering if baptisms would help generate an income for the church. You know...babies.'

As the laughter from Josephine's comment receded, playfully, Vicar Charlotte put on a serious face as she said, 'No money in baptisms. Now, funerals, that's a different matter. Very lucrative.'

Edith giggled as she said, 'We'd have to change our name to the St Mary's Hatch, Match and Dispatch Agency.'

'Ladies and John,' intervened Catherine. 'This is Pi-Ski, not an episode of Midsomer Murders, and that's a reference to a British TV series if you didn't know.'

She peered around the hall.

'If we've finished discussing John's romance,' Catherine continued, 'Can I return us to the Parish Council meeting and the repair of the church roof?'

***

The meeting over, the councillors milled about, chatting before they prepared to leave. Josephine hung back, waiting for an opportunity to speak to John in private. As he left the hall, she followed him outside.

'John, do you have a minute?'

'Sure Josephine. What's on your mind?'

'Are you back at work?'

'Not until next week.'

'Would you mind if I dropped by in the morning, say ten o'clock?'

John was tempted to ask her why she wanted to speak to him but he didn't, instead saying, 'I'll have the kettle on.'

As Josephine started to walk home, she heard Edith call her name eagerly.

Josephine turned.

'I know it's late Josephine, but I'm so excited I couldn't wait to tell you.'

'Tell me what?'

'I'm going to be the benefactor of a will, a substantial amount of money.'

Not again, Josephine thought. 'Somebody you know?'

'Oh, no.'

'Did they email you?'

'Yes, how did you know that?'

'I'll walk home with you and you can show me. Okay?'

Edith's laptop was where she'd left it, open on the kitchen table and they positioned themselves in front of the screen. Edith displayed the message, but before showing Josephine, she said, 'You must promise not to tell about my windfall. It's a lot of money

168

and I want to become an anonymous benefactor, like the person who gifted the repairs for the church roof.'

'When did the message arrive?'

'Earlier today. Promise you won't tell?'

'My lips are sealed.'

Edith pushed the laptop in front of Josephine, who started reading.

Dear Edith Kelly

I am sorry if you find this email unsolicited. I hope that you will have the patience to read thought my message. My name is Maya Hodtsev, a career woman and an entrepreneur. I am a childless widow who was diagnosed of breast cancer 7 years ago. I have gone to many hospitals but my health keeps failing. I have lived a carefree and selfish life throughout my healthy days. No thanks to my inability to have a child for my loving husband before he died. I had to siphon all his wealth and made them mine. I did a lot of things that will make every man feel hurt. I hurt both God and man. Just last week, a Pastor came to conduct service at the Hospital where I am being observed by doctors. His teaching touched me after he left and I had to repent and give my life to Jesus.

My Doctor told me that I have few days to live. Now, I might die any moment and all this wealth will all be gone. I prayed and made up my mind to will all the money that I inherited valued at US$15,000,000 equivalent in Canadian Dollars in the family vault in a Bank in Canada. I prayed that I will be led to someone with a good heart outside my country United States who can invest this money into Charity. I have to give back to the Charity.

So, yesterday, I saw a directory on the desk of my Doctor and I had to copy your name and email address (this I apologize). So, I had to follow my heart and write you without knowledge of my Doctor, I will want you to stand as the beneficiary of my funds and having them used for Charity and humanitarian services in my honor. I will give your details about everything when I hear from you. Please don't reply me by phone because I don't want this dream of mine to either get to my Doctor or Husbands relatives who keeps coming and hoping when I will die and they will lay hands to my inheritance. Just write me on my email:

maya@hodtsevfamily.com

I will be using my last strength to be checking my email and hoping I will receive your reply. You are truly

blessed and may good God bless you and may this our
contact be a great one.

Regards.

Maya Hodtsev.

Josephine looked at Edith who had been watching her eagerly. 'Have you replied?'

'No, I wanted to show you first.'

'It's a scam, Edith!'

Edith's heart sank as she said, sheepishly, 'But it's addressed to me. I thought the scam emails just said Hi. How can you be so sure?'

Not wishing to insult her friend by her response, Josephine thought for a moment before saying, 'It's getting harder and harder to know and I've almost fallen for their tricks myself. Some of the really good email scams are almost flawless.' Josephine decided to lie. 'This one is very good and I can see how you were taken in. If you read it carefully, the English is,' she paused to choose her words wisely, 'less than perfect, and then, why would a doctor in the USA have your contact details? Edith, as a general rule of thumb, if it sounds too good to be true, then it is. The second rule is that legit companies don't request your sensitive information via email. I know, this time Maya didn't ask for your details, but if you respond she will. I'm really pleased you shared it with me; scams are easier to detect when you read them with someone else.'

Edith dropped her head. 'You must think me stupid.'

'On the contrary, if you were stupid, we wouldn't be here right now.'

Edith smiled. 'Thank you.'

***

Next morning, walking to John's home, Josephine considered her dilemma. She needed to raise her suspicions without making John defensive, rejecting her concerns before hearing her out. *I can't break Edith's trust, but I could pretend that I was the victim of a romance scam. That will do it.*

Arriving, she knocked and entered, shouting to John as she walked down the hall. Josephine had the same impression each time she visited John's home, a typical bachelor dwelling, even the ornate clock hanging on the dining room wall and a scattering of antique furniture seemed dull and uninteresting. A dwelling occupied with the necessities of life, shelter, cooking, eating, and sleeping. *If this was a woman's home*, she thought, *the lady would have opted for furnishings in decorative soft colourful palettes, a tasteful rug on the floor, art would hang on the walls and welcoming cushions would complement the furniture, making the rooms feel homely, a comfortable place in which to live and relax. Knick knacks would be on display, items that reminded her of her childhood home, the wonderful warm and safe place where she had grown up.* Some single men Josephine had known weren't tidy housekeepers, John's house was clinically clean to the point of creating a sterile environment. If Lucy was his true love, she wondered how he would adjust to the woman's touch and hoped Lucy understood it isn't possible to teach an old dog new tricks.

'A cup of tea?' John said, greeting her in the sitting room, which also doubled as his dining room.

'Yes, that would be nice. Thank you,' Josephine answered.

Left alone, Josephine churned over how to introduce the topic, just as she had when lying in bed the previous night. There the words had come easily. *I wish I'd written them down*, she thought, because on the walk over, her mind had muddled the sentences. Waiting for the drink to arrive, the words that tumbled in her mind were a jumble, like clothes folding over each other in a dryer. Nervously straightening her dress, she watched as John returned with the tea. He sat in the chair opposite.

'You wanted to talk to me?' he said.

Josephine thought for a moment before she commenced.

'I'm struggling to find the right words, so please give me some latitude for my clumsiness. Where to start? Let me tell you this in confidence.'

Josephine glanced at John as his face developed a look of surprise. Realising that she was expecting a response, John nodded and Josephine continued.

'I once succumbed to an online romance scam, an unpleasant experience, I can tell you. Unlike myself, you've met your match, but there are similarities between my situation and the one you related to us, your experience in Saint Moritz.'

Josephine paused, glancing at John, gauging his reaction. To her relief, he appeared to be giving her a hearing.

John thought for a moment before saying,

'I'm sorry to hear about what happened to you, Josephine. I've read about romance scams in the paper and believed they happened in cyber space, where the victim never met their supposed lover, probably someone operating from a Nigerian internet cafe.'

'Yes John, I did fall victim to the textbook internet scam and as a result lost a considerable sum of money to a person I never met. Other and perhaps more sophisticated scams operate similarly, but differently. Could yours be one of those?'

John smiled, remembering Lucy. To him, it was impossible to imagine that she could be anything but genuine. 'Is that where the idea for the St Mary's Dating Agency originated?'

'Yes. After my experience, I began researching online romances. Do you remember the Scammers' Cookbook I gave out at our first meeting? Have you read it?'

'No, I've been rather busy,' he said, folding his arms in frustration. 'Wasn't it you ladies who sent me on the trip? Now you're trying to tell me I've fallen for a scam?'

Josephine was losing the argument, so she interjected, 'I understand, but will you allow me to explain?'

'Okay,' John said, a blunt tone developing in his voice.

'Some of the conversations you recounted between Lucy and yourself, well, they may not be in the book word perfect, but they could have easily come from it. Another similarity, the speed at which things progressed between you. After a single day, she's leaving Australia to move to England. Possible, I suppose, but one would think improbable. I'm sorry, that sounds a little clinical and harsh.'

John gave a dismissive shrug as his disgruntled mien developed, lips pursed, face and eyes tense, exposing his wrinkled brow. Josephine wondered how he was going to respond but needn't have worried for, after a moment, John softened his demeanour and said, 'You're beginning to sound like Catherine.' Then he paused before adding, 'It developed quickly, I'll grant you that. We met on the last day of our holiday, what else were we supposed to do? Don't you believe in love at first sight?'

John, however, was perturbed by Josephine's concerns, though he was trying not to show it. People did fall in love at first sight, he knew that, but secretly he struggled to understand how a beautiful woman like Lucy could fall for him.

Josephine gave a nervous laugh. 'Love at first sight, I suppose I do. I'm not saying categorically that this is a scam, just that it would be prudent to be careful. Do you mind if I ask some personal questions?'

John raised his eyebrows. 'It depends.'

'Not that kind of personal,' Josephine said with a smile.

To prove Lucy's authenticity, John wanted to explain that it had been Lucy who'd donated the money for the restoration of the church roof. That would confirm to Josephine that the encounter wasn't a scam, but he resisted, instead saying, 'No, I don't mind.'

'Has she asked you for any money?'

'No, none,' he said.

'John, promise me, if she asks for financial help to move from Australia, for example, that you will come and talk to me before sending any.'

'Sure.'

If only you knew she is rich, he said to himself.

Josephine continued, 'Often with money scams they fake wealth, sending gifts, then suddenly they experience a financial difficulty and ask for help.'

Unsettled by the revelation John said, as he moved uncomfortably in his seat, 'Yes, I've read that.'

Josephine noticed the change in his body language.

'Other times, the scam isn't about money. They establish trust, then invite a person to fly and meet them under the pretext of love or a job. The unwitting target is asked to bring something back into the country, often drugs. You'll have heard the term Drug Mule. Did Lucy give you anything to bring to England, something that she'd want back, or that you were to give to somebody else?'

John's heart skipped a beat and his face dropped.

Noticing the change, Josephine raised an eyebrow as she said, 'What was it?'

'A gift she brought for her uncle.' He smiled, remembering how he came to have it. 'It can't be anything sinister because I was there when she bought it. Wait, let me get it.'

John left the room, returning two minutes later, holding the gold wrapped box with its distinctive red bow.

Taking it from John, Josephine asked, 'What is it?'

'A pen. We went to the jewellery store together and I saw the sales assistant wrap it.'

Josephine thought for a moment before saying, 'She gave you the wrapped box at the jewellery store and you've had it ever since?'

The moment Josephine asked the question, John knew what she was implying. As the circumstances played out in his mind, his mood became sombre as he said, 'Yes. There would have been ample opportunity for her to switch the contents but I just don't think she did.'

The room was silent for seconds that seemed longer before John said, disappointment resonating in his voice, 'Josephine, it felt, so... so right.'

'I understand, I really do. Just because she asked you to bring this to England doesn't necessarily mean that you've been used as a mule.' Looking directly at John, Josephine asked, 'I think the cheque for the church roof came from Lucy. Am I right?'

The question caught John by surprise and when he didn't answer, Josephine continued. 'Remember, I told you that scammers send gifts, grooming to build trust and credibility'

'It was Lucy,' he said, shaking his head in dismay, 'And she asked me not to tell. Now I'm getting worried, I can't believe it. How can she have set this up when ours was a random meeting on the ski-slopes?'

'I don't know, John. She may well be genuine, but it would be prudent to exercise caution. I'm sorry to sound like an armchair expert, but from what I've read, these scam artists are practiced at faking sincerity, the difference being their evil intent. It is difficult to distinguish between the two. If she is grooming you by sending, let's say thirty-thousand pounds, it must be something big and potentially very dangerous.'

'From what you've read?' repeated John, becoming frustrated with the conversation, as he continued, 'The truth is you don't know, and all you're doing is trying to turn a wonderful experience into a cheap script from some penny-dreadful book.'

Having witnessed Edith's exploitation, Josephine was willing to push the boundaries with John, for his own sake, as she saw it.

'I know how it must seem and perhaps my anxiety comes from my experience, but remember, this could be the biggest decision of your life. Don't you think it's better to be safe than sorry?' She was going to add, you could end up dead, but stopped herself, thinking the statement too melodramatic and therefore counterproductive.

John pondered for a moment before saying in a voice laced with misgiving, 'I suppose you're right.'

With an air of optimism in her voice, designed to encourage John, Josephine said, 'There is a way to find out'

'Do you mean we should open the gift box?'

'I suppose we could but no, I was thinking more along the lines of you giving it to me for safekeeping. When Lucy comes, you tell her it's been misplaced. If she becomes agitated, angry even, you will know the truth. If, on the other hand, Lucy is truly in love with you, she will be disappointed, but love will prevail. And besides, it's just a pen after all.'

A very expensive one, John muttered to himself before saying,

'If I've been lured into being a drug mule, won't I be in danger if I say I don't have it?'

'I've thought of that. If she becomes agitated, you give her a kiss and say that you haven't really misplaced it but didn't want to leave it in the house while you were at work, in case someone broke in and it was stolen. Tell her you gave it to your friend Josephine for safekeeping until she arrived. Offer to fetch it, suggest that I'm looking forward to meeting her.'

'You think she'll come?'

'Oh, yes, I do. Most certainly.'

'I don't know, Josephine. I understand what you're trying to do and appreciate your concern, but it's so deceptive.'

'There's something else we could try first, and I wouldn't be at all surprised if it's close to the truth.'

John looked at her curiously as he said, 'What?'

'I assume you email or talk to each other every day?'

'Yes.'

'You could write, tell her you're worried that your romance happened too quickly and, if she comes to England, that she won't find happiness here. Tell her that people grow into love, not fall in love, that kind of stuff. If, as I suspect, Lucy is using romance scam techniques, she'll challenge your concern. We can compare what she writes to the Romance Scammers' Cookbook.'

John was in two minds as to what to do and Josephine waited patiently as he considered her suggestion until finally he said, 'Alright, I'll say I'm getting cold feet. Come back tomorrow. How does ten o'clock suit you?'

When Josephine left, John agonised over what, or if, he should write. Despite his qualms about the deception he was considering, he decided to proceed. He wrote, then deleted the email six times before pushing... "Send."

The time for indecision has passed.

* * *

Next morning at ten o'clock on the button, the doorbell rang. John's laptop was already setup on the kitchen table.

'Sit,' he said, offering the chair next to his so that both could see the computer screen.

Josephine was feeling nervous. Secretly, she hoped that Lucy had written something obviously suspicious, justifying her scepticism. She also wanted John to find real love and if Lucy was real, she'd seem like a fool.

'Alright,' he said. This is what she said.'

> *My dearest John,*
>
> *I do share your qualms; our relationship has happened so suddenly. If you wish to say goodbye, I'll understand, however the truth is every journey starts with a single step so I ask that you let me come to England, for to share my world with you, I need to be willing to be part of yours. I feel helpless wanting you to know that you are loved, yet we're separated by so many miles.*

Whatever the final outcome, I will respect and honour your decision. With no promises, I would like to see what happens next.

Thank you for listening, for sharing my doubts and fears.

Love, Lucy.

John looked at Josephine and said, 'Well my "Armchair Detective", what do you make of that?'

Josephine studied the text, frowning as she read. 'Oh, to tell you the truth, John, I'm not sure. It seems too vague. From the Romance Scammers' Cookbook, I've printed some scripts they use when the target gets cold feet.' Josephine placed a piece of paper on the table saying, 'I will start reading aloud the extracts and let's see if anything jumps out.'

'You can see we are good people meeting at the best time of our lives.'

'I wouldn't be scared away, because truly, love is not about finding the right person, but creating a right relationship. It's not about how much love you have in the beginning, but how much love your build till the end.'

'Don't just think it will happen in an instant, it will surprise you before you know it, but it will be the most rewarding experience you will ever have.'

'Many people spend so much time thinking they can create love. The truth is, a journey of a thousand years starts with a single step. The best we can is....' Josephine paused in her reading, saying,

'There, it's not exact, but similar. Lucy wrote, "the truth is, every journey starts with a single step". The script reads, "the truth is, a journey of a thousand years starts with a single step." What do you think?'

'Vague,' John said, slightly annoyed. He took a deep breath and added, 'Sorry, Josephine.'

'That's alright.'

John smiled as he said, 'I don't know, Josephine. In Lucy's email, she is letting me choose whether she travels here or not. These feel different.'

'You're right,' Josephine said, but not wanting to admit defeat added, 'Please John, at least give me the gift for safe keeping. You have nothing to lose and so much to gain. If I'm wrong and she doesn't become angry, I will promise to be her best friend.'

'Ha! Is that a promise or a threat?'

'A promise,' Josephine said, chuckling.

John's mind was filled with contradictions.

What to do?

'Okay, I'll go and get it.'

CHAPTER 9

Melbourne

After a morning five-kilometre run, Lucy and Penny returned to the flat sweaty but invigorated. 'I'm going to take a shower,' Penny said.

Lucy nodded. 'Okay.'

When Penny left, Lucy retrieved her laptop from the bedroom, carrying it to the kitchen table. She wanted to see whether John had replied.

Well I never, she thought as she read his message.

Lucy waited for the shower water to stop running before calling out to Penny.

'Yes?'

'Here, I want to show you something.'

'Give me a minute.'

Penny wandered into the kitchen, a white towel in her hand, drying her hair. Noticing Lucy peering at the computer screen, she said, 'Is that a message from John?'

'Yes, listen to this.'

Penny grabbed a chair and joined Lucy at the kitchen table as she read out the email message from John.

Dear Lucy

I was dreaming of you last night and woke concerned that our romance happened too quickly and if you come to England, you won't find happiness here. I fear that one day was not enough for us to know each other. I believe that people grow into love, not fall in love. The distance between us is more than miles and I bid to set you free, if that is your wish.

Love, John.

'Your opinion?' Lucy asked.

Penny considered for a moment before saying, 'I don't know the man, but the writing and expression don't seem...' Penny paused, searching for the right words, and Lucy filled the space.

'Natural?'

'Yes,' Penny agreed, 'Natural. It reads as if it's staged. There's apprehension in the message but it feels like a test, you know, to see how you respond. Do you think Lucy, that he might suspect?'

'Yes, it's a possibility. There's a distinct shift in his style of writing. He's not been suspicious before. Maybe someone else is wary, another member of the St Mary's Parish Council, perhaps? In the reply we must be careful, be cautious in our choice of words. Whoever is with John will be watching; we need to pass the scrutiny of this assessor's eyes. Suggestions?'

Penny mulled over the possibilities before saying, 'It's difficult Lucy. He has what you want and you need to travel to England to collect it. Would it be right for you to profess your undying love?'

'If someone else is reading my messages, then perhaps not. We should start by acknowledging his concern; let John believe that I'm genuinely listening. In the art of manipulation, we call this faking - "listening to understand". We'll replace his narrative with an alternative, one that puts me in the UK. I'll finish by letting him believe that the success of our relationship is in his hands, which it isn't, of course.' Lucy started typing, speaking the text as she went.

My dearest John,

I do share your qualms; our relationship has happened so suddenly. If you wish to say goodbye, I'll understand, however the truth is every journey starts with a single step so I ask that you let me come to England, for to share my world with you, I need to be willing to be part of yours. I feel helpless wanting you to know that you are loved, yet we're separated by so many miles. Whatever the final outcome, I will respect and honour your decision. With no promises, I would like to see what happens next.

Thank you for listening, for sharing my doubts and fears.

Love, Lucy.

'What do you think, Penny?'

'Brilliant. How could anyone say no to that?'

Lucy pushed the send button and closed the lid of her laptop. 'That's one job done. After breakfast, I would like us to do a practical run through our plans for next week and if all goes well, I'll give the go ahead for our Russian hacker friends to instigate internet chatter for the Australian Signals Directorate to pick up.

We want the intelligence agencies to believe there is a credible threat to Melbourne. Just enough chatter, because we don't want to spook the stock market, not until we are ready. The threat will become specific when the authorities view our disruptive activities through the prism of an anticipated terrorist attack. We, Penny, are to be the catalyst, but the security services and the public will do the rest. A week's time Thursday, D-Day, will be a moment that will live in the memories of Melburnians for a long time.'

That afternoon Lucy gave the team of hackers the go ahead, commencing the count down. The following two days were spent putting the finer components of the plan in place and ferrying equipment to the cars. Sunday and Monday were to be rest days, with Tuesday the start of Operation Chaos, as they had named it.

***

Tuesday started as a normal day. Penny and Lucy rose early going for their early morning run and, as agreed, with no discussion about the forthcoming attack. The morning dragged for Penny, while Lucy relaxed in a chair and read a book. At mid-day, Lucy changed into her operational clothes, ate a light lunch and, at 1.00pm precisely announced, 'Let's do it.' The two women shared their memorised checklist for the last time, Lucy confirming as Penny spoke.

'Two-way radios?'

'In car one.'

'Pram?'

'Car one.'

'Mobile phones.'

Standard practice now, Lucy and Penny placed their mobile phones on the kitchen table.

'No phones on person,' Lucy said.

'Wardrobe?'

Lucy touched the shopping bags containing today's disguises and attire. 'Check.'

Finally, Penny said, 'Good Luck.'

Lucy smiled while retrieving a set of car keys from the table and the bag containing a dress, wig, glasses and gloves. Today's mission was to deliver items to the Airbnb house they had rented for the week, only five kilometres from Melbourne airport.

Holding the car keys, Lucy stared at Penny, who said, 'Keys for car one?'

Lucy examined the keys and said, 'Check. Do you have the spare boot key?'

Penny held up the boot key for car one. 'Check.'

Lucy nodded. 'Okay, we are good to go,' and left the flat.

The hire cars, booked using false driver's licence and credit cards supplied by the Mafia, were parked a kilometre away. By using back streets and cutting through a quiet park, one with a toilet block where they could change their clothes, Penny and Lucy knew they could walk from the flat to the car unseen by surveillance cameras and safe from prying eyes.

As expected, transporting the remaining items from the flat to the car had taken Penny a further two trips and at the end of each journey, Penny placed the items in the car boot.

As Penny ferried the goods, Lucy enjoyed a leisurely coffee. At the appointed time, she commenced her journey to the park. Once there, she put a jacket over the one she was wearing, donned a wig, gloves and glasses, and proceeded to the car. Her disguise was a woman in a floral jacket and beige gloves. Under the clothes, Lucy wore a full white suit made from a disposable papery plastic protective material called Tyvek, the kind crime scene investigators wear on TV. They wear the suit to stop their own clothes from contaminating the scene. Lucy intended to eliminate the chances of leaving DNA or fingerprints behind at the house. The short blond wig she wore provided some protection too, preventing any strand of her own hair from being left behind. Once inside the target house, she would pull the hood of the protective suit over her head. To ensure that no evidence was left behind, the safest option was to burn down the house when they had finished. This was not an option for this operation; no one was to be injured and no collateral damage caused. She'd need to be careful, leaving no evidence of her presence.

Reaching the street where the cars were parked, Lucy hesitated before approaching the vehicle, scanning for anything out of the ordinary. Before driving off, she checked the trunk, everything was there: folding pram, disinfectant, sleeping bag and meals. *Penny's done a good job.*

Checking her watch, Lucy found she was running ten minutes behind schedule but still inside the safety window. She started the engine and the car moved off, commencing the thirty-five-minute drive north of the city to her base in Westmeadows, a suburb eight minutes from Melbourne Airport. A kilometre from the Airbnb rental, to be certain that she was alone, Lucy turned off the main road and zig-zagged through the back streets, regularly checking the rear-view mirror. Confident she wasn't being followed, she pulled into the driveway of the 1930s detached weatherboard house.

The house key was in a locked steel box next to the front door. Entering the supplied combination number, Lucy opened the safe and removed the key. She checked inside the house before unpacking the car. To the other residents of the street, Lucy was another Airbnb renter moving in; her comings and goings would draw little attention.

In keeping with their plot, Lucy remained at the house over Tuesday night to assemble five drones and program flight plans into their GPS-controlled navigation systems. Each was fitted with flares that could be ignited remotely.

Having slept in the white suit, on Wednesday morning, Lucy meticulously cleaned the bathroom and toilet with disinfectant. She picked up and then sealed her paper dinner plate, breakfast bowl, cup, utensils and meal packaging into a plastic bag and placed it in the boot of the car. Returning to the house, Lucy carried one of the drones to the back garden, placing it in standby mode, ready to take off when commanded. Lucy made a final inspection of the house and, once satisfied that it was clean, took the remaining drones to the car to be delivered to locations identified on their reconnaissance missions, all in the vicinity of Melbourne airport.

Meanwhile, a disguised Penny drove the second hire car to the transition spot in Greenvale, ten minutes' drive from the airport and an eight-minute walk from the Greenvale Reservoir, the place where they would dump Lucy's vehicle on the day of the operation. After parking the car, Penny walked to the Roxburgh Park railway station and caught a train into the Melbourne CBD. The trip home was a confirmation of Thursday's escape plan, catching two trams, then walking the route they knew was free of CCTV to the park. Once in the park, away from prying eyes, Penny pulled off the outer layer of clothing, revealing the clothes she'd worn as she left the flat that morning. The wig and glasses were stuffed under her top and the discarded clothing was placed into a rubbish bin that Penny knew was emptied at seven o'clock every morning.

The placement of drones near the airport had proceeded without a hitch. With the day's mission completed, Lucy returned the car to the safe street, ready for the next day. Following the same safety protocol as Penny, Lucy made her way back to the flat. Both women knew that when the post operation investigations started sloppy reconnaissance often brought people to heel. They had been meticulous.

Penny had been home for an hour, waiting expectantly for her partner's return. She heard the sound of a key opening in the front door and glanced at her watch.

'I'm home,' Lucy called out.

'I'm in the kitchen,' Penny replied. 'How did you go?'

'As smooth as silk,' Lucy said, adding that she needed a shower. She returned half an hour later, refreshed, carrying the white Tyvek suit. Holding it up she said, 'Effective, but I can tell you, after twenty-four hours it's sweaty.'

Penny nodded as Lucy continued. 'After dinner we'll go for a walk and dispose of it and the other clothes that I wore today in a bin. Then, it's an early night. We have a big day ahead of us tomorrow.'

Penny nodded again, before replying, 'I've everything laid out in the bedroom for you to check.'

'Good.'

***

Waiting for her first mission to start, Penny had a restless night and was already awake at half-past three in the morning when her alarm went off. Rising, she went to the kitchen to make a cup of coffee. Lucy was already there, dressed and ready.

'Did you sleep well?' Lucy asked.

'Not bad.'

From experience, Lucy knew the truth and smiled as she said, 'Nobody sleeps well before a big day but it doesn't matter because we will be too busy to be tired. Breakfast?'

'I'm not that hungry.'

'Have a couple of slices of toast anyway; we won't get time to eat later.'

'Okay.'

Lucy smiled. 'Sit down and I'll make it for you. Coffee?'

'Yes, please.'

The two women ate in silence. For Penny, time seemed to drag on, while Lucy was comfortable with her own thoughts.

At four o'clock Lucy said, 'Time to dress and double check everything. Are you ready?'

Penny nodded.

The day's plan was set to unfold with military precision. At four thirty precisely, hats pulled over their heads, shrouding but not concealing their identities completely, Lucy and Penny left the flat. The backpacks which held their disguises for the operation were on their fronts, over which they wore oversized coats. The other items needed for the day's operation had been left in strategic positions. At four-thirty-eight, they left the footpath and entered a park and, under the cover of darkness, they changed into their disguises.

Lucy was dressed as a man, an officer of the VicRoads Transport Safety Services, an agency whose primary focus was enforcement of traffic rules for heavy vehicles. The service has a role similar to the Police and failure to obey lawful instructions of a Transport Safety Services officer is an offence. Along with the uniform, she wore a brown wig, black-rimmed glasses and she sported a neatly shaven beard. Lucy's other clothes from the operation were under the uniform with the backpack, giving her the appearance of a mildly overweight man. In one hand she carried a Transport Safety Services officer's high visibility vest, bright yellow with a VicRoads emblem on it. Her other hand gripped a torch. A two-way radio and a taser were secured to her belt. Transport Safety officers didn't ordinarily carry tasers, also called electrical control devices. They'd been used by law enforcement agencies since the mid-1970s to subdue suspects by zapping them with an electrical shock. Lucy checked her pocket; the syringe and vial were there.

Penny wore a black beanie and was dressed in blue tradesperson's overalls, the concealed backpack underneath giving her the appearance of a man with a potbelly. To hide her facial features, she'd donned a black moustache, large round glasses and painted a brown mole on her right cheek. A two-way radio was concealed in a pocket.

A scan revealed that the street in which their car was parked was deserted. Lucy checked her watch as Penny pressed the engine start button at four-fifty-five precisely. Their destination, a truck stop north of Melbourne on the Hume Highway. Sunrise was at six-fifty-five.

Lucy said, 'It will start getting light about six o'clock. We need to have finished part one of our operation by then.'

Penny nodded.

***

'See, I told you,' Lucy said, as they pulled into the truck stop. 'People are creatures of habit, more predictable than they like to think. You should always watch for their patterns.'

'Another lesson?'

Lucy laughed, 'No, just an observation, a useful truth.'

The B-double cattle truck they had been monitoring, a prime mover hauling two fully loaded semi-trailers, all twenty-five metres or eighty-two feet of it, was parked in its regular Thursday spot, twenty metres away from the other heavy vehicles. They knew the driver, a man in his fifties with a pot belly bigger than any near-term pregnant woman, was inside the road house buying a burger and coffee, which he would consume in the truck before driving off. They waited patiently for him to return. 'Here he comes,' Penny said.

Lucy nodded.

They waited for the driver to climb into his cabin and close the door, then Lucy said, 'Do you have everything?'

Penny held the two-way radio for Lucy to see, ready to put it on the passenger's seat as she left. 'Yes.'

'Good, and remember to speak only Russian over the radio. Wait for my call before coming over.'

Penny nodded.

'One last thing,' Lucy said. 'When we are driving on the motorway, I will be right up your arse so nobody is able to slide between us. Are you ready?'

'Yes.'

'Let's do this.'

Climbing from the car, Lucy slipped on her high visibility vest, then walked towards the truck, using the torch to shine its light into the cabin. The driver looked down from the window and, seeing a VicRoads officer, opened the door.

Lucy smiled and in a deep male voice said, 'Good morning Sir. May I see your log book please?'

'Sure mate.'

The driver leaned across to the passenger side of the truck to retrieve his paperwork. While his back was turned, Lucy removed the taser from her belt, climbed up onto the truck step and zapped him. The man convulsed, unable to control his muscles or defend himself. Lucy filled the syringe from the vial she carried and stuck the needle into the driver's backside to tranquillise him. Moments later he was unconscious.

Speaking in Russian, Lucy said into the radio, 'здесь – Here.'

Retrieving a jacket for Lucy, Penny opened the car door and strolled across to the cattle truck. Working together, the two women secured the driver's hands and legs with cable ties before moving the sleeping body across to the passenger side of the vehicle. While Penny returned to the car, Lucy removed the high visibility vest she was wearing and slipped on the jacket to hide the Transport Safety officer's uniform. Checking her watch, Lucy said to herself as the truck's engine sprang into life, *Perfect*.

'Идти – Go,' Lucy said into the radio.

Selecting a gear, the vehicle started moving.

As the first shafts of light ignited the dawn of a new day, stage one of the operation was complete. Penny positioned the car in front of the truck as they drove away from Melbourne on the Hume Highway towards Sydney. Had they wanted to maximise traffic chaos, they would have blocked the Tullamarine motorway during the morning peak hour, but their mission was to cause the share market to suddenly drop. The timing of the disruption needed to coincide with the opening of trading, so twenty minutes north of Melbourne, they pulled into a roadside truck stop to wait.

The Australian Signals Directorate were on high alert monitoring communications following the bogus internet chatter created by the Russians. At eight forty-five precisely, Lucy said into the radio, 'Операция Orange включена – Operation Orange is on.'

Penny responded with what sounded like a nonsense word, 'Альбатрос – Albatross,' acknowledging Lucy's communication. It was time to head back to Melbourne and the motorway.

Traffic was still congested when Penny, with Lucy following, edged her way onto the Tullamarine motorway. Keeping to the inside lane, they drove towards the Airport. As pathfinder, Penny's job was to determine when and where to stop. Two hundred metres before the Airport slipway, Penny picked up the radio and said, 'остановка – Stopping.'

She applied the brakes, bringing the car to a standstill. As Lucy slowed the truck, she turned it right, positioning the front across the lanes to block all the traffic. When she brought the twenty-five-metre B-double to a halt, nothing could pass.

Lucy glanced over at the truck driver, he was still unconscious. Stuffing the high visibility jacket into her pocket, she removed the keys from the ignition and clambered down from the cabin to walk to the rear trailer. Unfazed by the watching eyes of those delayed in their cars, she climbed onto the back of the truck and opened the gates, which kept the cattle secure.

'Hey what the f..k do you think you're doing?' she heard an angry male voice call out.

Holding on to the back of the truck, Lucy turned her head to look at the person.

After the September eleven attacks, she thought, *everyone's a hero*.

'Mate, animal health and safety regulations, the cattle are becoming distressed.' Lucy said, jumping down, landing near a muscular man in his forties. He took a step towards Lucy and, at one hundred and ninety-six centimetres, he towered above her.

This is going to be interesting. Just my luck, a bikie, Lucy whispered to herself, while staring at his bulging biceps covered in colourful tattoos. The word REBELS was emblazoned on his forearm, an Australian outlaw motorcycle club, Lucy surmised.

Pointing he snarled, 'I meant the f..ken truck.'

'Not me, mate. Take a look out front. It's bloody lucky they weren't all killed.'

Annoyed, the man huffed as Lucy directed him around the truck to see the imagined obstacle. She slowed, allowing him to walk in front. As he passed her...

WHACK!

She struck him with a single blow, a karate chop to the neck. Lucy expected him to collapse; it didn't happen. Instead, he stopped walking, flexed his head and neck, unharmed but riled by the attack. Lucy exhaled a loud growl of frustration. *I haven't time for this, he's built like a brick shithouse.*

WHACK!

She hit him again, with a force capable of snapping an ordinary person's neck, but seemed to succeed only in making him angrier. He turned, eyes set with rage and Lucy smiled, shrugging her shoulders as he clenched his fists, ready for an all-in brawl. Dropping her right leg back while bending her knees, Lucy took a side-on stance, ready for a fight. Before she had a chance to strike, the big man's face shadowed with shock as his legs finally wobbled then gave way. As he crumpled, Lucy leapt forward to slow the collapsing body, preventing his head from hitting the road and killing him.

Gee, you're heavy, she groaned, as she pulled her hands free of the now prostrate body. Coolly, Lucy stepped over the frame and continued her journey around the truck and into Penny's waiting car.

Noticing Lucy's flushed face, Penny said, 'All good?'

'The bigger they are, the harder they fall.'

'Did something happen?'

'No, let's go.'

Penny accelerated hard, speeding along the clear road in front, to leave the unfolding turmoil behind.

'Take it easy,' Lucy directed. 'We don't want to attract unwanted attention to ourselves.'

Penny backed off and, as the car slowed, she said, 'Sorry.'

Removing the two-way radio from her belt, Lucy switched channels, tuning to the police frequency, wanting to monitor their communication from the outcome of their handiwork.

'Any units available?' the radio crackled. 'We have a report of a truck blocking all outgoing lanes on the Tullamarine motorway, about one hundred metres before the Melbourne Airport entry.'

'VKC, Broadmeadows 300.'

'Go ahead Broadmeadows 300.'

'VKC Broadmeadows 300. We're currently at the Airport and will take a look at that one for you.'

Monitoring the police channel on the drive to the next waypoint, Lucy and Penny smiled at each other, knowing that behind them, traffic was at a standstill. If all was going to plan, the cattle being transported, finding the rear trailer gate open, had meandered onto the road and were amongst the vehicles, creating an additional headache for the authorities. The traffic travelling in the opposite direction, inbound on the motorway, seeing what was occurring on the other side of the road would slow, causing a self-reinforcing chain reaction, their braking amplified until the traffic came to a complete standstill. Lucy estimated it would take three minutes before both inbound and outbound lanes stopped moving.

With cattle wandering on either side of the road and the keys removed from the truck, it would take hours before things returned to normal. And this was only the beginning.

'VKC, Broadmeadows 300.'

'Go ahead Broadmeadows 300.'

'Traffic in both directions on the motorway is at a standstill. We can see cattle, at least twenty, wandering on both sides of the road. There's no access to the Airport from the motorway, and outbound access from the Airport is also blocked.'

'Roger, Broadmeadows 300.'

Lucy looked at Penny. 'They're trying to work out what's unfolding.'

'VKC to all units, standby.' Silence fell over the police channel.

'What's happening now?' Lucy said. 'Because we created the internet chatter, counter-terrorism agencies are in communication with the police trying to decide what's developing. Expect a full emergency management response. They will determine that if they don't act promptly, the traffic jam we've created will spread, isolating the airport, limiting their ability to control the incident and counter any further happenings.'

'VKC Keilor 200.'

'Let's see if I'm right,' Lucy said.

'Keilor 200.'

'VKC Keilor 200, our first priority is to maintain emergency vehicle access to the airport. Proceed to the Arundel Rd, Keilor Junction and stop all northbound traffic.'

'Keilor 200, Roger.'

A three-second pause.

'VKC Keilor 307.'

'Keilor 307.'

'Proceed to Sharps Road and Airport Drive. No northbound traffic.'

'Keilor 307, Roger.'

'VKC Air 470.'

Lucy switched off the radio. 'Perfect,' she said, 'Now they are calling in the Air wing, the groundwork for the next part of our plan is set.'

'Will they deploy troops and tanks at the airport, like they did at Heathrow?' Penny asked.

'Once we launch the drones and the illusion of a specific targeted threat is created, they will want to act, however the gridlock will cascade faster than they can control, making it difficult if not impossible for them to deploy the resources they need. By the time they employ counter-drone tactics our exercise will be over. Were this a real attack, it would be too late,' Lucy said, laughing. 'Maybe we should send the Australian Government a bill for providing vulnerability testing of their security measures. I can guarantee that they'll make changes to their procedures when we're done.'

Melbourne International Airport, known as Tullamarine Airport, is located on the western fringes of the city and is the primary airport serving Melbourne and the second busiest airport in Australia, after Sydney. Fourteen minutes after leaving the disabled truck, travelling through the outskirts of the city, Penny and Lucy turned left on to Greenvale Park Drive, a quiet suburban road that runs parallel to the Greenvale Reservoir, an off-stream water storage dam holding 27,000 megalitres. As the crow flies, they were only four point nine kilometres or three miles from the airport, but they may as well have been on the moon, such was the difference. Five hundred metres later, Penny turned right into Greenvale Short Cut Road, then, almost immediately, left on to a dirt road that runs parallel to Green Park Drive. Travelling a further hundred metres, Penny stopped in the deserted spot, concealed by trees, chosen during their reconnaissance mission. They were alone.

'Everything we don't need stays here,' Lucy said.

'Okay,' Penny replied.

Before stepping out of the car, Lucy removed the jacket she was wearing over the VicRoads Transport Safety Services uniform, throwing it onto the back seat. Like each of the disguises they used, the uniform had been constructed like that used by a quick-change magician. Various layers were connected using a mixture of Velcro, magnets and fish bone pull fasteners. Within seconds, Lucy had shed her VicRoads officer's uniform and was now a business man. From the glove compartment she collected a black wig, a beard with a moustache, and a pair of stylish silver-framed glasses. The collection that formed the old disguise joined the discarded jacket in the back seat. Penny changed her appearance too, becoming a redheaded lady in a floral skirt. Before adding shoes to her outfit, Penny's backpack containing the abandoned costume, was tossed into the back of the car.

Looking at Penny, Lucy said, 'Very tasteful.'

'And you're a very smart-looking young man,' Penny replied, chuckling, then adding, as she held out a set of keys for the vehicle, 'For you, Sir.'

It was time to go, and the women nodded to each other. They opened their car doors simultaneously and walked to the open boot where Penny removed and unfolded a pram before pushing it five metres away. Lucy took out a brown leather briefcase, one with decorative twin buckles and push closure for quick access. Closing the trunk, she walked to the passenger side rear door and, placing the satchel on the ground, opened the door. Inside was a canister of petrol, which she removed. Opening the container, Lucy swished the flammable contents about liberally, giving the backpacks and discarded disguises a generous soaking. Finding it empty, she dropped the canister on the floor of the car. From her satchel, Lucy took two incendiary ignition devices fitted with timers set for seven minutes.

Placing both carefully on the floor of the vehicle, Lucy said, so that Penny could hear her, 'Having two of them is a failsafe. If the car fails to burn, it's all over for us.' She looked at Penny, who acknowledged her with a nod.

Lucy locked the car and threw the keys into the storage dam. 'Ready?'

The couple, pushing the baby's pram along the road, joined Greenvale Road, following it over Yuroke Creek, where they cut across a reserve and into the grounds of Aitken College, the school where the getaway vehicle was parked. It had taken six minutes to reach the car, the plan was still on schedule. As Penny put the pram in the boot, Lucy removed the remote controls for the drones.

The traffic chaos they had caused would by now be spiralling outwards, engulfing the surrounding roads. With their next destination being the Melbourne CBD, they needed to make haste if they were to avoid being caught in their own labyrinth of disruption. Penny started the engine.

'To our observation point, if you please,' Lucy directed, smiling.

Penny reversed to a position where they had a clear view of the area where their first car had been left. Lucy checked her watch:

seven minutes had passed. Thirty seconds later, they witnessed black smoke rising into the air, a confirmation that the car was on fire.

'Stage two is go! Let's drive,' Lucy said.

They had allowed forty-five minutes for the drive to the CBD, the route taking them across the northern suburbs of Melbourne, through Campbellfield, dropping down to Thomastown, Preston, Fitzroy, and finally the CBD. Lucy would awaken the drones as they drove, their flight plans programmed to menace Melbourne Airport. The moment the first drone penetrated the five-kilometre airport exclusion zone, the Australian Signals Directorate would conclude the airport was a terrorist target.

Penny turned on to Cooper Street.

'As quick as you can without speeding,' Lucy said. 'We need to be through the Craigieburn By-pass and Hume Highway Interchange before our antics cause it to clog.'

'So far so good. The traffic is still flowing well,' Penny said. 'When will you launch the drones?'

'Right now,' Lucy replied.

She switched on the remote-control unit for the first craft. In the garden of the Airbnb they'd used, a drone received a signal, moving it from standby mode to active, an unseen green LED flashing. Taking to the air, it followed a programmed flight plan, rising to an altitude of one hundred and twenty metres before slowly flying towards the airport exclusion zone. To minimise the risk of collateral damage, the drone had been instructed to hover on the outskirts of the airport, giving the authorities four minutes to divert incoming planes and close the runways. It was a delicate balancing act, affording a margin of error for public safety, yet giving the appearance of a terrorist attack without permitting time for the authorities to deploy counter drone defences.

With Lucy monitoring the aircraft, Penny provided regular updates on their progress.

'The traffic is still flowing well.'

'Nothing in the rear-view mirror.'

Finally, Lucy heard the words she was listening for. 'We're through the Hume Highway Interchange.'

'Excellent Penny, you know where to go next.'

As the first drone hovered at the prescribed altitude near Melbourne Airport, Penny turned into the Epping Plaza shopping centre. She parked near the Post Office and their designated public phone booth.

Lucy checked her watch and said, 'We are still within the operational window.'

'I agree,' Penny answered.

Lucy left the car and walked to the public phone where she dialled the news centre of the Australian Broadcasting Corporation (ABC), a number she knew would be answered.

'Good morning,' said the voice on the other end of the phone. 'Australian Broadcasting Corporation, Peter speaking, how may I...'

'Listen carefully,' Lucy interrupted in her disguised male voice. 'Melbourne Airport is under attack.'

There was a pause as the recipient of the message assessed the validity of the call.

To muffle her next announcement so that anyone nearby could not hear, Lucy wrapped her hands around the mouthpiece of the phone and screamed down the receiver, 'Allahu Akbar.'

She hung up.

Back in the car, Lucy checked her watch. It was five minutes precisely since the first drone was airborne. In thirty seconds, the attached red flare would self-activate. It would descend and fly low and fast over the gridlocked Tullamarine motorway, making a low altitude run, trailing a vibrant display of intimidating colour and smoke as it sped towards the airport. Inside the airport perimeter, it would gain altitude and hover above the two intersecting runways, then descend before flying around menacingly and crashing into the window of the control tower. Before it struck the control tower,

Lucy would activate the other four drones; they were also programmed to penetrate the no-go zone of the airport, then fly low and fast over the stranded vehicles on the motorway, leaving in their wake a trailing tail of flare smoke. Their final target was the airport's terminals.

As they left the shopping centre car park, Lucy activated the drones and said, 'We have everything airborne.'

'Excellent, I'm about to turn right onto High Street for the run into the city. The share market is open. Now it's up to the panicked public to spread our misinformation.'

'Yes, a dose of TV, radio and social media hysteria,' Lucy said, as she leaned forward to switch on the car radio, selecting 3AW, a Melbourne talk back radio show.

'What can you see?' she heard the commentator ask.

In a panicked voice, a man said, 'It's a missile and it's heading towards the airport. I can see the flames coming out of the back. It passed over us, really low. Oh, my God! There's another one.'

The commentator interrupted, 'Are you saying there are two?'

The caller, in distress said, 'Yes, I can see two. Are we at war?'

Lucy smiled at Penny. 'If this hasn't already sent jitters through the Australian stock market, our next little escapades certainly will.'

'Police,' Penny said, her voice raised an octave in pitch 'In my mirror and gaining fast.'

'Ignore them,' Lucy said calmly. 'It's too early to be worried. Even the best security services in the world wouldn't be on to us yet.

'Okay,' Penny replied.

When the car had passed, Lucy said, 'Stage three of our plan is the dangerous part, with the police already on heightened alert.'

Penny nodded and then asked, 'If the stock market crashes, do we need to execute stage three?'

'Unless we have a compelling reason, it's safest if we stick to the original plan. Besides, it's part of the deal I struck and the Russians will have started their short-selling plan to make money from the mayhem by now. We stay the course.'

For the next twenty minutes they drove in silence. Penny slowed the car, indicated right and turned onto Victoria Parade, followed by an immediate left into Nicholson Street. Two hundred metres later, another right onto Little Bourke Street for the stop-start run through the city, heading for a car park near the Southern Cross railway station.

Waiting for the traffic lights to turn green, Penny broke the silence as she said, 'How much money will the Mafia make from their short selling?'

'I don't know exactly. At a guess, it will be hundreds of millions.'

'The transactions, can't they be tracked?' Penny asked.

'Of course, but Monya is in bed with the Kremlin. Australia will identify who made the money, just as they knew the Chinese hacked into the Australian National University and stole its student records, or that it was North Korea who perpetrated the ransomware attack on the hospitals. We're in an era of State-sponsored criminal terrorism and diplomacy has yet to catch up. Short of war or sanctions, neither of which is going to happen, the Australian government is helpless. In reality, our international players are sending a message, flexing their muscles, telling the world that they can target anyone, anywhere, whenever they wish.

'Penny, after today you will be guaranteed acceptance into my old network with access to their worldwide resources.' Lucy glanced at her watch.

'By now the security services will have assessed that our charade at Melbourne Airport isn't a serious threat - an inconvenience undoubtedly, but not a deadly terrorist attack. The public, however doesn't know that, so as phase three unfolds, the authorities will face a conundrum; is the new activity part of a coordinated attack or another charade? They'll be wondering whether the airport incident was a diversion from the main event, but in the end, for us it doesn't matter. Until they know otherwise, the security services have little choice but to respond to our activities as a credible threat.'

'You're good,' Penny said.

'Experience! This is the easy bit; the getaway isn't state sponsored, we'll be on our own. Our CBD activities will be captured on CCTV, giving the police and spooks a good look at us. You can guarantee they'll be hunting for us as we make our escape. It's important that we stick to the agreed plan.'

Penny nodded, 'I know. Strangely, it makes me feel excited rather than afraid.'

'Adrenaline is either a friend or foe,' Lucy said.

'Is it addictive?'

'I like to think so,' Lucy smiled. 'Can you taste it on your lips?'

'Oh, yes.'

To dump the vehicle, the women had chosen a multi-storey car park in Little Bourke Street, one block from the railway station.

As they pulled in, Lucy looked at her watch; ten minutes behind schedule, but still within the operating window. 'We are good to go,' she said.

Penny nodded, reversing the car into a reserved parking spot on the third floor.

Lucy said, 'Let's hope whoever is allocated that place doesn't turn up now. Check the surroundings.'

'It's clear.'

Lucy nodded. 'Let's do it.'

Penny removed the pram from the boot. It would carry and conceal some of the items needed for the next stage of the operation.

Following the same routine as they had at Greenvale, Penny pushed the pram away from the car while Lucy made preparations for another fire. Before setting the ten-minute timers on the incendiary devices, she tossed the two-way radios, fake credit cards and drivers' licences onto the floor of the car then doused them in petrol. She covered the emptied petrol canisters with a beach towel, hiding them from anyone peering in the window. As Lucy closed the door, she noted the time; the ten-minute countdown had started.

'Let's go,' she said.

Following their plan, they left the carpark and split up, independently travelling to the railway station. The Southern Cross railway station is a major interchange for Melbourne, acting as the terminus for V/Line, the regional railway network, and the interstate links to Sydney and Adelaide. It also services Melbourne Metropolitan trains and the Underground. Country and airport coach services also operate from Southern Cross. Eighteen million passengers use the station annually, it is a bustling transport hub and the perfect target.

Penny reached the terminal first and pushed the pram through the throng of people, like worker ants scurrying about their business. She walked to her selected position, an aluminium bench seat adjacent to the main thoroughfare and, before seating herself, she removed a piece of hand luggage like that used on airlines from the pram. It was a black travel bag and, unseen by passers-by, a velcro strip held a flap of material to the front of the bag, concealing what was underneath. Placing the bag next to her on the ground, she waited.

It's a busy place, she thought, secretly scanning back and forth.

There were no signs of any increase in security, the authority's attentions drawn to the airport currently, as they had hoped. Penny knew that time was of the essence. Within minutes, the net would start closing in on them.

Briefcase satchel in hand, Lucy joined the other ants at the Southern Cross station, making her way to WH Smiths

Newsagency, a vendor stall to buy a newspaper. Her designated position was another bench seat thirty metres from where Penny was seated, with a view to the outside of the station.

Disguised as a man reading a paper, Lucy checked her timepiece; ten minutes had passed. They had allowed seventeen minutes. The mission would be aborted if the trigger failed to occur within that window. Four minutes later she heard the sound of wailing sirens outside and seeing fire engines rushing to a blaze in a multi-storey car park, said to herself,

That's it, we are good to go.

Lucy waited a further minute before placing the newspaper in front of the satchel to mask her actions, unclipped it and removed a packet of M500 Jumbo firework crackers, which she placed inside the newspaper, then folded it in half to conceal them. The fuse on the crackers would be ignited by a simple ignition device, one that Lucy had constructed at Penny's flat, using a D-cell sized battery, a Christmas tree light with its end cut off and filled with powdered match heads. The homemade device was connected to a timer Lucy had purchased at a hobby store. After building three ignition units with timers, all evidence of their construction at the flat was removed. Lucy disposed of the left-over material, the tools used in the construction, a soldering iron, pliers and screwdriver. She even went as far as dumping the unused matches and glue. Not a trace of her work was left in Penny's apartment; she'd been meticulous.

The makeshift incendiary device was to be placed in the metal rubbish bin next to the escalator leading to the mezzanine concourse. After activating the timer, Lucy deposited the newspaper and its explosive contents into the waste bin as she walked past, catching the escalator to the next floor. The timer was set with a ten second delay but it would take another three seconds for the fuse to burn and the cluster of crackers to begin exploding. As Lucy stepped onto the mezzanine concourse, the crackers ignited, replicating a series of gunshots.

BANG - BANG - BANG - BANG.

Their threatening sound was amplified by the echo from the building. Screams of panic rang out across the railway station as people looked about in horror, unsure of where to run.

The explosions were Penny's cue. In the confusion that followed the firecrackers, she stood and ripped off the material flap from the travel case, exposing red and black wires leading into the hand luggage.

She yelled out in mock fear, 'A bomb, help! It's a bomb.'

To focus the minds of already frightened travellers, Penny pointed to the abandoned luggage with its exposed wires and, still screaming, fled in apparent dread, the pram veering from side to side as she hurried from the scene.

Time was tight and with the structures already in place, Lucy understood the police would soon be swarming over the CBD. Those coordinating a response would know that the attacks were designed to split their resources. A dedicated team would be deployed, assigned to identify and hunt Lucy and Penny before they struck again.

The women knew that the emergency services would need to contain the fire in Little Bourke Street, evacuate, then secure the railway station. They still had time, but the window of opportunity was closing. Their next target was Melbourne Central, four city blocks away.

The Melbourne Central was a contemporary multi-storey shopping mall offering a variety of upscale retailers, plus restaurants and a large food court. Inside the complex, Christmas shoppers, looking like a busy colony of bees, went about their tasks, unaware of the mayhem on the motorway, at the airport, in the multi-storey car park and at Southern Cross station. The mall was its own domain, sheltered from the outside world.

Carrying the business satchel, Lucy made for the hectic food court, buzzing with people. After queuing to be served, Lucy reached the head of the line and said, 'I'll have a Big Mac and a medium Coke please.'

'Would you like fries with that?' said the acne scarred boy on the counter.

'No, thank you.'

'Eat in or take away?'

'Take away,' Lucy said, as she really wanted the box containing the Big Mac and the paper carry bag.

Waiting for the meal, Lucy knew law enforcement operatives would be viewing the CCTV footage from the railway station. There being little time between putting the fireworks in the rubbish bin and the explosions, they would identify her quickly and Lucy was certain that a description of her would be distributed soon, and of Penny not long after. The shopping centre was a risky place to be.

It took an age for Lucy's order to arrive. She became annoyed because she had to stop herself from inspecting her watch twice.

This is stupid, she thought. *I'm never on edge.*

She was relieved when the Big Mac and Coke arrived and glanced around the food hall, spotting an empty table near a trash can. Casually, she meandered over to it, pulled out a chair at the table and removed the Big Mac, first from its paper bag and then the box. Penny lingered nearby, glancing in shop windows while keeping a watchful eye on her partner.

Hungry, Lucy took a bite from the Big Mac.

Not bad. They always taste better than I'm expecting. I just wish they weren't so unhealthy.

She took another, then a last bite before stuffing the half-eaten burger into the paper bag. Reaching down, Lucy picked up her satchel and placed it on the table in front of her. Before reaching inside, she finished the Coke. Yuk. Lucy activated another device timer, setting it for two minutes, then placed it inside the Big Mac box, then the box inside the paper bag. She squished-up the Coke container, a signal for Penny. Rubbish in hand, Lucy stood, moving to put the fire bomb package in a nearby bin. As she approached, a security guard patrolling the food court stopped in front of it.

Bugger.

Lucy scanned the area. Nearby were plenty of alternatives but insufficient time until the device ignited. Calmly, she walked to the three-quarters full bin.

'Excuse me,' she said to the guard, lifting the rubbish for him to see.

'Sorry, Sir,' came the reply as he moved aside.

Lucy deposited her contents and strolled away as the guard moved on.

Penny, waiting for the signal, removed a paper bag from the pram containing more M500 Jumbo firework crackers. When smoke started to billow from the rubbish bin, she flicked the timing device, initiating a thirty-second delay. She placed her bag into another garbage bin then, pram in front of her, she strode purposefully away. As Penny exited the building, crackers, sounding like gunshots, rang out. People screamed in panic and a fire alarm sounded. Resisting the urge to look back, Penny kept walking, soon joined by fleeing shoppers.

It's time for you to vanish, young Penny, she whispered, her destination the Carlton Gardens, two blocks away.

Using a different exit from that of Penny, Lucy had taken longer to clear the shopping centre, stopping to allow heavily armed police officers to rush past. Walking to the next waypoint to commence the journey home, Lucy imagined the decisions being made at the command and control centre for the situation they'd caused. The Melbourne Central incident would have drawn emergency vehicles to her part of the city; a police incident response team was on site before she'd left. With traffic at a standstill and authorities unsure whether another strike would occur, she knew that a decision would be made to close down the CBD. Traffic chaos would cascade outwards in all directions from the city. Lucy understood they needed to clear the city or they risked being trapped. By now their descriptions would have been circulated. The net was closing in.

For Penny, the stroll to the Carlton Gardens was without incident. Following their plan, she walked to a park bench that was free of CCTV surveillance. From the pram, she removed a bag containing a new disguise and a cream jacket. Collapsing the pram, she pushed it neatly under the bench; it had served its purpose. She then walked to the public toilets where, in a cubicle, she pulled off the clothes she was wearing to reveal a new set underneath. Swapping her wig and spectacles for alternatives, she stuffed the old items into her jacket pockets. In a different part of the same park, Lucy was repeating Penny's actions.

All that remained for Penny was to catch a tram away from the city, back to near where they'd parked the cars at the start of the mission. From there, she could wander back to the apartment unseen by CCTV.

The traffic in front of the Carlton Gardens was at a standstill and gridlocked on Victoria Parade.

She's good, Penny thought. This *is exactly what Lucy said would happen.*

Melbourne's tram system is an iconic part of the city's identity, playing a vital role in the city's transport system, particularly in linking the CBD, inner and middle suburbs. The performance of the ageing tramway system had been eroded by low speeds on the majority of the network, which is located on congested arterial roadways or suburban streets. The trams operating on Victoria Parade carried their passengers on a light rail system, a dedicated transit lane, separate from cars, which is why

Lucy chose that route. As the police cordoned off the CBD, the unfolding traffic chaos elsewhere in the city would eventually limit the supply of trams reaching the Parade. Lucy knew that there would be a narrow window to make her escape from the city.

Using her newly learned meditation techniques, Penny brought her racing heart under control as she waited patiently for the next tram to arrive. Peering to her right, she could see that a tram was struggling to cross a choked intersection. She willed it on; *come on, you can make it,* but it was stuck.

Now what should I do?

She took a deep breath.

Options Penny?

You could wait or start walking.

If I walk, do I follow the tram route or head north away from the congestion?

Glancing at her fellow travellers, she could see that they were making similar calculations.

An older woman, in her seventies, standing next to Penny said, 'It's going to be difficult to get home.'

'I think so.'

Over the traffic noise came the sound of wailing sirens.

'Do you know what's going on?' asked the woman anxiously.

'No.'

'Look, that's good,' said the woman pointing. 'The police are clearing the intersection to allow the fire brigade to get through.'

Penny nodded as she watched the tram edge its way forward. Three long minutes later, it pulled up in front of her and opened its doors. It was a sardine-tin, packed tight with patrons trying to reach home.

'Oh dear, there's not much room,' the older woman said.

'You go first. I'll be right behind you,' Penny said.

'I might need a push.'

Penny giggled. 'A shove more like it, if we are going to fit in there.'

'The joys of city living,' said the woman, 'squashed like a pancake.'

Along with six other patrons, they squeezed on, pushing forward so that the door could close behind them. With a jerk, the tram moved off, making its way tentatively down Victoria Parade, stopping often to allow passengers to disembark and, for the lucky ones, allowing some to embark. For Penny, fleeing the city felt like an eternity, but she was relaxed, observing the world about her. It was odd that even with the occasional emergency vehicle passing through, sirens blazing, rushing towards the CBD on the tram it was as if nothing had transpired. The people around her seemed oblivious to the happenings outside, sitting or standing, cheek by jowl, talking quietly, a world away from the bedlam of the city centre.

The tram, once it crossed the Hoddle Street intersection, again shared the road with cars. Penny decided that if the traffic was gridlocked, she would walk. With little congestion evident, the tram rumbled on and with more people leaving than entering the tram, Penny found a seat. Reaching the Barkers Road - High Street intersection, Penny changed trams, taking a near empty one, the one-oh-nine tram north towards Kew Junction and, after crossing it, she disembarked at Cotham Road for her walk to the park. She was almost home and safe, but the sound of an approaching police siren caused Penny to momentarily freeze as it raced past.

During the planning, Lucy and Penny had debated changing clothes one final time in the park, dumping the discarded objects in a rubbish bin en-route to the flat. Instead, they decided to remove their facial disguises only. At home they would shower, bag the left-over items from the day and deposit them at an industrial waste bin on their way to the Dandenong ranges, a low mountain range, thirty-five kilometres east of the Melbourne CBD, where they were booked into a restaurant for dinner.

'Made it,' Penny sighed, lifting the door mat for the key to the flat.

'What kept you?' she heard Lucy call from the lounge.

Penny wondered how Lucy had made it back ahead of her as she smiled and said, 'You know this and that.'

Lucy was already showered and changed.

'Get a move along, slow coach, I'm hungry,' she said.

'Ha! You're hungry. At least you ate a Big Mac. I've had nothing.'

'All the more reason to shake a leg.'

Fifteen minutes later, Penny was back, looking refreshed, bag in hand. 'I'm ready.'

'Are you?' Lucy asked, raising an eyebrow.

Penny looked at herself, saying hesitantly, 'Well, I thought so.'

Lucy pointed at her own wrist saying, 'Watch! You wore that today. In the bag with it.'

Penny nodded.

'It's the small things that can bring you undone.'

On the drive to the restaurant, Penny leaned forward and tuned the radio to the non-stop news channel.

Authorities are still unsure of the motive behind what they believe were well-coordinated hoax terrorist attacks. Police have confirmed they have examined CCTV footage from Southern Cross station and are seeking two unknown suspects spotted on the footage. It's not known if the two suspects were responsible for the events at Melbourne Airport, but they have been linked to the fire at Melbourne Central. Authorities believe all the events are connected.

According to ABC sources, it is unlikely that private individuals would have access to the sophisticated drones used to close down Melbourne Airport. An act of state sponsored terrorism hasn't been ruled out.

Penny turned the volume down and asked, 'What happened on the stock market? I haven't had time to look.'

'Down a whopping three per cent, recovering later in the day but, by then, our friends would have made an absolute killing. You're set.'

'Thank you,' Penny said, pondering for a moment before adding, 'Can the authorities trace us?'

'Unlikely, and even if they could, nothing will stick with the courts. No mobile phone tracking, nothing on computers, fake driver's licence and credit card, no motive, no evidence at the flat, not even a match head to examine. At best, our build and height will be similar to people on the CCTV, though I doubt that, too. They'll not have a clue, Penny. Welcome to the wonderful world of international espionage.'

'Didn't we do this for the Russian Mafia?'

Lucy laughed heartily, 'It's the same thing Penny, the same thing.'

From her pocket, Lucy produced a business card, holding it up for Penny to see. She said, 'On here is a phone number that gives you twenty-four-seven access, in any country in the world, to whatever support and equipment you need.'

'Do I memorise the number and then destroy the card?'

Lucy laughed as she said, 'It's no use without a password. Keep it in your purse.'

'What's the password?' Penny asked.

'Claudia.'

CHAPTER 10

The Protector

Following the "cold feet" email, John and Lucy continued corresponding daily and Skyping twice a week. Since Josephine's intervention, John started analysing each word Lucy spoke in their calls and wrote in her emails. He was searching for evidence of entrapment, but his suspicions were fading with every contact with Lucy. On several occasions, Lucy had asked whether everything was alright, questioning John, making sure that he wanted her to come. He had answered positively, but was puzzled.

Why would a beautiful woman like Lucy be interested in a boring person like me? Damn you, Josephine!

Three weeks had passed in a flash and John was in the church hall, enjoying a cup of tea and biscuits, following the Sunday communion service at St Mary's. It was the day before Lucy was due to arrive in England.

'You're not meeting her at the airport, are you?' Edith asked, while nibbling on the ears of a biscuit shaped like a teddy bear.

'That was my intention,' John said, 'but Lucy wanted to hire a car and drive herself. She told me she needs her own transport, to help in finding somewhere to live.'

Edith swallowed, hiding her disappointment, as the conversation awakening memories of Paul. She'd travelled expectantly to the airport to meet the love of her life, the man that never came. She felt sorry for John because, other than Josephine, no one else knew how much of a fool she had made of herself. For John, if Lucy didn't show, everyone would know that he had been taken in by a scam.

'Wouldn't it have been better for Lucy to hire a car locally?'

John shrugged his shoulders. He would be glad to be heading home, away from the well-meaning but interfering women of the Parish Council. 'Can I get you another cup of tea?'

'That would be lovely.'

Later, opening the front door of his house, John was struck with a feeling of unease, a penetrating chill and a shiver running up and down his spine. Someone had been in the house, he was sure. Standing in the doorway, he paused, frightened to enter, searching for signs of an intruder.

Tick, tock.

Except for the ticking of the dining room clock, nothing stirred; looking down the hallway, all appeared as it should.

This is nonsense, you're being paranoid. Lucy has arrived a day early, that's all.

Instead of rushing in to greet his guest, John's feet were frozen to the spot.

He called out, 'Lucy, is that you?'

Thirty seconds later, he repeated the enquiry, but the house remained silent, except for the clock; tick, tock. *Should I call the police?* he questioned. *How can I, when I'm not sure anything is wrong.* Nervously, John stepped across the threshold and into the hallway. The single drawer of the antique Scottish oak carved lamp table was slightly ajar; John knew it hadn't been opened in weeks. Now his heart raced; if someone had been in the house, perhaps they were still here, he couldn't be sure. Tentatively, he opened the drawer, but nothing had been disturbed. Doubt drenched him, wanting to believe he was imagining the intrusion. His angst told him otherwise.

Hesitantly, he entered the dining room. Nothing was missing, everything was in its place, or was it? He found himself straightening a place mat on the table, wondering whether it had been moved. Meticulously, room by room, he combed the house, seeking clues. As far as he could tell, nothing was missing. The feeling that someone had been in the house was inescapable. He was sure of it. A book moved here, a pen, not quite aligned, a bath towel hanging crookedly, all conclusive to him. His privacy had been violated. John knew his house had been searched carefully and thoroughly.

Alone in the kitchen, his mind began to race.

People don't break into a house without a reason.

His conversation with Josephine about being a mule came rushing back, filling him with dread.

It's the wrapped gift, the pen. That's what they were looking for. Why?

With Lucy arriving the following day, John felt a tightening in his throat as fear gripped him.

What am I mixed up in, an international drug smuggling syndicate? What if it was the Mafia who had been in the house...or the police? God knows who else. I could be arrested and I've done nothing wrong.

He panicked.

How would I prove that I wasn't complicit in a crime and that the St Mary's Dating Agency isn't a front? What if Lucy is an assassin and she cuts my throat in the middle of the night?

Catastrophising, beads of sweat ran down his face, his heart pounded and his breathing was rapid.

Stop this, he yelled to himself. *You're being stupid. Take deep breaths, inhale, hold it, now exhale; that's good, John.*

Settling, he said, aloud, though he was alone, 'I want you to count slowly from one to ten.'

His body relaxed as he counted.

That's better, John. Why don't you make yourself a nice cup of hot tea, England's answer to everything.

As he filled the kettle with water, John's nerves settled and he considered asking Josephine if he could stay the night at her house, but changed his mind.

If someone wanted to hurt you, they would have done it. You're quite safe, for now.

That night, sleep eluded John as he tossed and turned, his mind ruminating over endless possibilities. The next morning, with a churning stomach, breakfast repulsed him. While waiting for Lucy to arrive, John tried to read but instead found himself pacing the floor, reading then pacing again, all the while watching the clock which seemed to tick interminably slowly and as the hour approached when Lucy was due to arrive, he repeated over and over to himself. *Act natural, John. Pretend that nothing is wrong and whatever you do—stay calm.*

Whilst seated, having completed a pacing cycle, John glanced at his watch, then through the window as a white Ford Focus pulled up outside. He could see Lucy staring at the house, checking the number. As John opened the front door, Lucy stood at the garden gate and, despite his apprehension, his heart leapt. She wore an elegant, navy blue, open backed, cap sleeved, lace skater dress. A red ribbon tied back her flowing blonde hair. She gave him a welcoming but weary smile, one from someone who had just completed a long-haul flight.

'Hi,' she called. 'Remember me?'

Lucy's beauty and grace were intoxicating, and John's fears melted away, submerged in the moment as he was consumed by her presence. Motionless, he stared in silent wonder at her smiling face.

'Are you going to invite me in?'

From his emails, Lucy knew John had been showing the warning signs of uncertainty, perhaps suspicion of her motives. His trust needed to be regained and Lucy anticipated a test of her genuineness, to see if her motives were pure. She had thought her plan through. Whatever he said or did, she would respond with concern, love, patience and understanding. In an arbitrary world, faith was a resource born from respect and she would earn it.

Momentarily mesmerised by her loveliness, John recovered and mumbled, 'I'm sorry Lucy, of course, come in.'

As she walked towards him, John speculated,

Do I kiss her hello?

Lucy answered the unspoken question by stretching her arms out towards him, inviting John to do the same. As they embraced, she kissed him tenderly on the cheek. Taking a step back while still holding him, Lucy stared deep into his eyes and, before planting a gentle kiss on his lips, said, 'Hello, Mr John Moss.'

'Come on in,' John said absent-mindedly, his passion rising, dreaming of another kiss.

John led Lucy into the dining room as she said, 'What a lovely home you have.'

'Thank you.'

There was a moment of awkward silence, broken by Lucy as she said, 'I would love a cup of tea. I've been awake for more than thirty hours.'

'Oh, sorry, yes, I'm not being the best host.'

I will have to deal with the elephant in the room straight away, Lucy thought. Misinterpreting his distraction as ambivalence rather than as a person besotted, she said, 'You're being a wonderful host John, although I sense that you're troubled. Is everything alright?'

The anxieties of the previous night flooded his mind.

John panicked. *What do I say? I can't tell the truth?*

'The house was broken into yesterday. It has unsettled me.'

The Chinese! They must have found the pictures of me with John. I wonder if they discovered the cube?

'I'm so sorry John. You must feel violated having your home invaded.'

Should I ask if they took anything? No, best to wait Lucy, but I will pay Mr Chen Li a visit.

'Would you prefer I stay somewhere else tonight? I would understand.'

Her genuineness was chipping away at his doubts. 'No, I want you to stay.'

Make him feel like he's protecting you, plotted Lucy.

'You promise to keep me safe?' she said.

John felt a lump form in his throat and, fighting it off, he said, light-heartedly, 'Who, me? I can't even ski. Not sure I'd be much of a bodyguard.'

Lucy smiled, taking hold of his hand as she said, 'How about that cup of tea you British are famous for?'

During the evening, as they shared an early dinner, John told Lucy that he was certain that someone had been through the house, though nothing had been stolen. Lucy was sure that the Chinese were behind the break-in, concluding that if nothing was stolen, the cube was safe, John having stashed it elsewhere. When the timing was right, she would ask him about it, suspecting that he would lie, suggesting he'd lost it to test her reaction. Lucy had anticipated staying two or three days, then vanishing while he was at work. If her conjecture was correct, it would take longer to earn his trust and the return of the package.

No bedding him tonight, she thought. *I will let him sleep on the thought of us making love.*

'John, I'm so tired after the flight. I have to go to bed. Would you stay with me until I fall asleep?'

'Sure, if that's what you would like.' His mind raced.

***

John pulled back the quilts, sitting fully clothed on the edge of the bed, waiting for Lucy to finish changing in the bathroom. A vision from heaven appeared and it stole his breath away. Lucy, an erotic angel of splendour, was wearing a silky translucent white nightgown, her red sexy underwear showing tantalisingly underneath.

'Thank you,' she whispered sweetly, slipping in between the sheets.

As John was tucking in the bedding, Lucy said, 'Hold me.'

He put his arm around her, feeling her body under the quilt.

'You can get under the covers if you like.'

John removed his shoes and slid in next to her. Feeling his presence, she nestled her back against his stomach.

'Good night,' Lucy whispered.

John's arm draped over her shoulder, his hand resting near her breast. As she breathed deeply in sleep, her chest rose and fell, brushing his hand in its rhythm. Her sweet fragrance was intoxicating, overwhelming his senses as he fought off sleep, wanting the moment to last forever.

***

'Hi, you stayed,' Lucy said the following morning, kissing him gently on the lips.

'I thought that if I moved, I'd wake you.'

'You're a sweet man, John Moss.'

John had taken the day off work and, despite her fears, Lucy found the village of Pi-Ski surprisingly pleasant and friendly. Having lied to John, telling him that this was her first visit to the UK, she welcomed enthusiastically his suggestion to visit a tourist attraction, though she'd been to Cornwall before on missions for both MI6 and the Russian Mafia. The winter rain didn't diminish their visit to St Michael's Mount, a historic castle and chapel built on a small tidal island in Mount's Bay. It was low tide and Lucy exclaimed with feigned surprise when the causeway appeared from the sea, permitting them to reach the Mount by foot, walking across an ancient cobbled path.

Pretending to be lost in the history, myth and legends that shape the Mount's story, Lucy asked, 'Is this where the fabled King Arthur lived?'

John squeezed her hand in delight as he said, 'Arthur was a Cornish king to be sure, but the folklore around here is that he held court and had his round table at Tintagel Castle. It's not far from Pi-Ski. If you like, we can visit at the weekend, a quest to find the Holy Grail?'

Lucy stopped, held both John's hands in hers and said, 'I think I've found my Holy Grail.'

He blushed in delight.

Why am I feeling sorry for him? This is business Lucy, just business. You are an actor playing a part.

After their day of adventure, Lucy wanted to fuss in the kitchen, preparing a culinary delight for their first dinner as a couple.

'Let me help you,' John said.

Lucy smiled lovingly. 'Out, get out of the kitchen. Tonight, this is my domain.'

Lucy had a menu displayed on the iPad, but to her dismay, following the instructions proved more complicated than understanding calculus. Because she rarely cooked, the end result was unlike the colour photo shown in the recipe. She watched expectantly as John took his first bite. If it tasted like poison, he gave no clue, proceeding to munch away. Raising a fork to her mouth, Lucy let the food pass between her lips.

Well, it's edible, she thought and smiled at her own accomplishment.

During their conversation at the table, Lucy asked if she could be introduced to the St Mary's Church Dating Agency team. John pondered for a moment before he spoke.

'There's a meeting Thursday night and you are welcome to come along; I know the ladies would love to meet you.'

There was a period of silence that John misinterpreted.

'Not if you don't want to. I wouldn't want you feeling like an exhibit.'

'John, I'm sure it will all be fine and besides, I'm looking forward to meeting the people you've told me so much about.'

'You're wonderful.'

Lucy's face developed a shallow smile as she said, 'Thank you. While you're at work tomorrow, I thought I would go shopping in Plymouth for some new clothes and to look for a car. I was also going to post the pen to my uncle.'

John was caught off guard. He'd had such a wonderful, perfect day that he had forgotten about the package.

Panicking he wondered, *What should I say?*

His conversation with Josephine wedged itself into his thoughts as he said, 'Oh, I'm sorry Lucy, I meant to tell you. I've misplaced it, but it can't be far, must be here somewhere.'

He watched for her reaction.

'Maybe it was stolen?' Lucy asked.

'I don't think so. Please forgive me, I'm sure I will find it.'

Is this my test, Mr John Moss?

Lucy smiled, holding his hand across the table as she said, 'It's fine John, it's just a pen. If you can't find it, your punishment will be to accompany me to the shops and buy another.' Then, wanting to change the subject, she said. 'Now, what would you like me to cook for you tomorrow night?'

'Wednesday evenings I volunteer at a community kitchen. We prepare, freeze and cryopak about four hundred meals for a food bank who then distribute them to those in need, the vulnerable, hungry and homeless.'

'You didn't tell me that. What a truly wonderful and kind man you are. Could I join you? I would love to help.'

'Lucy, that would be great. We start at five thirty and finish at eight o'clock. I'll write the address down for you. All the food is donated; St Mary's used to contribute, but that hasn't been possible for a few years. I volunteer my time instead.'

'I'll meet you there. It will be something we can do together,' Lucy said. 'Kindness is the key to happiness.'

***

If Chinese State Security were snooping about in Pi-Ski, Lucy needed to buy some practical clothing whilst she was in Plymouth. She had to conceal a firearm and other weapons; slacks, jacket and a business suit would suffice. She wanted to contact the "Agency", to update them on the cube-shaped, black metallic object she'd retrieved and place an order for the equipment she needed: a pistol, Scotland Yard warrant card, and a car. Following her run-in with the Chinese in Germany and their search of John house, she desired authorisation to visit Mr Li. She also wanted an explanation. What was the radioactive signature given off by the cube?

When John had left for work, Lucy called her Agency contact, Rosie, at the East Dart Hotel in Postbridge, Devon. At the end of the conversation, Rosie said that the goods she wanted, along with the responses to her questions would be waiting at Postbridge on Friday.

Hanging up the phone, Lucy said to herself, *I will delay my trip to Plymouth until then.*

***

Later that day, the community kitchen was a hive of activity, with people working diligently, rushing about in ordered chaos under the skillful direction of a chef. The one thing louder than the clashing of pots and pans was the laughter filling the room, enthusiastic volunteers enjoying their tasks. Working side by side with strangers, Lucy found that warm hearted chatter flowed easily. She felt comfortable. John and Lucy had been put to work in separate parts of the kitchen, each engaged in their own tasks. Lucy spotted John only twice during the evening and on each occasion he was beavering away, chopping vegetables, stirring soup, packing meals, all done while lost in banter. To her, he seemed a shy, awkward, unassuming man, with a poor taste in clothes and glasses that rested crookedly on his nose. Here, amongst these volunteers, he fitted like the two sides of a dovetail joint. Lucy observed that in this kitchen, people's differences were submerged; a group of diverse people, united in a common purpose for the betterment of others. The shared happiness in the room was contagious; she felt a strange sensation of contentment and satisfaction, a rare awareness for Lucy. Without thinking, her eyes sought out John. He saw her and smiled warmly.

He's a good man. What does that make me?

Lucy dismissed the reflection, concentrating on her cooking.

At the end of the evening, Lucy and John, hand in hand, left the kitchen and walked to their cars, which were parked next to each other.

'Your England is chilly,' Lucy grumbled, condensation seeping from her lips as she spoke.

Rubbing his hands together to warm them against the evening chill, John said, 'You do look beautiful, but you're meant to wear a coat, then layer up against the cold.'

In the dim glow of a streetlight which cast a long shadow over their cars, Lucy spotted movement at her driver's door. Someone wearing a black hoodie was trying to break in. John saw it too.

For Lucy, her reflexes kicked in.

I don't think so, Mate. You're not having my car.

'What are you doing? Don't, it's dangerous,' John said in distress, as Lucy broke free of his hand, striding resolutely towards the robber.

If she heard him, his plea for caution failed to register. John remained transfixed in shock, pondering her stupidity. She'd already reached the thief before he made an attempt to catch up.

Confronting the assailant, Lucy said coolly, 'Good evening. Can I help you, Sweetie?'

Disturbed, the crook's attention was drawn to her.

'Piss off, lady,' a male voice spat.

Why is it always men?

Lucy took a step closer. In the dark and because of the thief's hoodie, she couldn't see his face, but what light there was bounced off the blade of a flick knife. It flashed at her and Lucy stepped aside just as the knife was about to strike. She brought her hand down sharply on top of the assailant's wrist, capturing and twisting it. In a flowing motion, the larcenist's arm was lifted into the air, pulling him towards Lucy, who, taking the opportunity and using the inertia of his motion and her own strength, kneed him in the groin. He groaned in agony, buckling over. Lucy was about to administer a killer blow to the neck but she paused, measured the impact, and stunned him instead. She let go of the assailant's arm and with her leg pushed him away. He fell motionless to the footpath, lucky to be alive, though he did not know it.

In the shadows, not far from where the thief had landed, Lucy spotted another, but larger person. They stared momentarily at each other, likes stags, each gauging the strength of the other. Lucy smiled invitingly as she beckoned with her hand and said, 'Come on, Sweetie...'

The figure turned and fled.

John, who now stood beside Lucy, mouth hanging open in disbelief, said, 'How did you do that?'

'I learned karate as a kid. Didn't get far, just enough to defend myself. Shall we go?'

'Shouldn't we call the police and an ambulance?'

'What's the point? He's just a druggy or a pusher, probably one of the people we've cooked for tonight. The police will only lock him up for the night, then he'll be back on the streets. Maybe he's learned a lesson from tonight. Once we are gone, his mate will come back and take care of him. I only stunned him; he'll be fine, just a little sore in the nuts.'

John weighed up the situation and hesitantly said, 'Okay.' Then, in a playful voice added, 'You're a woman of mystery. Remind me never to get into a fight with you.'

Lucy found his hand and squeezed it as she said, 'Karate makes a woman very flexible. When we get home, I'll show you some moves.'

'Promise?'

She kissed him on the cheek and whispered, 'Promise!'

***

For the meeting with John's friends from the St Mary's Parish Council, Lucy donned her innocent, girl-next-door appearance. Her conjecture was that John had entrusted the package with the cube to one of his church colleagues. Winning their confidence, without appearing arrogant or pushy, was now part of the game; helping the church would serve in gaining their trust.

The Parish Council members were already seated around the table, talking merrily as they entered the church hall.

'Hi, everyone,' John announced, 'This is Lucy.'

They all looked up and Lucy gave a reserved but confident greeting. 'Hello.'

Automatically Lucy glanced from one person to the next, assessing them, evaluating the faces of the people present. The moment her eyes settled on Josephine Carter she recognised her from Florence five years earlier, when she had been sent to watch a retiring agent, Harry Carter. Lucy hadn't made the connection before, between Harry and the Josephine Carter of John's stories. Preventing her eyes from lingering, Lucy scanned each of the participants, her appearance neutral as her gaze rested on Josephine fleetingly. In her peripheral vision, Lucy could see Josephine's puzzled countenance, trying to work out why Lucy seemed familiar to her.

I wonder if Josephine knew the truth about her husband? What secrets would a husband and wife share?

'Welcome,' Vicar Charlotte said. 'Thank you for joining us. John, why don't you do the introductions?'

As John spoke a few words about each person in turn, Lucy looked each in the eye and, when it was Josephine's turn, her years of practice ensured that her demeanour gave nothing away.

'How are you settling in?' Catherine asked.

'Wonderfully, thank you. I joined John at the community kitchen last night and tomorrow I'm off to Plymouth to buy a car and, next week, I hope to start looking for a job and a place to live.'

'What do you do?' Josephine asked.

'I'm a pre-school teacher. I checked before I came, my qualifications are accepted in the UK.'

Josephine continued, pondering why she recognised this woman. 'John told us you are from Australia?'

'Yes.'

'How wonderful, and have you been to the UK before?'

'No. When I met John, that was my first trip overseas.' Lucy said, a smile on her face. 'Well that's not quite true. I've been to New Zealand, but in Australia, that doesn't count.'

Josephine was about to ask another question when the Vicar interrupted. 'We don't want to make this young woman feel like we are the Spanish Inquisition.'

'That's okay,' Lucy said. 'John told me all about the St Mary's Dating Agency and your plans to grow your congregation and save the church. I'm pleased to be your first success. I will be an open book and you are welcome to interrogate me, to help refine your skills for whoever is next.'

Marrying people off may help put bums on seats,' Catherine said gruffly, 'But what we need is recurrent income to pay the bills.'

'God is answering our prayers,' Vicar Charlotte said excitedly. 'He has given us Lucy and the roof of his house will be repaired next week.'

Lucy stayed poker-faced during the meeting, listening to the well-meant, but ridiculous chatter that passed as a considered way of raising money for the Church. By the end of the gathering they'd reached an agreement. Edith would be the agency's next client and was tasked with writing her dating profile.

With the meeting finished, people gossiped in little groups as they moved towards the door and home. Lucy remained at the table observing the committee members as they left. She noticed John whispering to Josephine, but couldn't quite make out what they were saying.

Was it that Josephine had to be Lucy's best friend? A bet of some kind?

Looking away, so as not to gain Josephine's attention, Lucy deliberated.

The pictures I encouraged John to send of us from Saint Moritz have made Josephine uncomfortable, though she doesn't know why.

Josephine... yes, it's her. She is the one who sowed the seeds of doubt in John's mind, convincing him to send the "cold feet" email. The package isn't misplaced, Josephine has it. Despite what John may say, I can sense her misgivings haven't been put to rest tonight; calming her disquiet will be challenging, a challenge, indeed. I will need to win over the other parish council members and John to do that.

Lucy, if you help grow the congregation and master being a loving partner for John, the package with the cube will return. You can have until the New Year. If you still don't have it by then, break into Josephine's house and take it apart brick by brick if you have to. If that fails, extract the information from her or John by any means.

Sneaking a look, John and Josephine were still talking. Lucy whispered to herself, *I would love to know what they are talking about*. It then occurred to her. If she had worked out where the package was hidden, then so might the Chinese agents and they would have no qualms about eliminating both Josephine and John. She needed to act, and soon. The seriousness of her thoughts was broken when she recalled that someone, and she couldn't remember who, had, in the mad ramblings that went around the table that night, mentioned that funerals were lucrative for a church. If she didn't push back against the MSS and limit their ability to steer events, St Mary's may get what they wished for, albeit, burying the Parish Councillors themselves. The irony made her smile.

'What are you smiling about?' John asked jovially, having finished talking with Josephine.

'Oh, nothing, I'm just happy.'

***

The next morning, acting like a dutiful wife, Lucy kissed John goodbye as he left for work.

'Enjoy your shopping in Plymouth,' John said.

'Anything you would like me to fetch for you?'

'Something red.'

Lucy put her hands on her hips and gave John a sideways glance as she said, a broad smile adorning her face, 'My John Moss, you are mischievous.'

CHAPTER 11

Quantum Cube

The East Dart Hotel

'Welcome back to the UK,' Rosie said, offering Lucy a chair in her office. 'I guess things didn't go as planned?'

'It would have helped if you'd told me that the item was radioactive. When I opened the container housing the cube, there were residual traces of its presence left on my hands. It would have also been useful to know its significance to the Chinese State Security; forewarned is forearmed. We operate on a need to know basis, I realise that but, on this occasion, I needed to know.'

'That was our mistake, Lucy. We thought less knowledge would be safer for you. It's not that we don't trust you, I don't want you to think otherwise.'

'I didn't consider that for a moment.'

'Indeed.'

'Now would be a good time to share some information, if you would be so kind,' Lucy said.

Rosie nodded in agreement before saying, 'In the course of world history, something sometimes comes along that is so revolutionary that if it is used for good will change the course of humanity, but if militarised, will dramatically change the global balance of power - to our disadvantage. The Janus Key was like that. When you were working for Monya and the Russian Mafia, you tried to capture the device from our agents Max and Olivia. You would have sold it to the highest bidder, irrespective of the consequences...' Rosie paused before saying, 'Did you know the whole story?'

Lucy shook her head.

'The Janus Machine, a biological weapon, was invented by Dr Von Erick Brack at the Majdanek concentration camp. He was moved to the Bergen-Belsen concentration camp when the Red Army liberated Majdanek. As you know, the machine was useless without the decryption key, and two were made. One was taken with Dr Von Brack to Bergen-Belsen and the other was to be destroyed when the Biological Weapons Facility at Majdanek was blown up by the retreating Germans. The Polish Resistance found the key, still intact in the rubble at Majdanek and smuggled it, via

Murmansk and the Russian convoys, to Britain. Max, as a young man, was the agent sent to Russia to retrieve it.

'The Janus Machine was a game changer because of its ability to attach diseases or viruses to individual body cells. If used for good in medicine, the technology would have allowed targeted treatment for almost any illness, especially the scourge of cancer. It would have revolutionised medicine as we know it, but militarised, as a biological weapon, disease agents could have been tailored to specific people, races, hair colour, or whatever you wanted. The consequences would have been unimaginable, dire.'

'Our British Government Agency which, as you know, works occasionally with MI5 and MI6 made a decision, gauging that the world wasn't ready for the Janus Machine. Towards the end of the Second World War we hid the key, waiting for a time when the word "humanity" was an accurate noun for our species.'

'Lucy, once again a scientific advance has come to our attention that we consider a potential danger; another for which the world is unprepared. The device you were sent to retrieve is a quantum cube and has the potential to revolutionise energy supply and use. It is more powerful and effective than a fusion reaction and would end the world's dependence on fossil fuel. For the first time since the Industrial Revolution, there is a realistic opportunity to limit the impact of global warming and irreversible climate change. You know, unless we dramatically alter course in the next thirty to fifty years, scientists believe CO_2 levels will exceed twelve hundred parts per million, pushing the earth's climate over a "tipping point". If that prediction were to come true, warming will then become unstoppable. What happens after that, well, we don't know, except that it won't be a good thing. Unfortunately, the Chinese State, like the Nazis before them, have focused on the weaponisation of the technology. We believe they have succeeded. The West isn't innocent, of course. We've done some research, succeeding partially, using a proton-antiproton collider but only with bottom and lighter quarks.

'I hope Lucy, that your knowledge of quantum physics is better than mine. The best I can do is to read to you from a briefing note. I asked our scientists to remove the jargon, keep it simple, and I hope it will help you understand why our government wants the device, and why the Chinese want it back.'

Rosie picked up the briefing note in front of her and started reading:

> 'Heavy quarks are a fundamental component of matter. All hadrons, such as protons, neutrons or pions, are made up of quarks. Up to now, six quark types have been observed: up, down, strange, charm, bottom and top quarks. The first three have a small mass, while the remaining three quarks are much heavier. The top quark is the heaviest.

'Until recently, it was believed that top quarks, because of their short-life time...'

Rosie paused and then snorted. 'I ask them to keep it simple and they write this. Here, take a look.'

Rosie showed Lucy the page with the formula 4.2×10^{25} displayed and Lucy said, 'I understand, that's 4.2 multiplied by 10 to the power twenty-five, representing seconds.'

'Very good Lucy, I'll keep reading,' Rosie said, as she continued...

'were not capable of binding together into strange hadrons with unusual properties and quarks zipping about inside them.

'There are some good examples of bound hadrons made up of two charm quarks and a lighter quark, formed when a hadron made up of two bulky bottom quarks and one lighter quark fuse together in a flash more powerful than the individual fusion reaction inside a hydrogen bomb. It was thought that the bottom quark fusion was militarily useless thanks to the heavy quarks' short lifetimes. We believe however this is no longer the case. Inside the Chinese cube is a tetraquark with a stable binding of top-quarks, the heaviest of the quarks. If any country were in sole possession of this technology and if it was applied militarily, it would be calamitous for any government who opposed them. A new type of radiation is given off by tetraquarks. While the quantum cube houses the energy, harmless amounts of radiation leak from it, at least we believe the radiation to be harmless.'

Rosie looked at Lucy. 'The pen shaped object you retrieved housing the cube is constructed of a new material that hides the tetraquark's radiation signature. When you opened it, tiny traces were left on you. If the quantum cube is still hidden within the pen, it is untraceable. The design was an inconspicuous way of moving something that doesn't exist.

'Our specialists tell me, Lucy, that what I've just read to you is an over-simplification. I've distilled it down to this: Inside the device you were sent to retrieve is the most powerful source of energy ever known to exist in mankind's history.'

Lucy pondered for a few seconds, and said, 'If this was the game changer, as you say, and you knew that it was in Saint Moritz, why not send in a military team to secure it?'

'When you were with the Russian Mafia, Claudia used her reputation as a weapon - compliance and obedience through fear of the consequences. We, on the other hand, are engaged in a delicate diplomatic dance. We aim to achieve our ends without rippling the water, plausible deniability to avoid a wider conflict arising. If we were heavy-handed, we would attract unwanted attention. You must see these most delicate of matters require subtlety that only the spy agencies can offer. The quantum cube has the same characteristics as the Janus Machine. The world, and that includes Britain, is unprepared and our job is to make the device disappear.'

Rosie stopped for a moment and gazed into Lucy's eyes as she said, 'Have you discovered what John did with it?'

'Not as such,' Lucy said. 'I believe that he's given it to a woman in his village called Josephine Carter. I've met her before, in the days before I worked for you. She may recognise me, or at least, I think she does.'

'Pray tell,' Rosie said, interested in the connection.

'Ordinarily, my work before the "Agency", is private. You don't ask, and I don't tell.'

'That is well understood,' Rosie said.

'On this occasion, our worlds overlap and I would like to exchange intelligence.' Lucy looked at Rosie questioningly. 'Do you agree?'

Rosie nodded her consent.

'Josephine Carter was married to a man called Harry Carter who held a privileged position in the UK Foreign Affairs Department.'

As Lucy continued, Rosie typed the name Harry Carter into the laptop on her desk.

'Harry was one of the KGB's long-term agents, recruited early in his Oxford days. When any of the KGB overseas operatives say they are going to retire, it is common practice to keep tabs on them for a while to ensure that we all part on good terms. Harry and Josephine were in Europe on holiday and the agent tasked with following them in Florence was taken ill. I was there for another matter and was asked to take over and followed them for a couple of days. Harry died.'

'It's not a good look when our services leak,' Rosie said. 'The inquiry following Harry's death raised the possibility of him being a mole.'

Rosie held back a sigh of despair as she looked at the screen and explained to Lucy what was in Harry's record.

'It reads that Josephine Carter told the police that she believed that she and her husband were being followed prior to his death. The person tracking them had a Louis Vuitton handbag and wore Dolce & Gabbana dresses. It made her stand out.'

Rosie looked at Lucy, then back at the computer screen.

'Josephine told the police that she noticed these things because she was an editor for a fashion magazine. The report concluded that Harry Carter was pushed to his death and did not fall from the lookout. Did you kill him Lucy?'

'No.'

'Are you sure?' Rosie asked again.

'Yes, I'm sure. Those in Russia thought it was you, the Brits, that terminated him.' Lucy paused before continuing, 'It explains why Josephine believes she recognises me. Winning her over will be challenging, especially if she makes the connection.'

Rosie said, 'If not Russia or the British, it may have been Josephine who pushed her husband to his death. It would be wise not to underestimate her.

Lucy nodded and then asked, 'Did she discover her husband was a spy for the wrong side?'

'She asked lots of questions. After his death there was a rumour in the Foreign Office that he was a spy, which she may have heard, so it's entirely possible,' Rosie said and then changed the subject.

'When do you expect to have the quantum cube?'

'Give me until the new year. I will have won her over by then.'

'Do you have a plan in mind?'

'Yes. Josephine is on the Parish Council of a church that is quickly running out of money. In six months' time they will no longer be able to afford to pay the Vicar. Saving St Mary's would probably do it.'

Rosie smiled. 'If you find a solution to that, I'm sure the Archbishop of Canterbury will recommend an honour for you, perhaps a title?'

'Dame Lucy. I like the sound of that.'

'Indeed. When you have a plan formulated, the Agency will see how it can help.'

'If I haven't succeeded by the new year, you may need to authorise more forceful means.'

'You know, Lucy, we prefer diplomacy.'

Lucy looked at Rosie. 'I can tell you that the Chinese Ministry of State Security doesn't respect your "delicate diplomatic dance".'

'You are right, Lucy, and we have been slow to respond to Chinese activism. The diplomatic disorder is spinning in all sorts of dangerous directions and starting to shape the twenty-first century.

"I agree,' Lucy said.

'Indeed, Lucy. The early warning signs were there, back in 2001, when a People's Liberation Navy J-8 fighter Jet collided with a US Navy aircraft off Hainan Island, an area which is now contested waters. While the economic rise of China has brought mutual prosperity, benefiting people in less developed countries, rather than seeking to balance security and trade, we believed that their economic liberalisation would inevitably lead to democracy. While we became inward looking, they grew both more mobile and authoritarian, seeking to influence and spread their ideology. We sat idly by while they built the islands in the South China Sea, then watched while they militarised them.'

'What has really caught us off-guard is how they weaponised our neo-liberalism against us. We've been taken as fools. Supposedly independent private Chinese companies operating overseas have been required to share their information and data with the central Chinese government. There is growing concern that the computer and communication equipment supplied by these Chinese companies are at risk of manipulation from their Government. Electronic eavesdropping and data theft, used to promote their propaganda, or worse, remotely take over the Chinese made equipment used in foreign countries.'

'We have evidence of significant state-backed activity; actors linked to the Chinese government are running covert information operations, you know, influencing, fake news, and so on, on Western social media platforms. The Chinese are mimicking Russia, with its use of large-scale government-backed fabrication and misinformation campaigns aimed at destabilising our democracies. The Chinese government is seeking to take over

Britain's political system through its insidious foreign interference operations. The number of foreign intelligence officers currently operating in Britain is higher than it was during the Cold War. Its effects might not present for decades and, by that time, it's too late.'

Lucy fought the urge to yawn, but it was impossible to resist. Her mouth gaped open before closing again. Rosie stopped speaking and gave Lucy a look that conveyed her displeasure.

'Jet lag,' Lucy said apologetically.

'Indeed. Can I continue?'

Lucy shifted uncomfortably in her seat before saying, 'By all means.'

'Good. Through the trillion-dollar One Belt, One Road, initiative, the new "Silk Road", and through other initiatives, the Chinese are buying and indebting nations, whereby infrastructure and economic aid is provided to needy economies in return for Chinese economic and strategic domination. Some countries involved are at significant risk of relinquishing their sovereignty to the Chinese State.

'Australia, our Five Eyes partner, faces the prospect of a Peoples' Liberation military base in Cambodia. China is on course to have other options in the Asia-Pacific region as well. The Australian government has leased the Port of Darwin to the Chinese, one which is used by the Australian and US Navy. They have also allowed a Chinese-backed company access to mines in South Australia's Woomera Prohibited Area, Australia's most sensitive military testing range. Britain is not immune, mostly because of our reliance on technology from Huawei. Nesting a dragon in our central nervous system will cost us dearly.'

'In our neo-liberal societies, we have the separation of church and state, justice and the government, we expect the same with private corporations but this is not the case with China; it has caught us off guard.'

'Other than lobby groups, political donations by companies, and other vested interest groups,' Lucy said, a shallow smile garnishing her face.

'Utopia doesn't exist,' Rosie said, as she sighed. 'We have the reverse situation. Multi-national companies like Microsoft, Facebook and Google, have, or desire to have, greater influence than government. The flip-flop of control is pluralism in action. Anyhow, as I was saying, we've been caught napping. If you look closer to home, the Chinese already have a military base in Djibouti on the horn of Africa with other African nations likely to follow. Pakistan is not immune either. Melting Arctic ice is making nations more accessible and the polar region is now, more than ever, a strategically important route. China has unveiled its "Polar Silk Road" desire, in which goods would be delivered by sea from Asia to Europe. They have already bankrolled three new airports in Greenland.'

'I work for the state,' Lucy said. 'I follow the instructions I'm given. China is behaving no differently from the gun-boat diplomacy days of the nineteenth-century period of imperialism. Didn't the UK intimidate other, less powerful states into granting concessions by demonstrating superior military capabilities?' Lucy hesitated... 'I'm just saying.'

'It is true, but society has matured since those times. We have a system of international laws and norms to prevent the mistakes of the past being repeated. That's why we need to develop a new plan to deal with the rise of China because you can bet that they're going to continue to ignore the international rules-based system when they believe it's in their interest, yet demand other countries abide by the basic norms governing international relations if they are criticised. We know of their brutal and secretive campaign in its western Xinjiang province. A "no mercy" crackdown against Uighurs, Kazakhs and other Muslim minorities, mass detention involving as many as one million people.'

Lucy nodded in agreement while Rosie continued to speak.

'It is safe to say China is not satisfied with maintaining the status quo, she is on the way to becoming a super power, but with it comes additional responsibilities, which means more is expected of her.'

'Their treatment of you in Germany broke the conventions that exist between the world's spy agencies; left unchecked, that will play out here in the UK too. I'm sure that I don't have to remind you of the Russian Intelligence assassination attempt on British soil of your colleague Jana with the toxic agent Novichok. We tolerate foreign agents in the UK, but do not look kindly on black operations that undermine our sovereignty. The MSS need to learn, and quickly, the behaviour expected of foreign agents working in our country under the guise of diplomatic staff, journalists or any other creative job titles they come up with.'

Lucy nodded. 'I hear German authorities suspect Russian agents of murdering Zelimkhan Khangoshvili, shot dead in broad daylight in a Berlin park?'

'Yes, another in the long list of targeted killings by the Russians over the past decade. The conventions that have governed spy behaviour since the Second World War are unravelling. The last time diplomacy collapsed in this way, we stumbled into the First World War. Peace is not a natural condition, it's a political construct.'

'Lucy, as you did with our Russian friends after the Novichok incident, we would like you to pay a visit to our new chum, Mr Chen Li, of the Chinese Ministry of State Security. A social call, perhaps?' She handed Lucy a piece of paper with an address written on it.'

'He and some associates are having lunch in London tomorrow and I've taken the liberty of booking a table for you. He will require a practical demonstration of how the intricacies of our diplomatic dance operate.'

From the desk draw Rosie took the pistol and holster Lucy had requisitioned saying, 'And Lucy, do try not to kill anyone. The Agency is more interested in a waltz with the MSS, not a rumba.'

Lucy smiled. 'The Police Warrant Card and badge?'

Taking it from the drawer, Rosie said, 'I take it you have something in mind?'

Lucy nodded, ignoring the question, instead saying. 'My car?'

Rosie held out keys towards Lucy, withdrawing them as she went to take them. 'Can we have this one back, and not in a million pieces?'

'Forewarned is forearmed?'

'You're warned Lucy. The MSS is very dangerous.'

'What do you have for me?'

'In your role as a country girl, in love, living in the beautiful village of Pi-Ski, we thought the practicality and versatility of a 5-seat SUV would suit. A family car.'

Lucy gave a look that would have frozen hell.

'Okay, it's a Jaguar F-Pace SVR, four hundred and five kilowatt, five-litre supercharged V8 and will do nought to a hundred in four point three seconds. In case you find yourself in a scrap, which we urge you to avoid, we have increased the stiffness at the front by thirty per cent and the rear by ten per cent, and added performance-focused anti-roll bars to decrease body roll by six per cent. It comes standard with an active rear-differential that can brake an inside wheel to help push it around corners. They tell me you will find the throttle response is exceptional across the entire rev range. Uncompromised performance is the by-line.'

Lucy smiled as she said, 'At a claimed three point eight seconds, the Alfa and Mercedes are both quicker to zero to one hundred.'

Rosie raised an eyebrow. 'Yes, but we're British. There's no pleasing some people.'

'Would you prefer me to say, oh that's wonderful, but what's the colour?'

Rosie laughed. 'Her Majesty's Government wishes colour was the only thing that interested you. It's red if you really want to know.'

Lucy laughed.

'What is it?' Rosie asked.

'It's nothing, just something John said.'

'Please take care of this one, Lucy. There are limits to our budget and patience.'

Rosie handed Lucy the keys.

Taking them, Lucy said, 'Thank you. Are there any special features?'

'Do you mean like revolving number plates, machine guns and ejector seats?'

'That would do.'

'Only in the movies, Lucy, but I do have this for you.'

Rosie handed Lucy a card. 'The number has been programmed into the voice activated telephone. All you have to say is, "Call Cliff", then follow the instructions I've given you.'

CHAPTER 12

London Rumba

After five days of driving an under-powered hire car, Lucy found it refreshing to once again be behind the wheel of a performance vehicle, a pleasure only kilowatts could deliver. She hoped that the Agency's choice of transport would reinforce her sophisticated yet humble persona; most residents of Pi-Ski being unaware that the Jaguar was one of the fastest SUVs in the world. She was going to tell John that the car was her "something red", a present for when they were married. She would add, *very racy*, knowing it would make him smile.

Lifting her foot off the accelerator, invigorated having sped over the Dartmoor Downs, the big cat's exhaust gave a snap, crackle and pop as it came to a halt.

Taking out her phone, Lucy sent a text message to John.

Hi Honey. The dealer in Plymouth found the car I wanted, but it's in London. They are detailing it for me and I can pick it up in the morning. Driving to London now and will stay the night. Will call later. Love you, Lucy.

That night, having called John from the hotel, Lucy was pleased with herself. Despite her absence, there was no suspicion in John's voice or the conversation. The progress towards rebuilding trust wouldn't be set back by the trip to London. When John asked Lucy about the car she was buying, she was amazed that he was genuinely interested and excited by her choice. He was knowledgeable about the Jaguar SUV. Lucy hadn't taken John for a man who knew his cars.

There's more to John Moss than first appears, but I suppose that's true of all of us. He's kind of cute, but it's more than that. John cares, he cares about many things.

When John had cautioned Lucy that she would stand out in the Jaguar, she'd responded,

'Who me?' They both laughed.

On Saturday morning Lucy awoke early, enjoying a long run, taking in Hyde Park and her other favourite places in the city before returning to the hotel for a hot shower. The exhilaration of intense exercise, followed by the cleansing of rejuvenating water hitting her body was how Lucy prepared for a difficult day. The rituals that once accompanied her showers, driven by a compulsive urge to be clean, were a memory that she persistently pushed into history.

Before leaving Postbridge, Lucy had placed an order for some items, gifts she told Rosie, that would encourage the MSS to abide by the established conventions. They were waiting in a sealed envelope at reception when she went for breakfast.

Mr Li and his associates were meeting at the prestigious Chinese Shark Fin restaurant in Soho. Usually, Lucy would survey her operating setting, evaluating the environment, learning its entrances, exits and escape routes. Today she'd inspected the building plans and performed a walk past, but time hadn't permitted an internal inspection, so she arrived twenty minutes before Mr Li and his party were due.

She was greeted at the door by a smartly dressed waiter, wearing black trousers, a white jacket and black bow tie. 'Does Madam have a reservation?'

'Certainly. It's in the name of Lucy.'

'Yes Madam, a table for one. Have you dined with us before?'

'No, but you come highly recommended.'

'Thank you, Madam. If you would kindly follow me.'

Subtly, Lucy assayed the layout of the room as she was being escorted to her table. From the entrance, they passed the bar to her right and, at the far end of the room, a door led to the kitchen. She estimated the restaurant to be eighteen to twenty metres wide, which concurred with the plans she'd viewed. The larger tables were located on the left-hand side of the room, surrounded by semicircular cushioned pods, which provided seating for up to ten people. In the middle were round tables offering seating for four and, on the right-hand side, where Lucy was being guided, were two-seater tables.

Her reserved table was discreetly placed in a nook off the side of the room; ideal for her purpose. She took a seat so that her back would be facing the targets.

'Would Madam like a drink while you look at the menu?' asked the waiter.

'A glass of champagne would be nice. Do you have a Dom Pérignon?'

'I'm sorry Madam. We do have a nice 1999 Bollinger.'

'Excellent choice. That will do nicely.'

'My apologies, Madam, but it is a bottle of Bollinger.'

'Thank you for your consideration. A bottle will do nicely. I hope it's not too cold.'

The waiter looked mildly affronted. 'Certainly not Madam!'

A mirror hung on the wall in front of Lucy, slightly off to one side, affording her a clear vision of Mr Li's table. That morning, Lucy had added a small fascinator to help with her disguise for the day, a jacket and pants, primarily to conceal the Glock semi-automatic pistol she was intending to carry. However, she hadn't liked her reflection in the mirror of the hotel room and so decided to change into a dress. She was now unarmed, but the fascinator stayed. In the restaurant Lucy carried a small purse, devoid of weapons, a risky strategy, but she considered the assailants when they saw her, would think her poorly equipped for a fight. After their clash in Germany, where Lucy had apparently not matched her ruthless reputation, Mr Li's team would be woefully unprepared for her.

British intelligence had been correct, at precisely five minutes past one, Mr Chen Li arrived, accompanied by six of his colleagues, one being Mr Yáyī, the repugnant dentist Lucy had met in Germany. Their supreme arrogance played out as she hoped. Not expecting trouble, they gave little attention to the other patrons in the restaurant. Lucy was unnoticed by the Chinese diners while she watched them.

As a precaution, she waited until they were enjoying their second course, imbibing wine, enjoying each other's company before deciding it was time to act. Lucy rose from her seat and walked towards the MSS agents, taking a chair from a middle table as she passed, placing it at the exposed edge of her target's table. Overconfidence on the part of the agents meant Lucy reached the table without being observed and the men were startled as she joined them.

Ensuring both of her hands were visible on top of the chair, so that they could see she was unarmed, Lucy said, 'Hello, Sweetie.'

Immediately, two of the MSS agents reached inside their suit jackets towards the weapons they were packing. Mr Li raised his hand and they paused.

'Do you mind if I join you?' Lucy said. 'I've brought my own chair.'

Before anyone could answer, she positioned the chair at the table and smoothed her dress before sitting. They watched in silence, their anger simmering.

'Mr Li, how good it is to see you again, and Mr Yáyī. You will be pleased to know that I brushed and flossed my teeth this morning, just for you.' Lucy grinned, showing her pearly whites, mocking his past treatment of her.

Chen Li said, 'You have let your pride obstruct your better judgement. There may be no one to save you this time.'

Lucy laughed. 'Sweetie, you're so melodramatic. The Shark Fin is a busy restaurant in the middle of London's Soho district. This is neither the time nor the place for your childish antics or your playground threats.'

'Your manners haven't improved, I see.' He paused, but when Lucy failed to answer, Chen Li sighed and said, 'To what do we owe this unexpected pleasure?'

Lucy brought her hand to her chin, holding it in place for a moment, mimicking an impression of concerned thoughtfulness before saying, 'Mr Li, operating in the United Kingdom and in Europe for that matter, requires that you adhere to rules of etiquette. How can I put it? There are behaviours that are expected of you, long established conventions, observed by the various spy agencies and their personnel working here. Foreign operatives are required to act differently to the Triads, Mafia or Yakuza. Intelligence agencies are not savages and an accord has operated since the end of World War Two, mostly respected by all sides. My employer describes this as a delicate diplomatic dance. When boundaries are breached, we end up with a messy international incident, something our governments are keen to avoid.' Lucy glanced at Mr Yáyī as she continued, 'Sweetie, a man of your talents isn't wanted here, although my former employer, the Russian Mafia, would welcome you.'

Chen Li snapped, 'For your sake, I will ignore your condescending remarks.'

As he spoke, Lucy picked up the chopsticks from the table and helped herself to the food on the plate of the person next to her. The man looked on in disgust as Lucy smiled.

'Your Western conventions,' continued Chen Li, 'came about to maintain balance, because each had spies operating in the other's country. I have heard it described as, "If you don't kill one of mine, I won't kill one of yours". Your agreement, like your visit here today, is both pathetic and weak.'

'The difference between the Chinese Ministry of State Security and other foreign parties with which you deal, is that your western agencies' presence in China is insignificant. You bring little to the negotiating table. When you meddle in the affairs of the People's Republic of China, like stealing something that clearly belongs to us, you must prepare for the consequences. They will be severe, uncompromising and merciless.' He raised his finger, pointing at Lucy and, as he lowered it said, 'How is John Moss, by the way?'

Lucy shrugged her shoulders. 'Expendable.'

Chen Li laughed. 'We know where you are and your time is running out.'

Lucy took another mouthful of food and said calmly, 'And we know where you are.'

Lucy placed the chopsticks on the table and opened her purse, removing six packages of heroin, placing them on the table. 'I'm told it's very pure.'

'You're trying to bribe us?' Chen Li snorted in disbelief.

Lucy gestured towards Yáyī.

'Mr Yáyī works at the Embassy of the People's Republic of China and tomorrow morning he is booked on British Airways flight 696 to Vienna. As he passes through Heathrow airport, sniffer dogs will alert customs to the presence of prohibited goods. A Customs search will find that he is carrying a trafficable quantity of heroin. A person at the airport is filming the incident on their smart phone. How they knew that Mr Yáyī worked for the Chinese embassy, well, we still don't know. Despite the British Government's best efforts, the video and story breaks on social media. Minutes later, all the major news agencies around the world are receiving reports that the People's Republic of China is using diplomatic immunity to traffic in drugs.' Lucy placed a USB stick on the table as she continued, 'He was also found carrying a USB stick that contains a PDF copy of a book entitled "The Secrets of Methamphetamine Production by Uncle Fester". A very informative read, or so I'm told.'

There was a tense silence as Lucy finished speaking. To fill the vacuum, she took a paper napkin from the place setting in front of her and began folding it into a paper crane, copying the calling card of a callous assassin used by the MSS whose true identity was unknown. The CIA believe the Crane works almost exclusively for the Chinese Ministry of State Security. Over the previous ten years, the assassin had eliminated people of annoyance to the Chinese State, including foreign agents, with brutal and ruthless efficiency. Their government kept the dirty work at arm's length, providing plausible deniability, although the international intelligence community knew who was paying the bills. Lucy sensed eyes watching her as she inspected her origami masterpiece. Pleased with the work, she placed it in front of her, mocking their most feared despatcher. Lucy nodded in satisfaction.

Lifting her gaze and staring at her opponent, Lucy said,

'A prophecy such as this is just one of many possible futures and the choice will rest with you, Mr Li.'

Lucy picked up the chopsticks again and took another piece of food from the person sitting next to her. 'This is great Chinese. No wonder you come here. I've always preferred Indian myself, a nice spicy curry, but I think you've converted me.'

As she replaced the chopsticks on the table, with a little sleight of hand, she hid one in her palm, its length concealed behind her arm.

Chen Li snorted in disgust as he spat, 'I like neither your tone nor threats. It is time for you to leave.'

'As you wish, Sweetie, but don't say I didn't warn you.'

Lucy pushed back her chair and stood, concealing the chopstick, as she strolled towards the front door. The waiter, who had been watching the exchange take place, rushed towards her.

'My apologies, Madam, your account.'

Lucy stopped. 'My associate Mr Li is paying and you will need to ask him.'

'The waiter glanced at Chen Li and then back to Lucy as he said, 'I think not, Madam.'

'A wise choice.' Lucy continued to the door.

At the table, Chen Li said, 'Finish her Mr Yáyī, now!'

From the reflection in the restaurant's front window, Lucy spotted Mr Yáyī as he stood and started following her. On the street, she turned right and took six steps before stopping. The street was busy at lunchtime, with people going about their business.

With the number of people about, Lucy thought, *he will try to stab me, then melt into the crowd.*

Lucy turned, positioning herself near the kerb between two parked cars; to passers-by and her attacker, she seemed to be hailing a taxi. She watched in the car windscreen, the reflection as Mr Yáyī approached her from behind, knife drawn, concealed, pressed against his leg. The blade glinted as he lifted it, ready to be driven home in to her back. He pulled back his hand preparing to strike. As he thrust forward Lucy swung around, grabbing the attacking hand, twisting it away. In the same movement, she flicked the concealed chopstick from behind her wrist, holding it in an attack position. Using momentum, she moved her body towards his, the forward motion adding to the force offered by her body weight. Lucy rammed the chopstick into his face, aiming for his nose where she wedged it firmly. As she felt resistance, she rammed it home using the palm of her hand. It made a sickening squelching noise, puncturing Mr Yáyī's brain.

As he died, Lucy released her grip on the chopstick, now protruding from his nose and Mr Yáyī fell towards her. Putting her hand into his suit jacket, she removed his pistol and stepped aside to let his lifeless body fall to the ground. Seconds later, with his gun held flat in her hand, Lucy heard a scream when a passer-by realised what had happened. Panic, followed by fear of an impending terrorist attack, rippled through the streets of Soho. Pistol in hand and finger away from the trigger, so that Chen Li knew she wasn't going to use it, Lucy walked calmly back into the restaurant. The commotion from outside had caused a brouhaha within the Shark Fin. Patrons were looking around, trying to comprehend what was happening outside. As Lucy entered, the restaurant went silent; the change in tone was palpable. All eyes followed her.

Feigning frustration as she approached Chen Li's table, Lucy said, 'Mr Li, were you not listening to me? What did I just say about acceptable behaviour?'

Now seated, she placed the firearm in front of her.

Mr Li, his tone venomous, said, 'That was a mistake and you won't be leaving here alive.'

Lucy laughed, 'Sweetie, this is London and, like me, the Police don't ordinarily carry guns. Nevertheless, they have one of the best armed response units in the world, known as SOC19. I am sure you've heard of them. Elite, specially trained, heavily armed, tactical officers.' She looked at her watch before continuing, 'From the moment when the first person dialled 999, Britain's emergency telephone number, to the armed response unit arriving at the scene is two minutes. If my calculations are correct, that is about now. When I defended myself against your operative and unfortunately he was liquidated, I ensured that those outside saw me come in here carrying his gun. You, my friend, are about to be faced with a dilemma.'

From her purse, Lucy removed a police badge and the warrant card, showing them to Mr Chen Li. He regarded it and a look of confusion spread across his face.

Armed officers burst into the restaurant.

'Nobody move,' they called, weapons scouring the space in front of them, looking to identify and eliminate any threats.

Staying perfectly still, Lucy called out, 'I am a Police Officer'.

She waited two seconds before repeating the statement to ensure they knew who was speaking, this time adding, 'I will lift my badge so that you can see it.'

Slowly, she raised her arm, holding it in the direction of a policeman.

'The men at this table are armed and dangerous. I am about to show you one of their weapons. I will pick it up by the barrel and then put it down again. Do I have your permission?'

As she spoke, the response officers took up strategic positions.

'Very slowly,' came the voice of the person in charge.

Lucy lifted the gun, then placed it down again.

The armed response officer said, 'All of you, including you Madam, place your hands on your head. If any of you make a sudden move, we are instructed to shoot.'

Mr Chen Li's four remaining colleagues looked at him for instructions.

Lucy smiled. 'As I was saying, Mr Li, you are about to face a dilemma. Your options are few. You could try to fight your way out, but imagine what your Government would think of a diplomat from the People's Republic of China being involved in a shootout with police in a busy London restaurant? On the other hand, you will be arrested. I can read the headlines now: *CHINESE EMBASSY OFFICIALS ARRESTED, CARRYING FIREARMS IN LONDON*. Equally, a poor outcome, I think you would agree. Alternatively, you could always agree to abide by our long-established conventions. If you were to comply, Sweetie, British Government officials will be waiting for you at the Police Station. They will be humbled and embarrassed that you were falsely accused, and by a person imitating a police officer. Her Majesty's Government will accept a reprimand from the People's Republic of China.'

'Mr Li, this is what we, in Britain, call the diplomatic dance a delicate waltz. The choice is yours.'

Chen Li contemplated for a few moments, then nodded as he said, 'We have been hasty. It may have been unwise to dismiss your long-established tradition.'

'Welcome to England, Mr Li. I suggest that we all remain perfectly still and follow the instructions of the officers. London has recently experienced some unsettling terrorist attacks; the officers will shoot first and ask questions later.'

***

It was nearing midnight when Lucy pulled up outside John's house. She remembered when a kill used to be an erotic aphrodisiac sending her in search of unfettered, gratuitous sex. There was a man waiting in bed and she felt desire, except this time she felt different. Lucy wanted to be held tenderly and caressed - sensual love making for both of them to enjoy. Taking Mr Yáyī's life hadn't energised Lucy but stolen from her. A necessity; no longer a pleasure.

CHAPTER 13

Church

Until meeting John at Saint Moritz, Lucy hadn't attended church, but in the time before travelling to England, she'd been each Sunday. She'd memorised the Order of Service, learning when to stand, sit or kneel, familiarising herself with church customs and learning the Christmas and Easter traditions. Lucy had read and studied the Bible during the time she learnt to speak English; her party trick was her ability to quote many of its passages.

In preparation for England, she'd attended a cathedral rather than a small church, where she would blend into the crowd, an unnoticed member of a larger congregation.

Lucy wasn't a religious person, having little spirituality and was neither an atheist nor agnostic. To her, life just "was", whatever that meant. On the first Sunday of her church reconnaissance, Lucy had been struck by the beautiful music that filled the cathedral, the singing of the choir echoing throughout the old stone building. The voice of the congregation about her was enhanced, encouraging the singers and amplifying their voices. Lucy found herself absorbed by the choral ensemble with its magical artistry that seemed perfectly aligned to the ancient architecture of the grand building. As she'd once said to Max, "this isn't my road to Damascus moment," but there was no question that at times, the voices and harmony she heard in this church made her body tingle.

Despite her late arrival from London the previous evening, Lucy arose early for a morning run, then prepared for her first service at St Mary's. For church, she'd adopt the appearance of the dutiful wife, enhancing her beauty without being overtly sexual. Mildly sensual was the look she sought, devout and obedient, yet intelligent and educated, John's equal. Importantly, she had decided that whatever the day threw at her, as the new person trying to fit in, she would appear as a woman of little drama, both unflappable and ready to adapt.

'Will I pass muster?' Lucy asked, giving a twirl in front of John.

'Absolutely, shall we go?' John said, eager to show off his lady.

Hand in hand, they walk to church, pausing in front of St Mary's to read the message board.

'That's interesting,' Lucy said.

'Someone's been playing with it again. It's supposed to read, "Just Love Everyone". The Pi-Ski prankster has added the phrase, "Religious Nuts".'

'Do you know who the prankster is?' Lucy asked.

'No. Not a clue.'

'How long has it been going on?'

'Since we purchased the board, a bit over four years ago. Someone on the Parish Council saw pictures of churches in America with notice boards on their grounds displaying witty but thought-provoking messages. The idea was to create some notoriety–attract people to the church. Instead it invited mischief.'

'Where do the quotes come from? Who makes them up?'

'They're free on the internet. If someone sees an interesting one, we copy it.'

Lucy considered for a moment before saying, 'You do know that the imp is one of your church Parish Councillors?'

John looked at her in disbelief and said, 'No way!'

'Of course it is, silly,' Lucy teased. 'It makes sense. A random practical joker from the village would have lost interest by now. To sustain the pranks for such a long time, the person would have a strong current or past connection to the church. As most of your past parishioners are dead, that leaves the Parish Council. It can't be the Vicar, so it's either you, Catherine, Edith or Josephine.'

John scratched his head as he said, 'I suppose it makes sense, but I can promise you, it's not me. Which one of them I wonder?'

'That, my dear Sherlock, is a good question, to which I haven't given any thought. If I did, I would have my suspicions, but things are not always as they seem. Besides, John, it's all a bit of harmless fun; uncovering the truth may prove disappointing. I'll wager that St Mary's needs a little mystery.'

'That is true on many levels. You don't think it's me, do you?'

Lucy shrugged her shoulders as she chuckled. 'You are a man of many surprises.'

John and Lucy were among the first of the congregation to arrive and, seeing them, a flustered Vicar Charlotte Foster rushed over.

'John,' Vicar Charlotte said.

'Yes, Vicar.'

'My apologies, Lucy. Can I borrow John, just for a moment?'

'Sure.'

'Honey, find a seat and I will join you in a minute.'

This was the first time Lucy had been inside the seventeenth century St Mary's Church. The dull stone of its exterior concealed the internal charm of a beautiful building. She found it quite grand, not matching the architectural wonder of the cathedral she'd visited, but a secret gem, with stone arches, wooden panelling and choir stalls. The altar was simple, set against three stained glass windows, a large arch window, with smaller rectangular windows on either side. They brought the carving etched into the altar timbers alive. She imagined that in summer, sunlight filtering through the stained glass windows would bathe the entire church in an enticing warmth.

St Mary's was virtually empty, Lucy counting four other people besides herself. John had told her that the church wouldn't be bursting at the seams when the service commenced. It was tempting to take a seat at the rear, hiding in the shadows, ready for a quick getaway, but she walked confidently towards the front. As the heels of her shoes struck the stone floor, the sound of their impact resonated around the building, creating a beat, and she imagined tap-dancing shoes striking the floor to form a percussion, echoing, reflecting off the walls and producing a distinctive repetition.

Lucy halted, three pews from the front.

Left or right? she thought. *Left, yes left.*

Catherine Hepburn, accompanied by Tina, her granddaughter, arrived, swooping into the church, a woman on a mission.

'What?' She exclaimed immediately when she saw Lucy seated in her regular place. 'I can't have this,' she muttered aloud. Tina, hearing her grandmother's complaint, put her hand on her arm reassuringly.

'Gran, it's alright. John's not with her, she doesn't know.'

Catherine huffed. 'That may well be, but she needs to understand that this is where we sit.'

Catherine strode with purpose towards Lucy.

Smiling daggers, Catherine said, 'Good morning, Lucy. I see John is not here to guide you in the way things are done at St Mary's. I hope you don't find me rude, but this is where I sit.'

'I know,' Lucy said, a warm and disarming smile drifting across her face. 'I was waiting for you to seek your advice and guidance. I knew I couldn't miss you if I occupied this seat.'

'Oh, I see,' Catherine said, her mood changing. 'How may I be of service to you?'

'John has been dragged away by the Vicar. Without him to guide me, I thought you would know the pew that has been allocated to me.'

'Lucy, my dear,' Catherine said with pride, oblivious to Lucy's sarcasm, 'We don't have allocated seating. You are welcome anywhere.'

Trying to hide her smile, Tina whispered into her grandmother's ear, 'Except here.'

'Nonsense,' Catherine said, raising her voice. 'Do you mind if we join you?'

'I'll shove along.'

Struggling to hide her amusement, Tina said, 'We should leave enough room for John.'

For the first time in ten years, Catherine occupied a different position, albeit on the same line of pews.

'Well I never,' John said, arriving with Josephine and observing the new seating arrangements.

'It looks like I've been kicked out,' Josephine said light heartedly, her face good-humoured.

Concerned, John replied, 'No, you sit with Catherine. I'll sit behind Lucy.'

'Nonsense, John. If we want new people, we have to be prepared to adapt. If moving a whole five feet is the worst of it, then bring it on.'

Watching Lucy, beautiful, comfortably chatting with Tina and Catherine, Josephine wondered if her fears were warranted.

Vicar Charlotte Foster entered the church from the vestry. The congregation stood as the service began.

'We will commence the service by singing hymn number 127, *Tis So Sweet to Trust in Jesus*,' the Vicar said.

Nothing could have prepared Lucy for the disappointment of a St Mary's service.

This is misery. That will teach me for doing my preparation in a cathedral, with its colourful procession and euphonic choir.

There was no musical accompaniment and the congregation of fifteen chanted the words or sang off key. There was no full, mellow or even strident tone of the cathedral. It was too pathetic to jar, yet the rasping gurgle masquerading as song was like someone dragging a nail down a blackboard.

Having my teeth pulled by the MSS wouldn't be as painful as this; truly a dreadful experience. St Mary's is a relic from history where they still practice the mortification of the flesh. The weekly service is used for self-flagellation; why else would anyone put themselves through this agony? It's unsurprising that few attend. Sorry John, but this would be grounds for divorce, were we married.

Four weeks of church attendance hadn't been sufficient time to form procedural memory of motor tasks through repetition - muscle memory, where the body switches into automatic pilot. Lucy couldn't sleep with her eyes open, while the reflexes react to the motions of the service. Lucy glanced at her watch, horrified that only ten minutes had transpired. It felt more like two hours.

At least I can doze through the sermon, she thought.

'Please be seated,' Vicar Charlotte said, preparing to deliver the address. Lucy started meditating, zoning out and in her mind, finding herself with Max, engaged in one of their religious and philosophical arguments. The words of Vicar Charlotte, however seeped through her reverie, dragging her back to the present, so she decided to listen in case John asked her a question.

> *'This story tells us much about the nature of true prayer. Prayer is not about the finding of easy solutions to life's dilemmas. It is not an alternative to the hard work and difficult decisions we still need to make about the complexities of life. Often those complexities are the product of ours and others' previous attempts at*

resolutions to life's dilemmas that have only made our situation worse. We cannot just walk away from those consequences. Prayer is not avoidance. It is rather a dual confrontation, with God and with ourselves and others, in the situations in which we find ourselves. In this sense, prayer at one level makes the struggle even tougher, because it involves a struggle with God and what we understand to be the demand of God in our life, as well as the demands of the circumstance in which we find ourselves.

Prayer brings new insight. That insight is wrought from the struggle that leads us to changed attitudes consistent with the claiming of our true identity. New patterns of response emerge from our struggle with God and with humanity in prayer that counter our usual patterns of response shaped by past experience, where often we have come unstuck because of our weaknesses and foibles. Instead of being bound by our past responses, we are opened up to new possibilities by our encounter with God. Prayer leaves an indelible mark on us.'

New possibilities, Lucy repeated to herself. *That's it, how to win John's and Josephine's trust and get the quantum cube back. New possibilities: bring music to the church. But how?*

Walking home after the service, John asked, 'Truthfully Lucy, what did you think?'

'Promise you won't be offended?'

'Promise.'

'It was awful my love, dreary and lifeless.'

Conscious of being over critical and fearful of harming their relationship, Lucy wanted to add a positive note.

'The Vicar's sermon was excellent, worth going for on its own.' She squeezed his arm within hers. 'The rest however, was like visiting a morgue. I thought you were a saint before, but now St Peter, move over, the gates of heaven are yours.'

John chuckled nervously. 'I get your point.'

'Music would help, John. The acoustics in St Mary's are wonderful and would be captivating, especially with a congregation in full voice. It would send a shiver down your spine, even if the hymn was from ten years before the birth of Christ.'

'Now you're exaggerating Lucy. Everything we sang today was from the nineteenth century. All very modern, by Church of England standards.' He took a deep breath. 'All joking aside, your observations are what we already know. You see, we can't have music without a congregation and you don't attract people without music. Even if we found someone to play the organ... how many attended today? Fifteen of us, that's all. Musical accompaniment still wouldn't help. Lily, our last organist, died last year, aged ninety-two and she played right up to the week before her passing. From eighty onwards, she became deafer and played slower. I miss her dearly; she was a wonderful, kind and generous woman but, if you thought the music today was dismal, believe me, it's been worse.'

Lucy was about to add that she knew someone who could help, but checked herself.

Before offering a solution, it's best that I contact the Agency and discover if there's anything the British Government can do to help. No point in promising something I can't deliver.

That evening, while John was taking a shower, Lucy phoned Rosie.

'Give me twenty-four hours' was her response. 'We might be able to offer something.'

***

On Monday evening, as John returned home from work, Lucy greeted him at the door, beaming.

'What is it?' he asked.

'How quickly can you call a meeting of the Parish Council?'

'Why?'

'I have a potential solution to St Mary's declining congregation woes and probably its lack of music too, all without producing a nude calendar. The only problem is that the Parish Council must make a decision by Wednesday.'

***

At seven thirty the following evening, a Tuesday, the Vicar, Parish Council members and Lucy were gathered around the table in the church hall.

Lucy spoke first.

'Thank you for inviting me and agreeing to meet at such short notice. I know John has told you I have a suggestion to help with the church's long-term viability and the reason for the urgency is that the window of opportunity is narrow, very restricted indeed. We need a decision to be made tonight.'

Josephine and Catherine regarded Lucy with sceptical eyes.

'I'm all ears,' Vicar Charlotte said, raising her eyebrows, the knowledge that the church was broke and that she would be out of a job in five months providing additional focus.

'Thank you,' Lucy said. 'A friend of a friend of mine knows a man called Sir Alex Wolf who is the conductor of the Vienna

Boys' Choir. You may have read in the newspaper that they have a new boy soprano superstar, Max Joseph, whose voice has been described as perfection, the finest of a generation, the voice of an angel. Earlier in the year, the choir recorded a Christmas album, to be released soon and they have been seeking a quintessential English village church to film a "Christmas Special", a promotional video for the album. The church they select must have exceptional acoustic qualities and when my friend told me of their need, I suggested that their location scout visit St Mary's. Sir Alex Wolf and the scout arrived yesterday and this is what they said...'

Lucy read from an email she had printed.

'The acoustics at St Mary's enhance the sound as it envelops, bounces and reverberates around the space. Music will reach the listener as a wonderfully clear sound with harmonics from many directions. An orchestra and choir performing at St Mary's would be... and these are his words... "enriching".'

Lucy scanned the faces of the committee members around the table, pausing to create an air of expectation before continuing.

'For the performance of their music, Sir Alex Wolf rates St Mary's church as one of the finest.'

The Parish Council members looked at each other in amazement and an air of excitement filled the room.

Lucy continued. 'If you were in agreement, the Vienna Boys' Choir wishes to film and perform at St Mary's. It will be the premier performance of their new Christmas album, orchestrated and stage-managed, as a promotional shoot. Sir Alex Wolf says that, as a part of any agreement, you would all be invited and have front row seats. The church would be filled with invited guests to give the promotional film atmosphere and authenticity.'

'That's all well and good Lucy,' interrupted Catherine dismissively. 'What makes you think that this will help St Mary's in the long term? Once filming has been done, they will pack up and leave. We will be forgotten and nothing will have changed.'

'A very good question, Catherine. There will be a modest payment for using the church.' Lucy paused, and a genuine smile spread across her face as she said excitedly, 'This is the thrilling bit. Sir Alex Wolf says that after their performance, St Mary's and Pi-Ski will shoot to international fame and recognition. The conductor believes that the acoustics of St Mary's are exceptional and that you will be inundated by requests from choirs of note wishing to practice in the church. He suggests, as payment for the use of the church, you require that they sing at your Sunday service. Imagine, the church will be filled with people.'

An energised murmur spread around the table.

Vicar Charlotte coughed a couple of times in an attempt to attract people's attention. When it failed, she shouted Lucy's name and the room went silent. 'When would the filming take place?'

'A week on Saturday. Everything is ready to go; the choir just need to settle on a site, they have a default which is Westminster Abbey. St Mary's is better.'

The table nodded in agreement.

Lucy said, 'This has all happened so quickly and I'm sorry for the short notice. We really do need to make a decision tonight because they need to know that we wish to proceed by tomorrow morning.'

Secretly, Josephine's spirit sank in shame. She had sown the seed of doubt in John's heart when all the evidence suggested that here was a woman of compassion and kindness. She'd viewed Lucy through eyes of suspicion; where there was genuineness, she had seen manipulation, where there was affection, she saw entrapment. If John told Lucy the truth, that Josephine persuaded him to give her the wrapped gift, for fear that Lucy was using him as a drug mule, or worse, the trust between John and Lucy could be irreconcilably damaged. Her doubts had risked John's happiness.

I must talk with John, she said to herself. *I've got to fix this.*

'Are you alright?' Edith asked, spotting a distracted look in Josephine's eyes.

'Sorry, the news is so exciting that I was lost in my own fantasies, thinking of a better future. We have to say yes to Lucy's suggestion.'

'I agree,' Catherine said, glancing at Lucy. 'What happens next?'

'Sir Alex and the Producer, will come here at seven on Thursday evening to meet with us and explain about the organisation of the event. I understand he may even offer some starring roles. Some of you will wear costumes and appear on camera.'

'Costumes?' Vicar Charlotte repeated.

'Yes, those people sitting in the front rows will need makeup and wardrobe, like in the movies.'

'Lights, camera, action,' giggled Edith.

'I'm confused,' said Catherine, ignoring Edith. 'Are they filming a promotional video or filming and recording their album?'

Lucy said, 'That's an excellent question. They will film the choir singing the entire album, from which they will create their Christmas Special promotional video. The album itself has been recorded in a studio already, before Max Joseph became an international celebrity. They want him to sing live as it will be worth millions of pounds to them in extra sales.'

'Are they a Christian choir?' Vicar Charlotte asked.

Lucy thought for a moment before answering, 'Secular, but they are to sing some traditional Christmas carols.' She paused for a moment, searching for a memory, before continuing.

'Away in a Manger is sung by the choir on the album; Max Joseph, the soprano, is the lead. It's been described as arguably the most beautiful rendition ever heard. It was these reviews that convinced Sir Alex that they should use a suitable church to promote their album and I imagine they will want a Christmas nativity scene. That's the sort of detail that Sir Alex Wolf will talk about when he visits.'

'How long is it since we've had a baby in the church?' Edith asked, her voice rising in tone as she spoke, 'They will definitely want to film someone holding a baby while they sing Away in a Manger, I'm sure. I'm sold on the idea. My vote would be "yes".'

'Those in agreement?' Catherine asked.

Everyone raised their hands, except for Lucy, who wasn't a member of the Church Parish Council.

Catherine said, 'The motion is carried unanimously.'

Edith clapped her hands in glee.

An exclamation of thanks to Lucy circulated the room, the mood upbeat compared to the start of the session.

'I close the meeting and invite everyone to meet again at seven on Thursday evening. 'With your permission,' continued Catherine, 'I would like to extend an invitation for Lucy to join us, as this has been her excellent idea.'

'Absolutely,' Vicar Charlotte said, and everyone agreed to the proposal.

As they were all leaving, Josephine called to John. 'Can I have a word?'

Lucy, her arm looped in John's, strolled over with him.

'In private,' Josephine said, glancing at her feet.

Lucy looked at John and then at Josephine as she said, 'I'll wait at the door.'

'John, it seems I've made an awful mistake with those things I said about Lucy before I'd even met her. I was wrong. I am so sorry.' Josephine bit her lip as she continued, 'The gift you left with me for safekeeping, the pen. I will return it on Thursday night, after the meeting. I will confess that I took it from you for the reasons we discussed. I will tell Lucy that you didn't know that I had it for sure, but were suspicious, which is why you didn't think the pen was stolen. I pray that you both can forgive me and hope I haven't ruined your relationship.'

John peeked at Lucy, who wasn't watching their conversation and said, 'That sounds like a wonderful idea, Josephine. I was beginning to wonder how we were going to return it. I wouldn't be overly concerned, Josephine. From what I've seen of Lucy, it won't surprise me if she considers the whole thing a prank. Can you imagine me as a mule? It's preposterous.' He gave her a reassuring smile.

'Oh, I do hope you are right, John.'

Lucy was on the other side of the room talking to the Vicar. From the corner of her eye, she watched the exchange between John and Josephine, spotting the despair spread across Josephine's face, followed by John's smile of understanding.

Softly softly, she said to herself. *Patience is paying off. My guess, the quantum cube will be back in my hot little hands very soon and by the time John arrives home from work on Friday, I will be history.*

No, I will wait until Monday, taking the device to the Agency on Friday, stay the weekend, then leave on Monday.

The conversation with Josephine over, John walked to Lucy, smiling radiantly; a man in love. He held a hand towards her, declaring chirpily, 'Shall we go home?'

Lucy took the proffered hand, returning an easy smile. She studied him surreptitiously. With his daggy glasses and old-fashioned jumper, Lucy found him cute in an eccentric kind of way. He radiated something she'd not experienced before and wasn't sure that she could describe it. Her emotions took her by surprise, they were overwhelming and confusing. Lucy felt sorrow; Monday night, in six days' time, he would be devastated to come home to a "Dear John" letter.

Stop it, she whispered to herself. *I must push the thought from my mind. His well-being is none of my business.*

It was a clear cold night in Pi-Ski as they walked home together. A light fog hung in the air, swirling as it was illuminated by streetlights. The chill was invigorating in a weird kind of way. Lucy stopped, letting go of John and dropped her hands to her side. She spun around several times and John laughed, then concern replaced his humour.

'Are you okay?'

'Perfectly. I'm happy, in a peculiar kind of way.'

'Aaaarrr, that's the magic of Cornwall, ghoulies and ghosties and long-legged beasties. And things that go bump in the night.'

'You're a funny man and I do love you.'

***

As she'd planned, after Thursday's meeting with Sir Alex Wolf, Josephine gave Lucy the pen, wrapped in gold and finished with a red bow. She explained why she had taken it from John's house and became tearful when Lucy displayed forgiveness, saying,

'What you did shows how much you care for John and his happiness.'

The evening however, wasn't without its surprises. To tug at the heartstrings, the Director of the Vienna Boys' Choir Christmas Special wanted a sentimental piece for the promotion. Her intention was to film a couple nursing a baby as the choir sang Away in a Manger, led by soprano Max Joseph. Sir Alex Wolf asked John and Lucy if they would play the parts. Even if either of them wanted to say no, the excitement of the moment and the expectations of the Parish Council removed the opportunity to reject the offer.

Lucy knew she would be gone before the filming and now, not only would she hurt John, his friends would also be devastated. By parting before the Christmas Special she would be leaving John holding the baby, literally and alone.

Don't get attached Lucy. This is only a job and not your problem. She sighed. *Why do bad things happen to nice people?*

CHAPTER 14

Crash Goes the Jaguar.

Home after the extraordinary Parish Council meeting and the briefing from Sir Alex Wolf, while John was upstairs preparing for bed, Lucy phoned the agency to tell them she'd recovered the quantum cube.

Rosie told Lucy that they had intercepted active chatter from Chinese Intelligence and that she wasn't to deliver the device to Postbridge, but instead to their Post Office Box in Exeter, Devon and the secret underground facility storeys below.

'We are still hoping to keep the operation low-key,' Rosie said. 'If we call for military assistance, intelligence agencies around the world, both friend and foe, will know that we have the cube. This is something we want to avoid, particularly a disagreement with an ally.'

'The Americans?'

'Yes, the Americans. Things however, are changing rapidly and for the moment you are on your own. The incident room is on standby and we are monitoring developments. Deadly force has been authorised, but remember Lucy, low key is our preference. Not your style, I know.'

Rosie paused... 'try to keep it discreet, Lucy.'

'Do the Chinese know that I have it?'

'We can't be sure, however our surveillance indicates they are planning something.'

'Good luck, Lucy. We will be watching your back.'

As Lucy climbed the stairs to be with John, she needed to behave as if the telephone call hadn't happened. She chuckled to herself.

Lucy, it's an interesting lie you live.

Lying on her pillow was a single long-stemmed red rose and John was already in a deep sleep. She kissed him tenderly on the cheek and before climbing into bed, whispered in his ear, 'Thank you, my funny man.'

There would be no sex tonight, only the company and warmth of someone who cared. As she listened to his rhythmic breathing, she pondered for a moment before snuggling down next to John.

I will always have a soft spot for you, she whispered to herself.

At nine thirty the following morning, with John at work, the Jaguar V8 rumbled into life with its traction control off and airbag fuse removed. No matter what happened next, Lucy would continue relentlessly until the drop-off was finalised. Although not expecting trouble, she was prepared, carrying a Glock in its shoulder holster. She would pull over for nobody, not even a local police routine check. With the quantum cube on board, the risk was too great to take any chances.

There were three ways out of Pi-Ski, all B roads, the lower class of road, often of poorer physical standard that linked to the better A roads. One of the B roads was a Cornish country lane, lined with hedges, barely wide enough for the SUV to fit. If she was being watched, it was unlikely that the resources required to mount an overseas operation would be big enough to cover all three routes. British intelligence would know if something of that scale had been deployed and would have told her.

To join the A30 and the one hundred and sixty kilometre drive to Exeter, Lucy chose the eight kilometre route, the narrow and twisty country lane out of Pi-Ski. Her assessment was that this route was the least likely of the three options to be patrolled by the Chinese MSS.

Lucy drove the big V8 cat swiftly but cautiously, taking each of the blind corners at speed with a narrow safety margin that would permit her to brake to avoid a head-on collision. Sometimes she could see over the hedges, across the green flowing fields and out to sea. Lucy mulled over the tranquil beauty until something caught her eye. Half a kilometre down the road, Lucy saw a black car parked off the road in a field. It was waiting at an open gate, poised. Lucy feared an ambush. If a vehicle was to come up from behind and the car ahead was to block the road, she would be trapped, hemmed in by the vehicles and the hedges on either side of the narrow road.

You need to go back; she thought, breathing deeply. *Better to face one of them rather than two.*

The road was too narrow for a U-turn so she slowed and scanned left and right, looking for a farmer's gate in the hedge-row. She spotted it, on her right, except the gate was shut and with no time to stop and open it, Lucy gunned the growling Jaguar through.

SMASH!

The gate broke free of its latches and sprung back by the impact of the collision, clearing the opening. The grass in the field was damp and the big cat slid as Lucy attempted to turn it around. She fought the steering wheel, mud flying from the rear wheels, as the V8 roared in anger, fighting for traction. The black interceptor, stalking her further down the road, saw the Jaguar launch itself into the field and started moving. Now facing back the way she had come, Lucy accelerated through the gate, turning towards Pi-Ski. Throwing caution to the wind, unleashing all the horses of the 5.0

litre supercharged V8, Lucy raced at breakneck speed, galloping down the road. As she rounded a corner, entering a rare straight section, a farmer's tractor meandered towards her, taking up the whole road. Suddenly, the black car zoomed into Lucy's rear-vision mirror. In a game of chicken with high stakes, she sped towards the obstacle, hoping the farmer would blink first and manoeuvre out of her way.

Staring out of the windscreen of her SUV, as the two immovable objects rushed towards each other, Lucy realised the driver of the tractor was wearing a suit; he was an ingredient of the interception recipe.

With no options left, Lucy stomped on the brakes, washing off speed, before hurling the big cat towards the hedge-row. A slight rise in the ground lifted the Jaguar from the road and, airborne, it struck the shrubbery, ripping a path clear through, leaving behind paint, a windscreen wiper and glass from a broken mirror. The Jaguar absorbed the shock as it landed, unfazed by the flight, biting at the bit for more action.

Come on Lucy, she whispered, scanning the field for an escape route. *There!*

She spotted, at the other end of the field, an opening that led back out onto the road and behind the tractor. Feathering the throttle so as not to spin the wheels, she pointed the cat towards the gate as the black car joined her on the grass. Reaching the gate, she used the Jaguar as a battering ram, smashing through and speeding towards Pi-Ski, the car's rear bumper dragging on the ground, the assailants in hot pursuit.

As she flew down the narrow winding country lane, Lucy went about her work, composed and detached. Speaking to the Jaguar's auto-dial system, she said, 'Phone Cliff.'

Glancing at the dash touch screen, a picture of a green phone appeared and Lucy heard the sound of a ring tone.

BANG!

The black car struck the rear of the SUV and she corrected a slide as the impact temporarily knocked her off course.

'How can I help you?' said a voice at the other end of the phone.

Lucy said, 'Can I speak to Robin?'

'She's not here.'

'I want to speak to her brother, Robin.'

'Certainly. May I have your number?'

'147 Echo.'

'One moment please...'

'Hello Lucy,' came another voice. 'Please state the nature of your emergency?'

'I have a priority one cargo on board and am being pursued. In need of urgent assistance.'

A volley of machine gun fire filled the air. A bullet struck and smashed the rear window. Lucy swerved left and right, trying to avoid being hit again.

'Putting you through to the incident control room.'

There was a pause.

'Hello Lucy. We have you on satellite visual heading towards Pi-Ski, where another bogey is waiting for you near the pub. Turn right when you reach there. A helicopter is en route and we are working on clearing the roads in front to rendezvous you with a rapid response team which has been dispatched. The Americans have two jet fighters in the area and they have been instructed to fly low and fast over your pursuers. We hope to intimidate them into calling off the chase. I'm afraid we have rather underestimated them; for the time being you are on you own. Rest assured that all means at your disposal have been authorised.'

'This was to be low-key, or so I thought.' Lucy said calmly.

'At nine thirty-one this morning, a major cyber-attack was launched which has crippled much of the UK infrastructure. We suspect the Chinese are responsible and that it is an all-out attempt to retrieve the quantum cube. We are not going to allow them to take it. Britain is counting on you; the world is counting on you.'

Edith and Josephine had finished preparing the flowers for the Sunday service at St Mary's and were walking along the road towards the Little People's Arms, Pi-Ski's pub.

Edith said, 'What's that? It sounds like gun shots!'

Lucy's pursuers fired again - Rat-a-tat.

Josephine took Edith by the arm, leading her off the road. The sound of roaring jet engines caused them to turn.

'What's happening?' Edith asked.

In the sky, two fighter jets were banking, lining themselves up for a low-level pass along the road on which they were standing. The squeal of tyres snapped Josephine's and Edith's heads back towards the pub. Sliding sideways, using the whole of the road, a damaged red Jaguar SUV came into view, immediately followed by a black car, also sidewards to the road.

Edith shrieked, 'Is that Lucy's car?'

The sound from the two United States Air-force F-22 Raptors preparing for their run was overpowering. Edith and Josephine watched as the first plane made its descent, their eyes following it as it swooped low, coming so close to them, the noise so deafening that they momentarily lost their balance. Everything shook in its wake as the jet rocketed skywards, having skimmed the vehicles. They heard the next plane approaching and, as they stared up at it, the bullet-riddled Jaguar raced by, its back window shot out and the rear bumper missing. Its pace was so rapid that they didn't see the driver. The next Raptor rocketed skyward as the black car and its foreign occupants sped through the village.

'They're chasing the red SUV,' Edith said. 'Look, here's another car, a silver BMW. Who is that one chasing?'

The BMW zoomed past, disregarding the Pi-Ski speed limit.

The jet fighters growled off into the distance before banking and heading back towards Pi-Ski.

'Are the planes chasing the cars?' Edith asked.

Josephine shrugged in amazement. 'I don't know, but something is happening, that's for sure.'

People living in the nearby houses, hearing the commotion, joined Josephine and Edith out on the street. In amazement they watched as one, then another, jet fighter roared low and loud overhead, the vibrations resonating through their bodies.

'Was that Lucy's Jaguar?' Edith asked again.

'It can't have been,' Josephine said, her eyes wide. 'Could it?'

Calm returned briefly, as people milled around, talking feverishly about what they had just seen. A minute later, the peace of the ordinarily tranquil Pi-Ski, a classic Cornish village with atmospheric old stone houses, was again shattered, this time by the distinctive beating sound of helicopter rotor blades as they cut their way through the air. Eyes drawn skywards, the population of Pi-Ski watched as the chopper flew above, heading in the direction taken by the cars. Whoosh!... and the helicopter was gone.

'Oh my goodness,' Edith said breathlessly. 'What on earth is going on?'

Another helicopter suddenly appeared, but this time it was a military looking one, although it carried no markings. It took the same route as the previous aircraft.

'That's an odd helicopter, no markings? You don't think it is chasing the first one, do you?' Josephine said.

'I don't know anything anymore, Josephine, completely lost my bearings. Should we ring John?' Edith asked.

Josephine put a soothing hand on Edith's shoulder as she said, 'Let's not worry him unnecessarily.'

***

'In four hundred metres you will come to a fork in the road. I want you to turn left,' said the voice on the phone.

Glancing in the mirror, Lucy saw that the black car was closing in fast. Lucy heard a helicopter, the distinctive chopping of the air by it blades betraying it. It was heading her way, as was a silver BMW. Slowing, she let the black vehicle gain on her.

Leaving the manoeuvre to the last possible moment, as the car positioned to ram into her, she swerved left, hoping her pursuers would miss the turn. The ploy failed.

'In one hundred...' said the voice, then silence. Lucy guessed the signal was being jammed.

Rat-a-tat. Another volley of machine gun fire commenced; with the winding road and uneven surface, a clear shot was problematic and the bullets passed by harmlessly. Lucy knew, however, if she couldn't deal with her assailants by the time they reached the main road, she was a sitting duck.

Glancing in the mirror, she flicked her eyes, searching for the helicopter. It was behind the black car, a marksman hanging out of the side, preparing to take a shot.

It's one of ours, she thought.

There was a flash of yellow, then the powerful sound of an explosion. The helicopter was missing from the theatre, blown from the sky. Seconds later, another chopper appeared through the smoke and debris, flying over Lucy before dropping low, hugging the ground, then vanishing over the sea cliff. In front of her, the fighter jets appeared as she whispered to herself, *They're hunting the rogue helicopter.*

She was on her own, the backup had evaporated.

Peeking at the speedo, she saw that it read one hundred and forty kilometres per hour.

I can't outrun them.

Praying that no one was coming in the other direction and using all the road, Lucy tipped the big Jaguar into the corner. At the apex, rather than accelerating, she eased back on the throttle, allowing the chasing car to close in. Once they hit the next straight, the occupants of the vehicle would have a clear shot at her.

As the road began to straighten, she accelerated to one hundred and eighty while allowing the two cars to stay with her, only metres away from her tail. WHAM!

Lucy jumped on the brakes as hard as she could and the nose of the Jaguar dug into the bitumen as it washed off speed. The following black car had nowhere to go and slammed into the rear of Lucy's SUV, then the silver BMW followed, crumpling into the rear of the BMW's collision zone. Lucy struggled to maintain control of the Jaguar during the impact. Her mobile phone, positioned on the centre console, was catapulted forward, smashing to bits as the dashboard stopped its trajectory. Lucy held on tightly to the steering wheel as the concertina of buckled metal slid to a slow halt.

Breathing deeply and slowly, Lucy removed the Glock pistol from its holster and went to open the door; however, the impact had twisted the Jaguar's chassis and the exit was jammed. Using both legs and all of her strength, she kicked at the door and on the third attempt it flew open. Determined, cold and calculating, she walked towards the black car, which was partially embedded in the SUV. Its two occupants were bloodied and still.

Bang! Bang!

Two shots rang out, a bullet lodged in each of their heads. She moved to the BMW. The driver was obviously dead, the passenger with blood streaming from his head was moving. Through half-open semi-conscious eyes, he watched Lucy approaching and tried to find his firearm.

Bang!

The assailant was gone.

Bang!

One for the driver, just in case.

Returning to the wreck of the Jaguar, Lucy retrieved the quantum cube from the glove compartment, still concealed in its gold wrapping and red bow. Hearing a vehicle approaching, she slipped the device into her pocket and slumped over the steering wheel pretending to be dead. When an electrician's van pulled up, Lucy decided on a change of plan, stumbling from the wreck and staggering towards the vehicle.

Alongside the driver's door, she called out, 'Help me, please help me.'

The door opened and a driver, in his twenties, peered out. From behind her back, Lucy produced the Glock and pointed it at a surprised young man.

'Out,' Lucy commanded.

'No.'

'I don't have time for this, Sweetie,' she said.

Bang!

Lucy put a shot between his legs, aiming to frighten the tradesman.

'I will count to three. One...'

In the rush to extract himself, the man fell onto the ground and Lucy stood on him as she climbed in behind the wheel. Pointing the Glock at his head, Lucy knew he had to die to prevent him from telling the MSS about the vehicle she was driving. The man closed his eyes as she squeezed the trigger.

BANG... went the van door as Lucy slammed it shut.

'It's your lucky day,' she said.

Putting the pistol into its holster as she selected reverse gear, the van shuddered, the spinning wheels clawing at the road. After thirty metres of driving flat-out backwards with the engine screaming, Lucy saw a siding where she could turn the van around. Wrenching the wheel, she flung the vehicle into it, then selected a forward gear, gravel spitting from the wheels as she sped away.

CHAPTER 15

Русская Мафия

Lucy, on reaching the A30, rather than turning right and heading to Exeter as the Chinese MSS would expect, went left in search of an alternative escape route. Wringing every last ounce of performance from the van, half a kilometre down the road, Lucy saw a signpost pointing to the village of Carbis Bay.

That will do, she said to herself.

Jumping on the brakes, obeying the traffic regulations in an effort not to attract attention to herself, she drove towards the village. Reaching the outskirts, Lucy turned left onto a local street. The road was sparsely dotted with houses, separated by vacant blocks and, moving slowly, Lucy scanned around, searching for anything useful.

I see you.

Up ahead, a man stood in a driveway, about to mount a trail bike. Lucy drove onto the wrong side of the road, bringing the van to a halt ten metres in front of him.

Lucy removed the Glock from its holster and smiling, wound down the van's window calling out, 'Hey, I'm looking for the Johnson place?'

With his motorbike helmet on, the man couldn't make out what the attractive woman in the electrician's van was saying. As he walked towards her, he began removing it.

Lucy leaned further out the window, letting her hair fall freely.

'Hi,' she said pleasantly, drawing him in. 'I'm looking for the Johnson place?'

The man, face etched with a smile, replied, 'I'm not sure I know the Johnsons.'

Lucy grinned as she said, 'Oh, that's okay, Sweetie.'

She lifted the concealed pistol and pointed it at him. The man froze in terror.

'Do as I say, Sweetie, and you will live to see another day. All I need is your motorbike and if you so much as blink...' She shrugged her shoulders. '... Unfortunately, it will be your last. Do we understand each other? You can nod for yes or shake your head for no, but do not speak, not a sound.'

He nodded.

'Very good, Sweetie. Listen carefully to my instructions. Please take off your motorcycle jacket.'

As he was undoing the zipper, Lucy opened the van door and stepped out. Keeping the pistol trained on him, she opened the sliding door in the side of the van and motioned with the Glock as she said. 'This way, Sweetie. Bring the jacket and helmet with you.'

As he approached, she said, 'Put the helmet on the ground and give me the jacket.' He did exactly as ordered.

'Excellent, Sweetie. Now get in the back.'

The man hesitated, and Lucy could smell his fear.

'Do as I say, Sweetie, and you will be fine. I won't hurt you. In you get.'

The van rocked under his weight as he climbed inside.

'Stop Sweetie, and don't turn around. Put your hands behind your back.'

She slipped the gun into its holster and let the jacket fall to the floor of the van. From one of the work shelves, Lucy took a packet of open cable ties and secured his hands. Taking the gun back out, she said, 'Turn around.'

'Sweetie, I want you to sit with your back against the wall.'

He sat down, then shuffled backwards.

'Very good.'

Lucy picked up the jacket and, searching through the pockets, she found his wallet and removed the driver's licence. Looking first at the photo and then at him, she said, 'Hello, Isaac Williams.'

Lucy took off her watch and placed it on the ground in front of him as she put on his leather jacket.

'Sweetie, I am with the Русская мафия.'

She repeated the statement in English for him to understand, 'The Russian Mafia. You have a choice to make, important for you, probably the most important in your life to date. I kill you now or you promise to sit here quietly for one hour, after which time you may call, bang and shout all that you like for help. When I leave, if I wás to discover that the police decided to intercept me on your bike and you hadn't waited the hour, then we will hunt you down and cut off your balls.'

Lucy held the driver's licence up towards him.

'So that I can remember who you are.'

She slipped the card into the jacket pocket and threw his wallet at his feet.

'I give you permission to speak, Mr Isaac Williams. What will it to be?'

Nervously he said, his voice stumbling, 'Not a sound for an hour and a half, just to be sure.'

'Excellent, Sweetie. Now, I will put a cable tie around your feet, but as I believe you to be a man of your word, there will be no gag. You know what will happen if you make a sound?' Lucy pointed the Glock between his legs as she continued. 'Do you remember the lyrics from that Beatles song, Yesterday?' Singing while laughing, Lucy recited: '*Suddenly I'm not half the man I used to be, there's nothing hanging under me.* A slight change of words there, but you get my meaning.'

Lucy softened her tone. 'Hey, that watch is worth more than your bike. Consider it compensation.'

She slammed the van door shut and locked it.

Inside the van, Isaac heard his trail bike start and as the noise vanished into the distance, he lifted his bound legs, ready to pound them against the side of the van. Glancing at the watch, he muttered aloud, 'I'll wait.'

From Carbis Bay, Lucy followed a route along the coastal track used by walkers travelling up the west coast to Lelant. From Lelant, keeping off the main roads, she rode towards Wadebridge.

Speeding on the trail bike, Lucy wondered how the MSS had known that she'd retrieved the quantum cube.

The only logical explanation is that they eavesdropped on the conversation with the Agency, she thought.

If that were the case and Agency data had also been compromised, it being a honeypot for malicious actors, Lucy considered that the MSS already knew Exeter was her destination. With communications out, Lucy was on her own.

She slowed the bike as she drew near to Padstow, bringing it to a standstill. Turning off the engine and looking around her, nothing appeared out of place. If anything, it was abnormally quiet.

Stick to the plan.

Lucy intended to ride across Cornwall, making her way to Plymouth where she would hire a car for the drive to Exeter. Reaching the Post Office was more problematic and would depend upon the resistance she encountered.

Kick-starting the trail bike, Lucy swung east onto the River Camel walking trail, a disused railway line once used by the London South West Railway, which follows the Camel Estuary from Padstow to Wadebridge before joining the route through the deep and beautiful wooded Camel Valley to Bodmin. Hitting speeds of over one hundred kilometres per hour along the well-maintained track, Lucy had to judge when to stand on the foot pegs, knees bent to absorb shock, or to be seated. Balancing the motorcycle on the uneven gravel surface at speed demanded concentration. Her aggressive riding was met with disdain by the trundlers, those sharing the walking trail. Lucy found she had to keep her thumb constantly pressed on the horn, warning the ramblers to move out of her way. Racing past, she showered them in dirt and dust as she left them in her wake.

At Bodmin, rather than following the trail inland to the edge of Bodmin Moor, Lucy decided to ride on the roads, knowing that the police would have received numerous complaints about a dangerous hooligan on a trail bike, terrorising walkers on the track. Obeying the road laws, she made her way first to St Germans before heading into Plymouth and a car rental firm. Having found one, she rode down to the docks, dumping the bike and helmet and, while walking back into town, she disposed of the jacket in a dump master.

'Good afternoon,' the lady behind the hire car company counter said. 'How may I be of assistance?'

'I'm in need of a car for a week. Mid-size if you have one available.'

'Certainly, Madam. May I have your driver's licence?'

While Lucy gave her details, which were dutifully loaded into the firm's computer, she imagined the data flowing into cyber space and wondered how long it would take for the MSS to intercept it.

'Lucy,' asked the lady behind the counter, 'Would you like to take out the collision damage waiver insurance?'

Lucy thought for a moment. 'Yes, I doubt I'll need it, but I find it's always better to be safe than sorry.'

'Definitely.'

Thirty minutes after walking in through the front door, Lucy was leaving the rental yard, driving two blocks before depositing the car in an underground car park. Next stop was a shop from which she purchased a plain carry bag and towel. In the women's toilets, she wrapped the gun and holster in the towel and placed them in the bag. While riding into Plymouth on the trail bike, Lucy had spotted a fancy-dress business. That was her next port of call.

'Hello,' Lucy said, appearing flustered, entering the fancy-dress shop and seeing the mid-thirties aged woman behind the counter, the proprietor she guessed.

The woman looked up.

Lucy sighed then said, 'I do hope you can help me. I'm meant to be at a charity fundraiser in an hour's time and totally forgot that it's fancy dress. I thought I could go as an elderly gentleman. Do you have anything?'

The woman thought for a moment and said, 'We have some bits and pieces, beards, bald head, but not a complete old man's costume, like we do for Batman or Wonder Woman.'

That's okay,' Lucy said, a fake smile shrouding her face. 'I didn't think I would be able to hire a complete costume, but was hoping you would be able to create it, you know, make me something. I have a budget of three hundred pounds.'

The proprietor's eyes lit up as she said excitedly, 'You won't need three hundred pounds. I do the make-up for our local theatre company and with what we have in the store, I can promise that you will be unrecognisable. I'm Toni Peters, the owner of this humble party and costume shop.'

'Lacy Braithwaite,' Lucy said, a grin spreading across her face. 'It's a pleasure to meet you.'

Toni pointed to a chair near the counter as she said, 'Take a seat, Lacy and I'll see what I can find.'

She vanished into the back of the store, reappearing three minutes later, her arms full and carrying a theatre make-up kit, which she placed on the counter.

'Now then, Lacy, I thought we could try this,' Toni said and held up a matt-finished, latex bald head cap, complete with a smidgen of grey hair on the sides.

'I just want to test it for size before I apply the adhesive,' Toni said, pulling the cap over Lucy's scalp. Lucy's long blond hair protruded, hanging down at the back. Using her fingers, Toni worked around the edges, pushing Lucy's hair under the cap until it was out of sight.

'Okay,' she said, standing back to examine her handiwork. 'Now let's see if we can tuck the back in,' Toni muttered, but no matter what she tried, the bulk of Lucy's hair caused the skull cap to lift.

'I was worried about that. Maybe if I pull your hair forward and pin it across the top of your head?'

'Do you have a pair of scissors?' Lucy asked.

'I do, but you're not thinking of cutting it, surely?'

'Sure, why not? I'm booked into the hairdresser tomorrow anyway and was going to get it trimmed to a little above the shoulders. Take a few centimetres off and no one will ever notice.'

'I can't. You're so beautiful, I'll wreck it.'

'Of course you can. Be wicked.'

'Are you really certain?'

Lucy said, her face betraying little. 'Snip snip, let's do it.'

With her hair cut, it folded perfectly under the cap. As Lucy held a mirror, Toni glued the hair disguise into place and set to work with the make-up. She managed to create a wrinkled, aged skin effect using only different coloured cosmetics and Lucy was impressed by Toni's ability; truly an artist. Even the bushy eyebrows appeared natural. The last addition were black-rimmed glasses.

'Let me dress you first before I do your hands,' Toni said. 'Otherwise, we may get some of the colour on the clothes.'

She held up a white shirt and said, 'I was thinking of this with a black tie.' She then selected a dark brown cardigan. 'Perhaps, the cardigan over the shirt, then this lighter brown jacket.' She pointed to a jacket laying across the counter. 'And matching trousers. To finish, I have black or brown shoes and, if they don't fit, there's a charity store in the next street. They will have something.'

Fifteen minutes later, Toni led Lucy to a full-length mirror.

'What do you think?' she asked.

'You're a master,' Lucy said, changing her profile so she that could see each side of herself in the mirror. 'What about some white whiskers under the nose?'

'A moustache?'

'Yes.'

'We have them, but they may look fake compared to the rest of you.' Toni paused before continuing, 'Maybe I could trim it and perhaps tone down the white, to make it look more natural.'

'Let's give it a go, Toni. If we don't like it, we can always remove it.'

Toni vanished out to the back, returning with a plastic package containing a costume moustache. Gluing it in place, she set about grooming and adjusting it.

'It's come up really well,' she said after five minutes. 'I think you'll be pleased.'

She held up a hand mirror for Lucy to see.

'Perfect.'

With her own clothing neatly stored in the plain carry bag and the Quantum Cube safely tucked into the inside pocket of the old man's coat, Lucy thanked Toni and started to leave.

'Wait! One more thing,' Toni called.

Lucy turned around.

'We forgot the stick. You can't be a dignified senior without a walking stick.'

Once outside the store, Lucy adopted the stance and behaviour of an old man, stooping slightly, conscious of not over-playing the role. With a shortened stride, a step akin to a man of her apparent age, Lucy walked to the railway station. In a cubicle inside the mens' toilet, she unrolled the towel, reloaded and secured the Glock, concealing it beneath her brown jacket.

Ten minutes later, Lucy boarded a train and was on her way to Exeter.

Despite the disguise, Lucy kept her head bowed as she left the Railway Station in case she was being watched. Carefully, vigilant, she made her way towards the mall where the Post Office drop off point was located. To reach the Post Office, Lucy had to walk through a town square, surrounded on two sides by shops, cafés and restaurants, the place where she would be most exposed. Nearing the danger point, Lucy stopped and purchased a newspaper, then meandered to the corner of the square before slipping into a café. From the window seat she had a clear view of the outside, a no-man's land which had to be crossed.

I see you, Lucy muttered to herself.

On either side of the street were two men that she recognised from the Shark Fin restaurant in London. Lucy anticipated having to slip past MSS sentinels, the reason for her disguise, but what surprised her was that they were both wearing the latest in facial recognition technology glasses.

Would the disguise fool the algorithm? Maybe a quick scan, thought Lucy, *but closer examination might see through the mask.*

With only a handful of pedestrians trickling through the space at any given time, the operatives would have ample opportunity to scrutinise her. A new plan was becoming essential.

Pretending to read the newspaper, Lucy considered the options.

The men were exposed and killing them wouldn't be difficult. Unquestionably, they were accompanied; other heavily armed MSS agents would be waiting to strike. Once inside the square, if a gunfight broke out, it would be a turkey shoot favouring those with the overwhelming advantage. I would be the turkey. Setting fire to the café would bring the fire brigade and the ensuing chaos could provide the cover needed to slip by. Today, with no crowds, the emergency would go unnoticed and the same would apply to a bomb scare. Outside was too quiet. Where are the queues when you want them? Calling for armed assistance was off the table; communications had been cut and the Agency compromised.

'Would you like another coffee?' the waiter asked.

From her pocket, Lucy produced a Scotland Yard warrant card and said, 'Could I have a chat with the manager, please?'

The waiter looked at the picture of the woman on the police badge and then back at Lucy. He glanced back at the ID photograph again.

'I'm wearing a disguise!'

'Really?'

That was code for "I don't think so".

Not quite understanding what was happening, the waiter watched as Lucy undid the top three buttons of her shirt and exposed her cleavage and red satin bra, then said, 'Are you satisfied?'

Flustered, he said, 'Certainly Sir, I mean Madam... I'll fetch the manager.'

Thank goodness I'm not a man pretending to be a woman, thought Lucy.

She watched the waiter hurry to the counter and talk to a woman in her early twenties, looking like a young girl to Lucy. They both came over to where the Police identity card was on display, lying on the table.

'Please, both of you have a seat,' Lucy said and gestured to the vacant chairs. They peered at her curiously as she continued, 'I'm in need of your help.'

'This costume is part of a counter terrorism exercise. I'm about to say something to you and I want you both to continue looking at me. Don't look around, do you understand?'

'Yes,' they answered in unison.

'Outside are two men.' Lucy raised her voice as she noticed the waiter's eyes and head move towards the window. 'I said, don't look.'

'Sorry.'

'They are wearing facial recognition technology glasses.'

'Cool,' said the young male waiter.

Lucy ignored him, resisting the urge to roll her eyes.

'My task is to deliver a package to the post office and put it inside a designated post office box.' She took the key from her pocket. 'This is the key. I would like to enlist your assistance.'

The manager shrugged her shoulders. 'What do you want?'

'Simply for one of you to take the package and put it in the box.'

'No problem,' said the manager, 'I get our mail from there every day. It's no big deal.'

'Ordinarily that's true. This however, is a serious exercise and my adversaries will be watching, expecting me to try this deception. I was thinking we should create a diversion.'

The waiter's eyes lit up at the thought.

'While you... my apologies, I haven't asked your names,' Lucy said.

'Samantha,' the manager said.

'Ian.'

'Hello, Samantha and Ian. Pleased to meet you. I'm Lucy. I'm an Inspector with the Scotland Yard Counter Terrorism Unit. As I was saying, we need a diversion. This is the plan. Samantha, you take this to the Post Office.'

Lucy took from her pocket the wrapped quantum cube, complete with its red bow and pushed it across the table to her.

Samantha looked at the package with suspicion and said, 'What's inside?'

'If I told you that, I'd have to kill you.'

The girl's face took on a look of fear.

'I'm teasing. This is a police exercise. It's a pen in the guise of a quantum cube.'

'Okay,' the manager said, the information comforting though not understood.

'Now where was I? While you take the quantum cube to the Post Office, Ian will take coffees to my colleagues and say that they are gifts from me.'

'Do I tell them where you are?' Ian asked.

'Absolutely. You're to point me out. Now, my recruits, timing is everything. Samantha, you will leave first then, thirty seconds later, Ian will take the coffees. You will temporarily distract my friends while Samantha enters the Post Office. I know people are in and out of there continually, but I'd like to take an additional precaution. Samantha, when you've successfully completed your mission, please bring the key back to me. I would imagine I'll have company by then, but you are to interrupt us. Are there any questions?'

'Do I hide the package?' Samantha asked.

'No, you're going to the Post Office to send it.'

'It's all a little boring,' Samantha grumbled.

'Let's hope so, because the real genius, the sign of a true master, is that no one should notice the deception.'

From her table, Lucy watched as the plan unfolded. Samantha left the café first and then Ian. As he delivered the coffee, Ian pointed towards the shop window and Lucy waved. Both men stared in her direction and the artificial intelligence worked its magic. With the delivery completed, Ian returned, followed twenty seconds later by Chen Li.

Where did you come from?

He joined her at the table and said, 'The reports were right and you are indeed a resourceful and dangerous woman. This, I take it, is a diversion. The Post Office box in Exeter drop a "red herring", as the British like to say.'

Through the window, Lucy saw Samantha returning, her hands free of the parcel and carrying the key.

'Not at all, Mr Li.'

The café door opened and Samantha came inside and approached the table.

'Any problems?' Lucy asked her.

'None,' the girl answered dismissively.

'Well done. The key if I may... Thank you.'

'Is that it?'

'That's it.' Lucy gestured towards Chen Li. 'This is Mr Chen Li, from the Chinese Ministry for State Security. He's part of this joint exercise. Say hello to Samantha, Mr Li. She works here.'

Hiding his displeasure, Chen Li asked, 'Do you go to the University here in Exeter?'

'Na,' Samantha replied, 'I just work here.'

Lucy smiled at Samantha and said, 'Thank you for your services.'

Samantha returned to the serving counter.

Lucy stood and said, 'It's been a pleasure Mr Li, but I do hope we don't see each other again, at least for a while.'

She was about to add that he owed her two new cars, but stopped herself. She'd killed five of his agents, one in London and four today; now wasn't the time for antagonising an opponent.

Inside, Chen Li was seething, but held his calm. 'The pleasure has been all mine.' As Lucy left the table, he called after her in Chinese, a language she didn't understand, '直到下一次,' (Until next time).

Before leaving the café, Lucy used the bathroom to wash the makeup from her face and hands and dispose of the old man's disguise. Her own clothes were in the plain bag, so she changed into them and threw everything else into the rubbish bin. The train ride to Plymouth took an hour, then she picked up the hire car and drove to Postbridge, the East Dart Hotel, and Rosie.

***

'It seems Lucy, that our communications have been compromised,' Rosie said, debriefing Lucy after the mission. 'We believe the problem is in the hardware. The contractor working with the Chinese government has slipped tiny surveillance chips into the motherboards. They were monitoring everything we were doing. That's how they knew you were in Saint Moritz, Pi-Ski, and that John didn't have the quantum cube. When you reported you had it and were instructed to take it to Exeter, they knew that too. They shut down our communications when we tried to help you. British intelligence has been well and truly compromised. Despite everything, you did well, although we have a monumental mess to clean up.'

'Yes, very unfortunate. What's the public message?'

'Unfortunate, indeed,' Rosie exhaled. After a pause, she said,

'There was a tragic end to a morning of reckless driving on the back roads of Cornwall with the death of four young people. A group of youths stole three high-powered sports cars and played chasey on the back roads of Cornwall where they came to grief. Regrettably, the pilot and film crew of a news helicopter were also killed when they clipped power lines while filming the mayhem. Police are searching for a fifth person who hijacked a van and fled the scene.'

'The jet fighters?'

'A routine low altitude training mission.'

'I see. What about Isaac Williams?' Lucy flicked Rosie his driver's licence.

'You must have scared the bejesus out of him. He's not going to talk, told us that he didn't get a look at whoever tied him up.'

Lucy sighed. 'It was my plan to remain in Pi-Ski until Monday, but I'm pretty sure I was seen this morning so it may be best if I just vanish?'

'No, that's not a good idea. It's best that you return. It will help with the cover story. I've already had the police ring John so that he knew what was happening before he heard or saw it on the news. They told him that your car and mobile phone had been stolen and filled him in on the events of the day, that youths were driving your Jaguar SUV, when it was involved in a fatal accident. You were supposed to be shopping when the car was taken. As you might expect, he is concerned.'

'I see.'

'Good. We want things to settle and you are to stay undercover until after the filming on Saturday week. If you were to leave now, having organised the Vienna Boys' Choir, it may raise some awkward questions. The drama in Pi-Ski will be forgotten in a week and replaced by the excitement of the visit of the Choir.'

Lucy nodded.

'Leave after that, when your connection to the events of today is less obvious.'

'The Chinese intelligence services?' Lucy asked.

'We won. It's all over until next time. I'm not expecting further trouble from them.'

Rosie looked at Lucy and said, 'What happened to your hair?'

'It's a long story.'

CHAPTER 16

The Last Supper

John knew Lucy was safe because the police had called, nevertheless, he repeatedly checked his watch in a state of worry. It was past seven in the evening and she still wasn't home. He'd seen the story on the news and had a visit from Josephine and Edith, who had described in excruciating detail what they had seen. This only heightened his anxiety, which he knew was silly.

Lucy had been shopping and wasn't in the Jaguar... This is Pi-Ski, nothing like that happens here... Would the events of today make her frightened? I pray she doesn't feel unsafe and return to Australia.

A flash of headlights lit up the front window.

Lucy's home.

Despite the cold, John rushed outside, tripping over on the footpath as he raced to greet her.

'Are you alright?' he asked as she stepped from a police car.

'Sure. It's just been a long day, that's all.'

John took her by the hand and said, 'Let's go inside. I'm so glad you're safe.'

'I'm fine, John. I never saw the thieves.'

'I know. It's just you were such a long time at the police station and they wouldn't let me visit.'

'Because my SUV was one of the stolen cars, the detectives wanted to question me. When the story was all over the news, they said they would call you, in case you recognised my Jaguar. They did, didn't they?'

He bit his lip, unable to stop himself as the words he was avoiding saying slipped out, 'I thought you might have spoken to me yourself, rather than the police.'

'Oh Honey, my kind and generous man, I wanted to, but they kept me in an interview room the whole time. I think they only called because I kept demanding to speak with you, saying how worried you would be. In the end, they relented and called you.'

A flash of guilt flowed through John's body and he became mute before saying, 'Sorry.'

'John Moss, you have nothing to be sorry for. For caring?'

They embraced and he whispered into Lucy's ear, 'Welcome home.'

'I'm so very pleased to be here, I can tell you.'

'What do you think of my new hairstyle?' she said, stepping away from John and spinning around to model the new design.

'It's lovely.'

'Ha, you didn't even notice, did you?'

'I was more concerned about you.'

Lucy chortled as she said, 'I really like it being a little shorter.'

'I think you're beautiful, however you style your hair. Have you eaten?'

'No.'

Over dinner, as they chatted, John recounted Josephine's and Edith's visit and how they had described in great detail her battered Jaguar SUV racing through Pi-Ski.

'They suggested, Honey, that we have a welcome party for you. Nothing grand, just a few nibbles and drinks before the Vienna Boys' Choir filming takes all our time.' John laughed, 'Sometimes I think the retired women of the church forget that I work.'

'That would be wonderful, John.'

John grinned. 'The only possible time was tomorrow evening at six; I hope you don't mind but, in your absence, I accepted.'

'Where?'

'Here.'

'Here?' Lucy repeated, surprised.

'Is that alright?' John questioned, concerned.

'Yes of course. It's just there's a bit of work for us to do.'

Looking perplexed, John said. 'Is there? I was going to buy some crisps, maybe some nuts and a couple of bottles of wine on my way home tomorrow night. What else is there to do?'

'My most handsome, darling man!'

Lucy was surprised how easily the words of affection flowed from her lips, almost as if she believed them.

'Please don't be offended, but that might be fine for a bachelor. When there's a woman in the house, things are different. Six o'clock means people won't have eaten, so we need something more substantial than a packet of crisps, and then there are the desserts. Do you have some nice plates and glasses?'

'I was going to use disposable paper plates and plastic glasses. If you want something more substantial to eat, let's buy a couple of roasted chickens. Keep it easy.'

Lucy flung her head back in sham exasperation.

'Men!'

She kissed him tenderly on the lips and he tasted good. She felt comfortable, at ease, the residual aura from the earlier killings falling away, supplanted by the demands and rigours of domestic life.

'I would like to make a good impression, that's all, John. Your friends care a great deal about you and I want them to see that I'm worthy of you.' She kissed him again.

'Worthy? I think I'm the luckiest man alive.'

What on earth am I thinking? Lucy said to herself. *I can't even boil an egg without a recipe.*

'Honey, I'll buy some cooked chickens in the morning. Your suggestion was a good idea.'

John laughed.

'What?' Lucy asked, giving him a look of curiosity and raising an eyebrow.

'They don't sell roast chickens in Pi-Ski and you don't have a car.'

'Oh, yes.'

'If you drive me to work, you can have mine. I'll ride home with someone.'

'I'll make it worth your while,' Lucy said, her eyes sparkling.

***

'What do you think?' asked Lucy, standing back and inspecting her handiwork.

The dreary dining room had been transformed, a white lace cloth adorned the table, on top of which were placed new crystal glasses, glistening in the room light. Flower-filled vases decorated the once bleak antique furniture, now alive with colour and vibrancy.

'I'm not sure the cushions are right.'

John shrugged, not wanting to give the wrong answer.

Lucy went to the couch and removed the cushions before re-joining John for another inspection. She breathed out heavily.

'No, definitely better with them.'

The doorbell rang and Lucy replaced the cushions as she faced John. She brushed down her dress.

'How do I look?'

'Stunning.'

'I'm ready then. Let's do it.'

John smiled, unsure what all the fuss was about, but pleased that Lucy was happy and at home.

The drinks and conversation flowed easily. Josephine and Edith retold the story of the cars racing through Pi-Ski.

'What wasn't in the news,' Edith said in a whisper, 'was that Lucy's Jaguar was bullet-riddled and there were two helicopters, not one. Also, two fighter jets flew over the cars. The Government is not telling us the truth.'

'A conspiracy? Everyone loves a conspiracy,' Vicar Charlotte said.

Catherine huffed, annoyed. 'Conspiracy! The government can't organise a cake stall, let alone orchestrate a conspiracy.'

'Maybe they were spies, like in James Bond,' Charlotte said. 'What do you think, Edith?'

At the mention of spies, Lucy saw a spark of recognition ignite in Josephine's eyes. A memory had been awakened and, at that moment, Josephine knew where she had seen Lucy. It was in Florence, before the death of her husband. If the revelation had happened a week before, Lucy's mission would have been compromised, but with the quantum cube safely with British Intelligence, that was no longer the case. Lucy considered her response. She could remain detached as she had at their first meeting or she could be open with Josephine about what they both knew. How Josephine reacted would depend upon her knowledge of her husband's activities or her complicity in his death. For John's sake, she wanted to remain mute, but unable to control her curiosity. When Josephine glanced towards her, she raised both of her eyebrows and gave an almost indistinguishable nod of acknowledgement. This time it was Josephine who remained impassive.

She's not frightened, thought Lucy, *and that tells me something.*

Edith nodded, 'We saw them, didn't we, Josephine? The planes were connected with the car chase, otherwise it would be too much of a coincidence.'

This was an opportunity for Lucy to send Josephine a coded message. With her eyes dancing from one to the other and finally settling on Josephine, she said, 'Some coincidences just happen.'

The meaning that she hoped would be conveyed to Josephine was, "I'm not here because of you."

'More wine?' John asked, passing around a bottle. With glasses filled, the conversation moved to the Dating Agency.

Edith frowned. 'Did we decide who was going next?'

Vicar Charlotte giggled, 'Edith, it's you. Remember, you were going to write your own profile?'

'That's right, it's me,' Edith said, her voice slightly shrill and starting to slur.

'I'm glad you haven't written it yet,' Vicar Charlotte said. 'I think we should assess what worked before we try again. Lucy, what was it about John's profile that attracted you?'

'I'm sorry to disappoint you, but we did it in the good old-fashioned way.'

Catherine snorted. 'We didn't put his profile on the dating site. Other than suggesting that he went to Saint Moritz, we did nothing. In fact, as far as I know, we haven't opened a single account.'

'You did Edith,' Josephine said, 'Purely for research purposes. Remember, you showed some profile examples?'

'I did?'

'That all seems such a long time ago,' Vicar Charlotte said.

'I know it was my idea,' Josephine said. 'However, I suggest we wait and see what happens after Saturday's performance. If as Lucy predicts, we have a voluntary choir for our services and people start attending St Mary's, then perhaps the old-fashioned way will be best, like it was for Lucy and John.'

'Even with the old-fashioned way, sometimes people need a helping hand, a gentle push,' Vicar Charlotte said.

Josephine smiled. 'Or a great big shove.'

'Ladies,' John announced loudly and they each stared at him. 'Have you forgotten the St Mary's naked charity calendar? I was to go in search of romance and you were to get your gear off. Imagine the potential sales when the Vienna Boys' Choir has performed and St Mary's is famous. Think of the money we can donate to charity– a mission from God.' He looked at them one at a time. 'An agreement is an agreement, is it not?'

'I'm not sure we actually agreed,' Catherine said.

'In spirit you did,' John said, a wicked smile on his lips. 'What we need is an interesting name for marketing purposes.' He thought for a moment, 'Perhaps the *St Mary's Full Monty Calendar*?'

'It does have a certain ring to it,' Lucy said, going along with John's game. 'Or, how about, *St Mary's exposed*?'

'That's not bad,' Vicar Charlotte said. 'Along the same lines, *St Mary's Uncovered*?'

'What about, *The Naked Ladies of St Mary's*?' Josephine chimed in.

Vicar Charlotte nodded. 'I like that.'

'And me,' agreed Lucy and Edith together.

'Catherine?' Josephine said, glancing Catherine's way, 'A deal is a deal. Think of the good we can do with the money.'

Catherine shook her head in defiance. 'We don't have enough people.'

'I'm in,' Lucy said, laughing. 'And so is John.'

'I am?' John said, his voice betraying his surprise.

Lucy nodded and smiling deeply said, 'You are.'

Looking bemused, John said, '*The Naked Ladies of St Mary's Plus John*, doesn't have the same appeal.'

Edith chortled, 'St Mary's is an equal opportunity employer.'

John shook his head in resigned submission. 'The Anglican Church should introduce a quota system with gender equality on Parish Councils.'

Smiling, Josephine said, 'We have equality; one naked, all naked. Isn't that right, Catherine?'

Catherine sighed. 'It's not really full-frontal nudity, is it?'

'No, you cover up, holding objects in front of your private parts. You remember, the Bishop with a lamb? Perhaps the Vicar with a Bible, you with a crucifix, me with a London bus and so on,' Josephine said.

Vicar Charlotte thought for a moment, 'When do we do it? It's too late for next year.'

'We should do the photo shoot in June,' Josephine said. 'Sorry, let me rephrase that. We WILL do the photo shoot in June, when the weather is a little warmer.'

Before anyone could question her assertion, Josephine lifted her glass.

'A toast to the *The Naked Ladies of St Mary's*.'

They raised their glasses and took a sip of wine.

'It's been a most remarkable couple of months,' Vicar Charlotte said.

'It has indeed been a most remarkable couple of months,' repeated Edith. 'Even the church roof has been repaired.'

Catherine looked at Lucy.

'Was that another coincidence?'

Lucy thought for a moment before she said, 'Good fortune in that case. What do they say, coincidence is in the eye of the beholder?'

'Well, do you want to know what I think?' Vicar Charlotte said. 'God answered our prayers. Not only with the roof, but by delivering Lucy into our presence. I propose a toast. To Lucy.'

'To Lucy,' they all repeated.

'Welcome to our St Mary's family,' smiled Vicar Charlotte.

Family? thought Lucy. *They're a peculiar assortment. Josephine Carter: highly intelligent, tender, caring, genuinely concerned for John's well-being. Other than being a potential murderer, she'd be an ideal friend and companion.*

Then there's Edith Kelly: naïve, gullible, vulnerable, the kind of person I would once have described as weak. After all, who wants to get hurt? Being emotionally guarded, protected against the unscrupulous whims of life is a strength–isn't it? Yet she's warm and inviting and sees life through a prism of positivity. There's the rub, the vulnerability paradox, as someone once said. It's "the first thing I look for in you, and the last thing I want you to see in me."

Catherine Hepburn: Attila the Hun, forceful, unafraid of expressing her opinions and wishes, but not necessarily in an empathetic way. She's a woman who's realised her strength and power and taken charge of her own life. If she sees something she wants, she's not going to wait for it to come to her. An alpha woman, possibly in the bedroom too. Probably what she needs right now is a good f--k to take her mind off who's sitting in her chair. A fiercely loyal woman, someone you'd want in your corner.

What can you say about Vicar Charlotte Foster? A true believer in her Jesus Christ, without being a wacky, nutty religious zealot. Authentic in her love. When she welcomed me to the St Mary's family, it came from the heart. How I envy that sincerity and certainty. If I were to seek to portray her within a biblical verse, it is to St Peter that I would turn, Chapter 1, verses 22-23.

> *Now that you have purified your souls by your obedience to the truth so that you have genuine mutual love, love one another deeply from the heart. You have been born anew, not of perishable but of imperishable seed, through the living and enduring word of God.*

Finally, my own John Moss. Before Saint Moritz, I associated quirky with someone who was weird or peculiar. John is interesting and unique, odd in an adorable kind of way, an enigma, socially awkward, yet he loves company but also likes being on his own. He's perceptive and able to savour the small things of life, finding their beauty and wonder. He's interesting with a soft heart and passionate about whatever he does, putting his soul into making it work, like our unlikely relationship. John Moss, you're a very unusual man, the kind I would normally avoid like the plague, but I'm glad I didn't.

I think I love you! No, I do love you. I love you, my John Moss.

Lucy reflected, *They're a weird mob, but strangely, I feel at home.*

Lucy drifted back from her thoughts and said, 'Thank you, each and every one of you.'

She raised her glass in return.

'To St Mary's!'

After the toast, Lucy excused herself and walked to the kitchen to fetch more food and wine.

'Guess what?' Vicar Charlotte asked.

They all looked at her in anticipation.

'Other than when they have played with the Church message board, I've had my first real encounter with Pi-Ski's pesky pixie.'

'What happened?' Catherine asked.

'I went into the church this morning and on the altar, someone had left a piece of origami, a beautifully crafted crane. I found its presence strangely disconcerting, as if it was left as a warning.'

By the time Lucy returned, the conversation had moved on.

CHAPTER 17

Voices of Angels

The news that St Mary's Parish Church of Pi-Ski was the setting for the filming of the Vienna Boys' Choir Christmas Special, with Max Joseph, the soprano super star, gathered international attention and was all that the quiet village could talk about. The car chase through the streets quickly became a distant memory. The local pub, The Little People's Arms and other businesses relished the thought of the influx of visitors that the soon-to-be-famous St Mary's would attract. Even the Sunday church service improved, with a feeling prevailing that the church was no longer on life support; the atmosphere of St Mary's was buoyed by a new sense of optimism. Things were about to change. A creature of habit, Catherine Hepburn turned up early, to make sure that nobody accidentally took her pew.

Lucy was surprised at how smoothly she slipped into a contented domestic routine. Using housework as exercise, the mundane tasks became a pleasurable experience. Cornish folklore has it that until someone has lived in a place for more than three generations, they're not considered a local. Pi-Ski inhabitants however, made Lucy feel very welcome.

Maybe it's because they know my connection to the Boys' choir, she considered, *and that's why they are giving me special treatment.*

Whatever the reason, Lucy was greeted warmly wherever she went in the village. Having lived a life of emotional separation, Lucy found in Pi-Ski a feeling of belonging that was foreign to her.

Extraordinary, she said to herself at the realisation and discovering the importance of belonging somewhere and having connections that care. Her feeling of well-being was more pronounced when John was with her and strangely, it persisted even when they were in separate rooms or together but silent.

When I leave, I don't want to go back to my old life she whispered to herself.

In preparation for the big day, the Parish Council agreed on the wording, a welcome to the world, that was to be displayed on the church notice board. It was to be a Christmas message of joy and hope: *SEE HIM LYING ON A BED OF STRAW*.

The support and film crews for the Choir arrived on Thursday and, in a matter of hours of unceasing activity, St Mary's Church was transformed. Cameras, cables, seating for the orchestra and an intricate and delicately carved nativity scene all found their places. John and Lucy were to be positioned in the front row to be filmed nursing a baby during the singing of the hymn, Away in a Manger. John took the Thursday afternoon off work, joining Lucy at the rehearsal and costume-fitting.

For the practice, the Director used recorded music and Lucy was given a baby doll to tend.

'Lucy, John,' the Director said, 'I can't express enough how important this scene is, the most important part of the choir's entire performance. It's the reason that we are filming in your church, why we've come to St Mary's. You understand?'

'No pressure then,' John said.

Lucy elbowed him caringly in the ribs as she said, 'We understand.'

'Good,' the Director said. 'When I start the music, I will walk you through what we are expecting. Look at the cameras in front of you. Ready?'

'Yes.'

'Music please,' she called.

A choral version of Away in a Manger filled the church.

'Looking at the camera, excellent... okay, now to each other. That's it, and smile... no, no, no!' complained the Director.

'John, Lucy, you are not at a comedy festival. I want to see a scene of love, a sincere smile, two people besotted with each other and with their baby child. Not the superficial smile you just gave us. You can understand the difference, can't you?'

'Yes,' they both said, too frightened and nervous to argue.

'Who knew that acting could be so challenging?' John whispered.

'Shoosh,' Lucy said.

The Director clapped her hands loudly.

'Start the music again please.'

The music started to play.

Away in a manger,

no crib for his bed...

'John, gaze into Lucy's eyes.'

...The little Lord Jesus laid down his sweet head...

'Smile at each other, that's good. Wait for the next line... here it comes.'

The stars in the night sky...

'Look at the baby.'

...Looked down where he lay.

'Stop! What on earth was that?'

The Director threw up her arms with exasperation.

'That's a baby you're holding in your arms Lucy. It is the most precious thing in the world to you... to both of you. You're holding it like a sack of potatoes. The people watching this at home must melt because of the love and affection you have for the child. Your devotion to the baby, it must overwhelm them so that tears roll down their cheeks at the image of you nursing the child as the beauty, majesty and magic of the music takes them. They will be overcome by a mix of ...'

She paused, wanting to emphasise the next words. Gesticulating with her hands, she found the phrase she was seeking.

'Joy! Compassion! Love!'

The Director went silent for a moment.

'Max Joseph is one of the best boy sopranos of our time, if not the best. As you look down at the child, he will be singing solo those stirring words from the Christmas carol.' The Director sang powerfully, *Looked down where he lay.*

'The Choir will be humming in the background, about to join in with three-part harmony. The viewers' visual experience must match the sheer splendour of the music. Do you follow?'

'Yes.'

'I want you to try it again, but this time, imagine, and let the music carry you. As it does Lucy, I want you to *feel* the child in your arms, show love in your eyes, and in the expression on your faces, both of you. I want to see your... physical yearning for the baby. The audience must ache at the sight of you holding the Christ child, accompanied by beautiful music. I want to create a feeling of longing, the urge to have a child. Can you do that for me? Do you understand what it is I need from you?'

'Yes.'

'Good, let's start again. Music please.'

***

If Josephine hadn't already placed Lucy, the outfit she was given to wear would have given the game away. A long sleeved, scooped neck Dolce & Gabbana, rose printed sheath dress, the bright colours and signature floral blooms striking against a black background. A compact Louis Vuitton handbag would be draped over her arm as she held the baby. Slipping into the dress, Lucy's skin tingled with rekindled memories, the feeling of the silk lining as it brushed against her body invigorating. As she prepared to leave for the church, the dress still felt wonderful. There was no question that it was a beautiful and expensive dress, but it was now an accessory, no longer the main event. Lucy realised that in her past, she'd become trapped in a world dominated by possessions. Connection to people was secondary.

John joined Lucy in the dining room. He was wearing a chalky and earthy near-black but dark-grey two-piece woollen Hugo Boss suit.

John Moss, you're strikingly handsome.

Seeing Lucy, John said, his eyes wide, 'Wow, you look absolutely stunning.'

He bit his lip, fighting back a sudden urge to propose, knowing that this wasn't the right time or place.

Tilting her head slightly to one side, then smoothing her dress, Lucy replied, 'Right back at you, kid.'

'Are you ready?' he asked.

'Wait, just one second. I bought you something.'

John raised an eyebrow in curiosity as Lucy rushed from the room, returning thirty seconds later with a pair of designer glasses she had purchased. She removed his quirky pair and slipped the replacements onto his face.

'What do you think?'

John looked at himself in the mirror.

'Pretty cool.'

Arm in arm, they left the house. As they reached the footpath, Lucy stopped abruptly.

'What's wrong, Honey?'

'I've got to fetch something. I'll be straight back.'

Lucy went into the house and when she returned, she turned him so that he was facing her and removed the designer glasses, flinging them into the garden. She positioned his old spectacles onto the bridge of his nose, carefully placing the sides behind his ears. Lucy stepped back to examine him.

'That's better, that's my John Moss... now I'm ready.'

Inside Lucy pined. *I will be gone by the time you come home on Monday, my precious man.*

A tear formed in the corner of her eye.

As they arrived at St Mary's Church, a crowd of people were gathered in front, laughing and taking pictures of the welcome message.

**ST MARY'S ANGLICAN CHURCH
PI-SKI**

SEE HIM LAYING ON A BED
OF STRAW

THE DRUNK

Lucy looked at John suspiciously.

'It wasn't me,' he said, 'but it is rather good. The timing is disappointing. Do you still think it's one of the Parish Council?'

'Undoubtedly.' Lucy paused before adding. 'It's not just the wording: THE DRUNK, that they are laughing at.'

John looked at Lucy inquisitively.

Lucy smiled. 'The sign should read, lying on a bed of straw, not laying on a bed of straw.'

John hung his head. 'Oh dear! That was me.'

She kissed him on the cheek.

***

The church was packed to the gunnels with invited guests for the filming and to hear the premier performance of the Vienna Boys' Choir Christmas Album. Scanning around, Lucy spotted the

377

Director near the front of the church standing next to a woman who was holding a baby.

'They are waiting for us,' she said.

'Hi Lucy and John,' the Director said, gesturing to the lady by her side. 'This is Adele and she is kindly lending us, or more to the point, you, her baby Sophie.'

Lucy held her hand out to Adele and said, 'I'm pleased to meet you.'

'If you're ready,' said the Director, pointing to Lucy and John's seats. Adele leaned forward and placed Sophie into Lucy's waiting arms. Receiving the child, a chill of both nerves and excitement travelled down Lucy's spine, making her quiver; this was the first time she'd held a baby.

'You're a natural,' Adele reassured her as she withdrew.

'Lots of nieces and nephews,' Lucy lied, to the sound of the accompanying orchestra warming up. As she looked down, the child met her gaze and smiled, then gurgled.

'Thank you,' said the Director to Adele. 'We have a place for you a little further back.'

As the Director started to leave, she turned to Lucy saying. 'Remember, let the music carry you. The rest will come naturally.'

A round of applause filled the church as the Vienna Boys' Choir entered and the clapping grew in intensity as the Conductor, Sir Alex Wolf, joined them. He gave a modest bow of recognition, turned and faced the boys, then lifted his baton. With a gentle flick of his wrist, music came forth, filling the church with harmony. A simple wave of his hand brought the voices of angels to life.

Lucy had lived the high life as the mistress of a Russian billionaire so had frequented operas, ballets, symphony orchestra's and rock concerts in some of the most prestigious concert halls throughout the world: Carnegie Hall in New York City, Wiener Musikverein in Vienna, Royal Albert Hall in London and Concertgebouw in Amsterdam. An all-boys choir in a little country church was a first for her, and it was the best. What struck Lucy was the intensity of the sound, particularly the trebles, as their voices were reflected in unblemished detail from the walls, reaching into her body and filling her with new-found awe and wonder.

The cameras focused on John moving to Lucy holding the baby. The soloist, Max Joseph, took a step forward, away from the choir. The orchestra started playing pianissimo, very softly. The perfection of the soprano's first words, '*Away in a Manger,*' merged with the music, yet towered above it:

Away in a manger
No crib for His bed
The little Lord Jesus
Laid down His sweet head

The stars in the bright sky
Looked down where He lay...

On cue, Lucy stared down upon her baby. The high-pitched voice of Max Joseph penetrated, an exquisiteness beyond anything she had known, rich, soulful and so melodic that a tear dribbled down her cheek. The innate desire for a woman to have a child was a myth and had no basis in science. Lucy knew that, but at that moment, comforting the baby in her arms, she emotionally and physically yearned for a child. Unconsciously, as she cradled the infant, she took hold of John's hand. He felt her connection, knowing that the time was right to ask for her hand in marriage. Lucy radiated tenderness, kindness, and love. Another tear formed and joined the other on Lucy's cheek. The Director, watching on the TV monitor, beamed in satisfaction; Lucy's compassion and beauty would sell them a million records.

The little Lord Jesus
Asleep on the hay

The cattle are lowing
The Baby awakes
But little Lord Jesus
No crying He makes...

The choir stopped its background humming in support of Max Joseph and started singing in three-part harmony. The hymn was building into a crescendo, gradually increasing in volume. Max Joseph's voice floated above the others, piercing the hearts of those present, the church vibrating as the melody blossomed.

I love Thee, Lord Jesus
Look down from the sky
And stay by my side
until morning is nigh

Be near...

The doubts that Sir Alex Wolf secretly held about being "required" to use St Mary's for the filming and the premiere performance of their Christmas album had been swept away by the time the Choir took its final bows. Sir Alex knew that he and the audience had just been part of something very special.

After the show, those present gathered in the church hall for light refreshments, milling around and talking excitedly. Lucy and John, having returned the baby to her mother, joined the festivities. Overcome by the events that occurred in the church, John's heart and mind were racing. Racked with doubt about whether Lucy would accept his proposal, he dithered.

Should I propose? Decide, John. Decide before the moment passes.

'I'm just going to pop home to get something,' John said to Lucy.

'What is it?'

'A surprise.'

He'd bought an engagement ring and was waiting for the right moment. He would take her into St Mary's to the spot where they had nursed the baby and listened to the choir, then drop down to one knee and say, 'Lucy, my most precious love, will you marry me?'

Smiling radiantly, Lucy said, 'Don't be long.'

Seeing Lucy on her own and glancing at the designer clothes that she was wearing, Josephine said, 'They suit you.'

'Why, thank you.'

Josephine smiled. 'Does he know?' She paused. 'Does he know that you're leaving?'

Lucy exhaled, her breath coming out as a groan. Try as she might to remain poker-faced, the corner of her lips gave away her quandary.

'Oh my goodness,' Josephine said, nonplussed, 'You're thinking of staying, aren't you?'

'Excuse me, Lucy,' Edith said, joining them. 'One of the choirboys asked me to give you this.'

She held out an origami crane for Lucy to take.

'That's funny,' Edith said. 'It's the same as the one Vicar Charlotte found on the altar the other day.'

Lucy called out, the panic and urgency straining in her voice. 'JOHN!'

The explosion rattled the church hall windows violently, the building shaking as if it had been hit by a severe earthquake. After the sound of the blast, for a few seconds, not a noise could be heard.

John's house had been destroyed, and he was dead.

The Crane would happily have killed both of them, but John leaving on his own was a bonus for the assassin. For someone like that, there was nothing more satisfying than inflicting permanent emotional scars on their adversary. Lucy would suffer.

By falling in love with John, she had condemned him.

This is my solemn vow and promise. In memory of my John, I, Claudia, will show you no mercy, Sweeties. Before you die, each of you will beg me to end your suffering.

She crumpled the paper crane in her fist and let it fall to the ground.

THE END

Coming Soon

The Ire of Claudia

MARK A. BIGGS

Hell hath been unleashed... **Claudia is coming!**

You shouldn't have done that, Sweetie, Lucy roared in pain and grief. In her mind, she pictured Chen Li and the colleagues he'd been dining with in London. I will start with you, Sweeties! Then, Crane, whoever and where ever you are, Claudia is coming for you next.

Max & Olivia are back.

LOVE LETTER FROM DRESDEN

MARK A. BIGGS

When Jacinta discovers a bundle of old love letters she embarks upon a journey of discovery. What unfolds is a touching story of lost but enduring love. A tale of death and heartbreak. But sometimes the truth is best left undisturbed.

This is a wonderful and moving story with a touch of Artōrius magic.

OPERATION UNDERPANTS

Book #1 Max & Olivia Series

MARK A. BIGGS

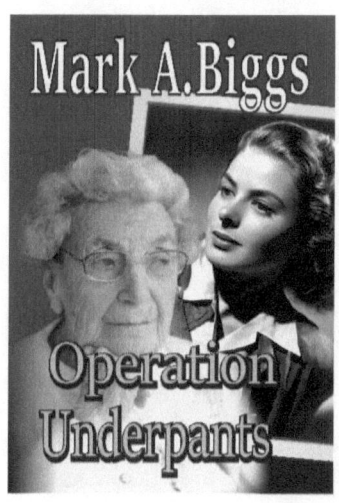

Unceremoniously dumped in a retirement home by their children, international ex-spies Max and Olivia languish forgotten and waiting to die. After finding a secret message in the newspaper they must escape and travel to the UK with the fate of London and much of the world hanging in the balance.

A wonderful action mystery with a little humour.

CLAUDIA

Book #2 Max & Olivia Series

MARK A. BIGGS

The adventures of our eccentric old spies, Max & Olivia continue in the exciting sequel to Operation Underpants. *Claudia* is an uplifting story full of danger, fear, good vs evil, never being too old, never giving up hope, and having ultimate faith in others.

Feared assassin Claudia doesn't kill Max but takes him with her - putting her at war with herself and a past she hoped to forget. Meanwhile, Olivia must escape the watchful eye of MI6 to track her beloved husband Max across Europe, leaving in her wake a delicious trail of chaos.

OPERATION OBE (Over Bloody Eighty)

Book #3 Max & Olivia Series

MARK A. BIGGS

Living out their days on board the Queen Mary 2, Max and Olivia are suddenly dragged back into the world of international espionage and an undeclared war with Russia

www.ingramcontent.com/pod-product-compliance
Lightning Source LLC
Chambersburg PA
CBHW030223120726
47903CB00005B/1335